Six for Gold

Also by Mary Reed and Eric Mayer

One for Sorrow
Two for Joy
Three for a Letter
Four for a Boy
Five for Silver

Six for Gold

Mary Reed & Eric Mayer

Poisoned Pen Press

*Poisoned
Pen
Press*

Copyright © 2005 by Mary Reed & Eric Mayer

First Edition 2005

10 9 8 7 6 5 4 3 2 1

Library of Congress Catalog Card Number: 2004117560

ISBN: 1-59058-145-8

Poisoned Pen Press
6962 E. First Ave., Ste. 103
Scottsdale, AZ 85251
www.poisonedpenpress.com
info@poisonedpenpress.com

Printed in the United States of America

For our parents

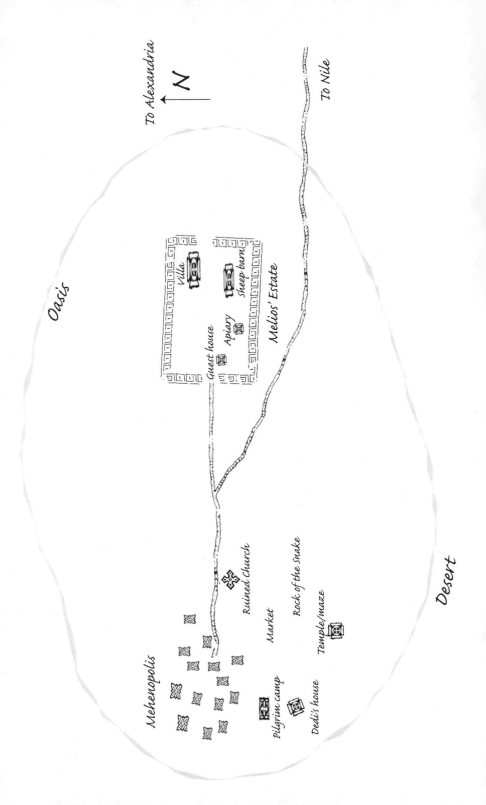

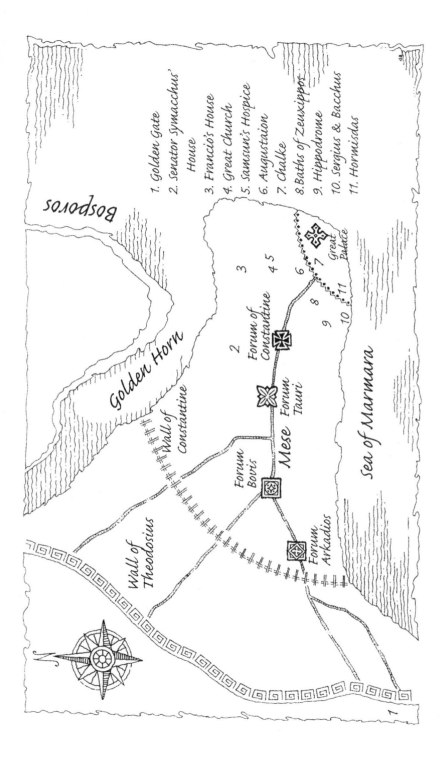

Bosporos

1. Golden Gate
2. Senator Symacchus' House
3. Francio's House
4. Great Church
5. Samsun's Hospice
6. Augustaion
7. Chalke
8. Baths of Zeuxippos
9. Hippodrome
10. Sergius & Bacchus
11. Hormisdas

Golden Horn

Wall of Constantine

Wall of Theodosius

Forum Bovis

Forum Tauri

Mese

Forum of Constantine

Forum Arkadios

Sea of Marmara

Great Palace

Chapter One

*J*ohn fled up steep tiers of marble benches.

Dusk had fallen over Constantinople. It was not dark enough to hide the hunted man. The setting sun filled the Hippodrome with light the color of blood in water.

The long shadows of the pursuers grasped at his heels. The distorted shape of a helmet sprang up in front of him, then bobbed away.

The excubitors were closing ground.

John glanced back. One line of guards snaked directly behind. Others climbed along the seating on either side, intent on cutting off his escape.

Above his head loomed the ornately sculpted facade of the imperial box. As Lord Chamberlain, John knew those seats were inaccessible to the easily inflamed crowds. He was just as familiar with the area directly below, used by the emperor's servants, musicians, and guards. As he reached the chest-high wall of the enclosure and pulled himself over, a spear hissed by his ear and rattled down onto the marble floor.

He thanked Mithra the door leading from the enclosure was for once unlocked. He leapt through the doorway into darkness and plunged headlong down a sloping corridor.

The sound of the pursuit echoed along the passageway as he emerged into the Hippodrome's concourse.

A beautiful, monstrous face below upraised wings smiled down at him. Dying sunlight flickered in the blank eyes.

John ran past the statue and outside. He was at the lower end of the Hippodrome. The shops lining its curved wall were closed, their gratings chained to rings in the pavement. He sprinted past them, keeping in the shadows as much as possible.

A hoarse shout told him he'd been spotted.

He dodged into a colonnaded street.

And fell.

The sprawled figure whose outstretched leg had tripped him winked.

No. Not a wink. Just a bloated fly skittering across the corpse's wide open eye.

John pushed himself upright. A ragged line of bodies in the middle of the street meandered to an overturned cart.

Plague victims.

Whatever the cause of the accident, the authorities had not picked up the remains.

John drew in a painful breath and ran.

Then, abruptly, the street dropped away. Below, John recognized the flickering lights of ships.

The docks.

There was nowhere else to run.

The guards at the imperial granary were intent on a game of knucklebones when the tall, lean man in a dark cloak burst into their midst. Before they could react, John was past them.

He reached the interior courtyard, veered through the nearest door, and raced along a dim hallway lined with narrow, rectangular alcoves—waist-high grain bins. The hallway intersected others with similar receptacles.

John zigzagged through the corridors. Skylights admitted only faint illumination. Rats scuttled out of his path.

Many of the bins were empty, others barely half full. The plague had disrupted everything, including the food supply.

His way was barred by a heaped grain bin that closed off the end of the corridor.

This then was the one Mithra had chosen.

John climbed in and burrowed under the grain. He pressed himself against the front wall and pulled his cloak up over his head to allow him to breathe.

The scrape and susurration of his effort gave way to a smothering silence. He fought off panic. The suffocating darkness was too much like being under water.

Loud footsteps approached.

"What do you mean where? Use your eyes!" someone said nearby.

John knew that voice.

"Here. Give me your spear," the man said.

John took shallow breaths. He strained to hear through the cloak and the stifling weight of the grain.

There was a dull thud, followed by silence and another thud. The pattern of sounds was repeated.

"Do the same with the others," came the order.

John understood.

His pursuers were thrusting spears into the grain piled in the bins.

There came the occasional scrape as a spear was deflected by a bin wall. Several curses. Footsteps. Someone emitted a coarse laugh.

Soon they would reach the bin in which John hid.

Each inhalation drew the fabric of the cloak toward his mouth, cutting off his breath.

"We'll be here all night," complained an excubitor.

"What's your hurry? Is Theodora waiting for you in the barracks?"

Now they were in front of John's bin.

He felt the grain move against his hip as the spear passed over and clashed against the back wall.

A grunt. Then flames seared John's shoulder.

He'd been grazed.

He had uttered no sound. Would they notice blood on the spear? Not in the near darkness.

"No one's in there either."

The men began to move away.

"Wait! Three times. Those were the orders."

The man addressed grumbled obscenely.

Again the spear sliced into the grain.

There was a piercing shriek. Rough hands grabbed John's arms and yanked him upwards. The screams rose into a gurgling screech.

A rat writhed and bled on the end of the spear.

Then the voice John recognized ordered the captive be bound.

"In the name of the emperor, I arrest you for murder."

It was Felix, captain of the excubitors and one of John's oldest friends.

He stared at John in astonishment. "John….Lord Chamberlain. I'm certain there is an explanation?"

John said nothing, but his gaze flickered briefly towards the floor. No one at a distance would have noticed. When Felix looked down, John quickly traced four lines in the dust with the toe of his boot. His expression remained stony.

"Captain, you see the situation. I know you will do your duty. I expect to be escorted to an imperial dungeon immediately."

Chapter Two

"We shall be merciful and allow you to keep one eye. We would not wish you to be unable to see what is in store after the torturers begin their work." Theodora's mouth curved into a scarlet scimitar.

A smile of anticipation.

John gazed over her head at the opposite wall of the torch-lit cell. He was chained naked to damp stones.

Although he avoided looking at his visitor, he could not escape her musk, a mixture of stale perfume, exotic spices, and sweat. He imagined she had been roused from sleep and instructed her ladies-in-waiting to dress her in the first robes that came to hand.

Theodora selected a pair of bloodstained pincers from a wooden table upon which were ranged a variety of instruments, many resembling physicians' tools. Her sharp, experimental click of the pincers drew John's unwilling attention.

Theodora set the tool down and picked up a wooden-handled razor. "Think of the damage this keen edge will do."

She looked John up and down. He could feel her gaze crawling over his body with a thousand insect-like legs.

"You are in fine physical condition. You will endure longer than most, once the work begins. Unfortunately for you, Lord Chamberlain."

She sighed. "That sounds like such an inappropriate title for one in your circumstances. Perhaps I should call you what the people in the streets do—John the Eunuch. Such a pity the Persians began our work for us. I am not without mercy. I like to give our special male guests a choice. Would you prefer to lose your eyes or...but that is an opportunity I cannot offer you. I give them a week to ponder the decision, just to be fair. What would you have chosen? Your eyes?"

John made no reply.

"Such a shame," Theodora continued. "I should have enjoyed seeing...but there are other possibilities. The skin can be removed piece by piece for some time before oblivion. Did you know that? Then again, we might do better not to pollute the flagstones with your blood, but rather break your bones one by one instead."

She tested the razor's edge with a slender fingertip. "This is sharp enough to have been used by a tonsor. Do you suppose the razor that trims the beard longs for the flesh of the throat? So near...but I notice you are strangely silent. You will soon have ample opportunity to test your discretion. I shall order that your inquisition be completed before your tongue is removed."

"I have nothing to say, highness."

Rage flared in Theodora's eyes. She lifted the blade. For an instant he thought she intended to slash him. Instead she struck him across the face with the flat of the blade. A thread of blood trickled down the concavity of John's cheek.

"You murdered a senator! Why? There is a reason and I will have it! Not even you can thwart me. It will be an interesting interview tomorrow and I look forward to it. Don't think you can escape our justice by biting off your tongue and choking yourself. You will be watched. You are a practical man and know your life is already forfeit. Why make whatever remains of it any more painful than it must be?"

John was silent.

Theodora's dark eyes glittered. "Very well. If you remain stubborn, I shall order the women in your household brought here. That one you call your wife…my servants will be able to offer her more, shall we say, intimate hospitality than you can, and you will witness it all."

She emitted a coarse laugh and opened the cell door. "Good night, dear Lord Chamberlain. While you're waiting for sunrise, you can consider what I've told you and count the passing hours until our next conversation."

***

As the door closed behind the empress, John allowed himself a thin smile. Then he leaned back against the rough stones. The scent of the empress remained, vanishingly faint yet discernable, an incongruous contrast to the malodor of the stuffy room.

His thoughts were not for himself but his family. His daughter Europa and her mother Cornelia, who had ill-advisedly set foot in this city where the scent of the empress who hated John was always in the air. There was also his daughter's new husband. That reckless fool Thomas.

What would they make of it all? What would they do now?

The door squealed open.

Two unfamiliar excubitors entered, removed his chains, threw a rough tunic over his nakedness, and shoved him out into the gloomy corridor. Other guards waited. He looked around, thinking he glimpsed Felix in the shadows at the back of the group. Strong hands forced his face forward.

"Watch where you're going!" A sword pommel jabbed hard in the back emphasized the curt instruction.

John was led along twisting passages, past nail-studded, iron-banded doors pierced with rusty, barred grates, up steep staircases, down, and along more corridors lined by other cell doors, then up once again. The measured tramp of his escorts' boots did not stir the black veil of darkness lying beyond the reach of their torches.

The party emerged into a soaring, echoing space he recognized as one of the emperor's reception halls.

It was not yet dawn. Tall windows held only a gray glow. Terra cotta lamps strewn across the dark marble floor illuminated the hall with hundreds of trembling flames. John had the impression of gazing down at the lights of a city. Smoke coiled up into a haze through which twinkled an enormous constellation in the shape of a massive cross, drawn in gold and precious stones on the vaulted ceiling.

At a hoarse command—he recognized Felix's voice—the excubitors came to a halt. Firm hands pushed him onward, into a curving lane of darkness between the lamps, leading toward a mountainous ivory throne from which Jupiter might preside. Or Jupiter and Juno, for there were two seats.

An indistinct group of figures moved in the smoke swirling behind the throne. John's keen eye caught a brief flash of gems on the hem of a cloak.

The emperor?

The wearer's pale, phantom visage coalesced for a heartbeat. John could not say whether it was smoke, his imagination, or the flickering light, but the face did not quite attain human form before it dissipated into darkness.

The misshapen, inhuman image floated in John's memory after the vision itself had vanished. He recalled wild tales told in the city. They claimed Justinian was a faceless demon who never slept but instead stalked the halls of the Great Palace all night.

As if summoned by the thought, Justinian approached from the shadows, his face not demonic, but as bland and round as a country farmer.

"Lord Chamberlain! Take care you don't trip! I do not usually receive visitors at this time of the night, but the lamps are kept lit for our nocturnal strolls. The emperor should never be kept in the dark." He spoke softly, his words intended only for John.

John said nothing.

"You are not in a humorous mood? But why should you be? Murder is always a vexatious matter, and the killing of a senator…. It has been a busy night. You realize you have given me no choice? Innocent men do not flee. That's what everyone at the palace will be whispering. One can think of a thousand reasons why a Lord Chamberlain might kill, but not a single one why he should then run away as if he were some common criminal."

Justinian waved his hand in exasperation. The movement of his heavy sleeve made the flames of nearby lamps tremble and sent shadows rolling along the walls.

"Powerful men may do what they wish, provided they are discreet," he went on. "For the emperor to pardon a man who has so plainly admitted his guilt…there would be grumbling, which so often leads to unrest. And what would the Patriarch say? There is nothing I can do but exile you." Although Justinian was already speaking quietly he lowered his reedy voice further before adding, "I see you grasped your opportunity, John. Well done."

"I did not kill Symacchus, Caesar."

"Oh, I'm not concerned about that. The important thing is you have arranged matters most conveniently."

"You will send me to Egypt?"

"Of course. Perhaps there you will find the answer that has thus far eluded you here in the city."

"It is difficult to investigate here without disturbing the empress," John admitted.

"You are aware the empress has a strong Christian interest in justice being done. She would prefer your tongue be exiled from your mouth, for a start."

"Have you elicited any new information regarding the situation in Egypt, excellency? I appreciate your informant has been vague, nevertheless, with so little known so far I have been chasing phantoms."

"Better that than faceless demons, wouldn't you agree?"

John gave a slight nod.

"My spies have given me the name of a certain landowner. A fellow called…ah…the name escapes me. Strange to relate, I granted him an audience in this very hall. There couldn't have been more than a hundred other petitioners that day. Last year?

Or was it before the riots? I believe the man's father also once visited the capital. Something involving taxation or possibly a property dispute. In any event, the family is not entirely unknown to me."

"Do they reside in Alexandria?"

"No. The settlement is some distance up the river. Most of Egypt is up the river, is it not? As you already know, those who oppose me—whoever they are—appear to believe there is something important to their cause in Egypt, and this location appears to be the place to begin your investigation."

He handed John an official document burdened by the heavy imperial seal. "This is your letter of introduction. One more thing. I have just learnt there have been a number of mysterious deaths on this man's estate. They should serve you as a starting gate."

John peered into the emperor's face. There seemed no life in the small eyes, except that lent to them by the lamplight's exaggerated shadows. He might have been examining a mask. "These deaths are mysterious, Caesar?"

"Oh yes, like nothing I have ever heard before. The man's sheep, although guarded and locked in a barn, are beheading themselves."

Chapter Three

Suicidal sheep?

No sooner had Justinian imparted this information than he ordered John escorted from the reception hall.

The party marched briskly away. Their route took them through one of the buildings housing the palace administrative offices, a warren of whitewashed walls punctuated by the dark doorways of empty rooms. From the entrance to one cubbyhole, where a lamp burned at a desk piled high with parchment, a pallid clerk peered out at them with the huge eyes of a startled nocturnal creature.

As the company turned a corner and exited into a small, tree-girded garden, John heard giggles. The sound turned to shrieks as three gaudily costumed court pages, who clearly had no business there, threw twigs and abuse at the excubitors and then raced away into the shrubbery.

The first red light of dawn illuminated the colonnade under which they walked. The harsh complaints of seagulls and a swelling chorus of birds greeted another day. Mist steamed off the dark vegetation.

John thought of his family. They would be informed he had murdered a man and would have to live with unanswered questions until he returned. There was no helping it. No one could be told the truth. Justinian was not the only person with spies everywhere, or torturers to elicit information from the unwilling.

As the party descended a series of stone stairways leading to the palace's private harbor, Felix ran up.

"John, I want to speak with you! I was detained. I fear there is bad news. Theodora sent for me. She's relieved me of the funds Justinian meant to be given to you for your journey."

"I see."

"It was a delicate situation, John. The empress said Justinian was being too kind, sending you into exile with a bag of coins. He would surely think better of it, were he asked to reconsider."

"She was right. He would have changed his mind," John replied as they arrived at the dock. A squat merchant ship bobbed on the swells of the harbor.

"The *Minotaur*," Felix remarked as they boarded. "There's more to this than it appears, isn't there? I realized that when you traced that seven on the granary floor. There are seven degrees in our religion and you were trying to reassure me. And how often does a man sent into exile be given funds as he departs?"

"I didn't murder the senator, Felix. I swear it as your brother in Mithra."

"You cannot tell me anything more?"

"I fear not."

"Mithra guard you always, John." Then Felix clattered off the ship.

***

John shivered in the brisk breeze and looked up past the sea wall into the city. An hour or two had passed since Felix and his excubitors had departed. The sun had risen, and now the dome of the Great Church stood out against an azure sky.

He turned at the sound of light footsteps.

A slim, deeply tanned woman whose dark hair held more than a hint of gray approached. She had the delicate, perfectly sculpted features of a patrician except for her lips, which were too thin for classical notions of beauty. They were now drawn into a determined line.

"Cornelia! Why are you here?"

"Felix came to the house not long ago and told us what little he knew," she replied. "Don't think I'm letting you go away on your own!"

"You must return home immediately." Though the words formed automatically he struggled to speak them.

Cornelia smiled, her expression halfway between laughter and tears. "I fear you will have to get used to not giving orders, Lord Chamberlain."

The deck planks creaked and for the first time John noticed Peter. The old servant appeared to be limping. "Don't worry, master. I haven't been hurt. It's just that…well…."

He placed the satchel he carried on the deck, bent unsteadily, and pulled off his footwear.

He held them out to John. "There was only time to pack one little bag and your favorite boots wouldn't fit in it. Though my sandals did so I have them. Captain Felix said you were being sent away in nothing but a tunic." His tone was outraged. He bent again to rub his feet. "Your boots aren't the right size for me, master, but I shall soon lose my limp."

Cornelia laid her hand on John's arm. "Before we left, I sent Europa to tell Anatolius. I'm certain between them, Thomas and Anatolius can take care of everything."

The ship moved under their feet. Timbers groaned.

Peter gave his satchel a few pats and then sat down stiffly on his make-shift cushion. "I've never been to Egypt, master. I hear it is a fascinating land."

A thought occurred to John. "How did you persuade the ship's captain to allow you aboard?"

The servant's wrinkled face assumed an innocent expression, but before he could reply Cornelia provided the answer.

"Peter insisted on paying for our passage with his savings."

"It seemed a good use for them," the old man smiled.

"I am very grateful, Peter," John said, and turned toward the bow. Wheeling gulls squalled. The noise reminded John of the shrieking court pages he had seen earlier. Thinking of them, he recalled a page now grown. Hektor.

Why should he think of Hektor? Perhaps because he was Theodora's creature. Like the empress, he would have delighted in seeing John suffer, particularly since not so long before he had been badly disfigured in an accident.

Hektor's once pretty face was now a demon's visage, akin to the one John had glimpsed in Justinian's reception hall.

"Mithra! Hektor was there!" John stopped himself from blurting out the rest of his thought—that his household had been left unguarded.

Chapter Four

Anatolius never heard the footsteps on the stairs.

He was concentrating on his task. One after another, he removed parchments from a reed basket on the kitchen table and dropped them into the brazier flames. He prodded the fire with an iron poker. A few half-burnt scraps spiraled upwards along with the sparks.

When a hand reached over his shoulder to catch one of the smoldering remnants, he turned in surprise.

"Francio!"

"I've been all over the palace looking for you. I was about to try the dungeons. I thought the emperor must've had you locked up. Then I heard you were at the Lord Chamberlain's house."

The visitor was short and muscular, with lumpy features, a narrow forehead, and cropped black hair. As usual he was perfectly turned out. This morning, he appeared in robes of variegated greens embroidered in pearls, and over all a short, yellow cloak decorated with a portrait of Dionysius.

He looked like a slave who'd stolen his master's clothes.

Anatolius, by contrast, was slim, his classical features framed by dark ringlets. He scowled at his aristocratic friend. "Where did you hear I was here?"

"You know me, my ear's always to the ground or the floor tiles. Nothing goes on at the palace that I don't know about."

Francio tapped the side of his nose with a stubby finger. The habitual gesture drew attention to the organ's flattened state. Anatolius had been given to understand it had been broken by a horse, but had noticed the explanations offered depended on the credulity of each listener. "What do you think you're up to, Anatolius?"

"I'm cleaning out my palace office."

Francio peered at the singed document in his hand. "Beauty More Stealthy," he read. "How could you possibly destroy your poems?"

"It's only ink and parchment, Francio."

"But it's about a woman!"

"She's gone."

"So you burn your memories of her?"

"My memory of her is part of me. I don't need poetry to remember." He snatched what was left of the poem from Francio's hand, crumpled it, and thrust it back into the brazier.

Finding the bundle of old poems had upset his humors more than he realized.

"Is the rumor true? Are you bent on becoming one of those lawyers?"

Anatolius grabbed more poems from the basket and consigned them to the fire.

"In times like these, writing poetry is frivolous."

"Homer might disagree, but what of your duties as Justinian's secretary? There's nothing frivolous about writing proclamations for the emperor. What will he say to the Armenian ambassador without you?"

"Obviously I'll still be at Justinian's disposal, not that he needs me. Remember, I was given the position because I'm a senator's son."

"Most of us at court are senators' sons, but we're not all as talented as you."

Anatolius took the basket and upended it over the brazier.

Francio flicked ashes from his garment. "A lawyer! I give your new occupation a month, and that's being generous!"

"What did you want to see me about, Francio?"

"I intended to ask you to dinner. I've planned a fine menu."

"With the plague still raging? I wouldn't have thought there was enough food left in the city to make a decent meal!"

"The shelves of the city may be empty, Anatolius, but nature's larder is still full. Yesterday it was venison. Tonight, we shall feast on pheasant."

"You've hired someone to poach in the emperor's preserves?"

"What do I know about hunting? For all I know the deer might have come out of the Marmara, and the delectable crane I had the night before could have been snared wandering the docks or crossing the Forum Bovis. I don't ask those who supply my needs."

"You're still trying to eat every creature mentioned in the Natural History?"

Francio wrinkled his forehead and tapped his ruined nose. "An excellent notion. I'll have to consider that after my current project. At present, I'm recreating Trimalchio's feast. You know the one. A wild boar stuffed with live thrushes, and wearing a liberty cap. A nice touch! I must not forget the liberty cap. First, however, I must obtain a wild boar."

"Isn't that somewhat ambitious?"

"Do you think so? If Justinian can reconquer Italy, I can manage to recreate a mere banquet. In connection with which, I am having some difficulty finding tooth powder." He coughed and waved floating ashes away. "I believe I'll return home and try my hand at composing verse. With all the smoke and ashes in here, I must have inhaled quite a bit of your genius by now!"

"You're welcome to try. Poetry never did me any good. Nor anyone else."

Anatolius glanced into the cooking pot set beside the brazier. The pot was filled with a mixture of honey and poppy seeds, now ruined by the flecks of ash that covered its glistening surface, not to mention rapidly gathering flies. Evidently it was one of Peter's confections, removed hurriedly from the heat and abandoned.

"Come to dine anyway," Francio replied. "I imagine you've worked up quite an appetite burning your past. But why skulk in here using the Lord Chamberlain's brazier? Isn't yours up to the task?"

"I thought it would be prudent to stay here in case someone has designs on John's house. I wouldn't be surprised, given the circumstances."

"What circumstances are these? Has something happened to the Lord Chamberlain? Not the plague?"

Anatolius offered his visitor a glum smile. "No. No, John is well. Or as well as possible, considering he's on his way to Egypt."

Chapter Five

John leaned carefully against the rail in the stern of the *Minotaur*. He did not look down into the swirling water. The sight of such depths made him uneasy.

Instead, he stared over the undulating and treacherous surface back toward Constantinople. Already the shapes of individual buildings heaped on its peninsula were becoming obscured by distance. Only the dome of the Great Church and the customs house rising from its tiny island at the mouth of the Bosporos were still recognizable.

He had come to consult Peter, who looked worriedly away from the birds swooping in the ship's wake. "I hope the morning meal was acceptable, master. Bread was all I could obtain. Plain fare to be sure, but nourishing enough. There's many in Constantinople would be glad of it right now."

John thought his servant looked tired. Peter's hands, gripping the rail, appeared more gnarled than they had while stirring the pots on the kitchen brazier. How old was Peter? John realized with some surprise that he did not know either Peter's age or where he had been born.

"It was perfectly acceptable, Peter, thank you. Now I wish to ask you a few questions. Did Thomas return to the house before you and Cornelia departed?"

"No, but we didn't expect him back yet, since he's working at night for Madam Isis." Peter's lips puckered around the name "Isis" as if it were an unripe olive. As a devout Christian, he did not approve of prostitutes, or even of those, such as Thomas, who served as doorkeepers for such establishments.

John's opinion of Thomas was darker still.

Peter made the sign of his religion and continued. "Forgive me, master, for speaking ill of your daughter's husband, but consider the job he holds. It's not a proper profession for a member of the Lord Chamberlain's family."

John didn't point out that Isis was a good friend of his, as Peter well knew. However rigid Peter's morality, he always found a loophole for the behavior of his employer. If John had been a Christian expecting to face the judgement of a demon tribunal on the ladder to heaven, he would have wanted Peter there to serve as his defender.

"You haven't noticed anything odd lately, Peter? Thomas didn't bring anything unusual into the house or perhaps mention unfamiliar names?"

"I try not to take notice of the personal affairs of those I serve, master."

"A commendable trait, Peter, but if you should remember anything out of the ordinary, let me know immediately."

"I will pray to remember anything useful I may have overlooked. It would be helpful if I knew what it was you suspected Thomas—"

John's sharp look cut him off. "Now, tell me what happened when Captain Felix arrived."

Peter frowned, adding another layer of wrinkles to the abundant creases in his brown face. "It was not long after dawn, and I'd risen to prepare the morning meal. There was a knocking at the house door that would have awakened the dead. At the time I didn't realize you weren't at home." He cast a reproachful glance at John.

"Well, as you now know, I had been unavoidably detained on imperial business."

"That's not how Captain Felix put it, master."

"What did he say?"

"Most of his comments I would prefer not to repeat. Captain Felix has an inventive turn of phrase when he's angry, and I say that as an old army cook. Anyhow, just as I was going downstairs to attend to the door, the mistress appeared. She looked very worried and said you had been gone all night."

There was no need to elaborate on what unexpected absences could mean at the palace. The gilded corridors at the center of the empire were more dangerous than the most squalid of the city's alleyways.

Peter continued his account. "Captain Felix almost knocked me down when he burst into the house. He was furious. He told us you'd been exiled for murdering a senator, and that you'd been caught red-handed with the body."

John was silent. He could feel the deck shifting with the swell, but kept his gaze fixed on the receding city. No doubt the murderer of Senator Symacchus was still there, as well as those who might be able to reveal the murderer's identity.

"Not that any of us believed the accusation, master," Peter went on. "I don't think the captain did either. He told us if we were fast enough we could catch this ship. The mistress instructed Europa to seek Anatolius' help, and then we left."

John was silent.

Peter frowned. "It is my opinion that if certain people knew Captain Felix had alerted us to your departure and the name of the ship taking you away, he would be in, well, a very difficult position."

"That would certainly be so."

Peter's eyelids narrowed in their nest of wrinkles. "Master, I suddenly remembered something! But now I'm sorry I did."

"What is it?"

"The pot I was using to cook honey and poppy seeds. I forgot to cover it before I left."

***

Cornelia was in a difficult humor. John had tried to question her about Thomas, but she could not enlighten him.

"If I were you, John, I'd have already read that letter of introduction."

John looked down at the document tucked in his belt. Addressed to one Melios, headman of Mehenopolis, the scroll was tightly tied by a linen ribbon with the gold seal of the emperor clamped over the knot. He had been waiting to explain his mission, uncertain what, or how much, to reveal. "Perhaps so, but you know quite well it is my duty to deliver it intact."

Cornelia perched on the rail of the *Minotaur*, her bare feet dangling above the deck. Just seeing her precarious position made John uneasy. A short length of rope was tied around her wrist and he wished she'd used it to tether herself to the ship.

"I would give a great deal to know what it says," Cornelia replied. "Particularly since if Theodora had had her wish, you'd be carrion by now."

"Even so, bearers of imperial letters with broken seals are seldom received in a friendly manner."

Cornelia scowled. "It might be best if we don't arrive at our destination at all. For all you know, that letter instructs the man Melios to have you killed on the spot. You have to admit it would be perfectly in keeping with Justinian's notion of a jest, sending you half way across the world to meet your end in some Egyptian backwater!"

There were creases around Cornelia's eyes now, but the fire that flared up in them was as hot as it had been years before, when John first knew her. "Yet if Egypt holds the end, remember it also saw the beginning!" he said.

They had met in Egypt under unlikely circumstances. John was Greek, Cornelia a native of Crete. As a young man, John had run off from Plato's Academy to see the world and subsequently become a mercenary, while Cornelia had abandoned her home to take ship with a traveling troupe.

Both had eagerly thrown away the settled lives awaiting them. They had had that in common when their paths crossed.

Thieves and cutthroats, pirates and kidnappers for the slave trade stalked roads and seaways. The band of performers and musicians to which Cornelia belonged had use for a man whose talents lay with the sword, so John joined the troupe and stayed at Cornelia's side.

Cornelia's displeasure seemed to vanish as swiftly as morning mist on the Bosporos. "It was a long time ago, wasn't it?" Her tone was wistful.

John smiled at her. "Indeed it was, Britomartis."

Her hand went to her eyes, as if to wipe away sea spray. "The Lady of the Nets. Who but you would've chosen such a name? Not my little thrush or sweet cake."

"I could never quite think of you as a little thrush."

"And you always remembered me?"

"Of course I did."

He did not add that he had tried to forget, during hundreds of nights, over all the years after he had strayed into enemy territory and his Persian captors had robbed him of his future. Reduced to slavery, he managed to catch the emperor's eye, win his freedom, and rise to a position of power.

Years after his forced abandonment of her, he and Cornelia met again, unexpectedly and briefly. Then he had sent her and his daughter away. The capital was a dangerous place, particularly for the family of a Lord Chamberlain.

He had never expected to see them again, but seven years later, they returned. He had not had time to send them away again before exactly what he feared had happened. Thomas, that supposed knight from Bretania, had become entangled in some sort of trouble and dragged John's whole family into it with him.

Annoyed, Cornelia tapped her fingers on the rail. "What is this you tell me about sheep killing themselves? What explanation can there be for something that must be nothing but a traveler's tale? What do dead animals have to do with a murdered senator?"

"I don't know if there's a connection."

John was being truthful. His investigations into amorphous rumors of a plot connected with Egypt had uncovered nothing. The only suspicious behavior he'd noticed belonged to Thomas, who seemed unusually thoughtful, and more guarded in his speech than usual. Then too Thomas had made more than one foray at an odd hour on what struck John as flimsy pretexts.

Finally John had followed him. He did not know what he expected, but it was certainly not to find Thomas standing over the body of a prominent senator.

"Besides, why should you be serving Justinian when he's just exiled you?" Cornelia went on.

"There's more to the situation than it appears," he told her. "The emperor could have sent someone from Alexandria to inquire about the livestock, but the fact is that he has discovered there is something of great value in the settlement, something connected with the matter I've been investigating. The problem is that to gain an advantage, he must keep his knowledge of the existence of the plot secret. Unfortunately Justinian, or rather his informant, doesn't know exactly what this valuable item might be. In a word, while I know nothing about what it is I am seeking, I have not been exiled. Which is not to say it may not be my lot if I fail to accomplish what I have been ordered to do."

She peered at him as if she might be able to see his thoughts if she stared hard enough. "So your exile is nothing but a story intended to throw smoke in the eyes of...who?"

John hesitated. "Everyone at court. The emperor can't be certain of the identities of those he needs to deceive because he doesn't yet know who might be plotting against him."

"But in that case why were you asking me about Thomas? Is he involved in this plot?"

"I cannot say," John replied, "although he and Europa are involved indirectly. Why do you suppose those really exiled do not need to be accompanied by guards or confined by bars? Because usually they have families who will serve as hostages."

"I see. Well, I hope you'll at least put Peter's fears to rest, not that I feel any better about the situation. I don't trust Justinian, and as for Theodora...."

Cornelia turned to look in the direction of Constantinople. When she spoke again, it was to change the subject. "Nikodemos has been showing me how to make different knots."

She undid the short length of rope looped around her wrist. Frowning in concentration she tied the rope into an intricate knot and displayed her complicated handiwork to John. "It's a sailor's skill I thought might have some entertainment value for those who never venture near the sea."

"And how did you happen to get into conversation with the ship's captain?"

"He's from Crete too, and naturally we got to talking. You'd get along well with him, John, since he's a former military man like yourself. He's given to wagering, I discovered. Not surprising, though, is it? As he observed, every sailor wagers his life on winds and tides."

"True enough," John replied uneasily. So far as he was concerned the knucklebones were rolled the hour he stepped aboard a ship, and kept rolling with the waves until his boots trod dry land again.

"I placed a wager with him myself. It hinged on whether or not he could extricate himself if I were to tie him up."

"Using that knot he showed you? Perhaps it's easily undone despite its elaborate appearance?"

"No. I was to tie him any way I wanted."

John looked thoughtful. "So you've been busy tying up the captain?"

Cornelia laughed. "Indeed! When he mentioned this trick had won him more than a few coins, I thought it would be useful to learn. An incantation or two and the captive is free. It would be most impressive. Magick is always popular."

John smiled to himself. They had only been at sea a few hours and already Cornelia was making plans. "You're thinking you can resume your old career, and Peter and I might join you? If only it could be so! And what happened with Nikodemos?"

"Oh, he escaped without any difficulty!" Cornelia clapped her hands and rocked backwards on her precarious perch. "I lost the wager, but it was a small price to pay for learning the trick."

"He explained how it was done?" John's mouth went dry as a large swell caused the ship to lurch and Cornelia with it.

"After I told him I wanted to use it for an act to be called the Nikodemos Mystery Escape. He was flattered, you see, when I explained the idea would be he was captured by pirates...."

The deck creaked as the *Minotaur* lurched abruptly. Cornelia gave a cry and began to topple backwards.

John leapt forward and grabbed her. Suddenly her weight was pressed against him. He staggered backwards, arms around her.

His heart was in his throat. "You almost fell into the sea," he managed to say.

She smiled up at him. "When you ride bulls you learn how to fall in whatever direction you wish, just as when you travel with a troupe, you learn to make a home wherever you find yourself."

Chapter Six

Anatolius lit the terra-cotta lamp on the table by the door of John's study. The flame illuminated what the gathering twilight beyond the diamond-paned windows did not. The room was sparsely furnished. A table, a scattering of three-legged stools, a desk, all guarded by a solemn-eyed little girl John called Zoe, who now glowered at him from her wall mosaic.

"Sorry to barge in when John's away," Anatolius said to the mosaic girl. "I suppose I'll end up talking to you myself if I stay in this house long enough. In fact, as you see, I already am."

He felt like a snail in a strange shell. He told himself to make a note of the image, then remembered he no longer wrote poetry.

The odor of burnt verse haunted the air.

Lighting lamps was a task for John's servants. Unfortunately, Peter had left with his master and Hypatia was assisting at Samsun's hospice, which was still overwhelmed by plague victims. The only person left in the house besides Anatolius was Europa. She had taken to her room as soon as her mother and Peter had left, according to Hypatia. If she had emerged during the day, Anatolius hadn't seen her.

He was aware of Zoe staring at him. The shifting firelight brought her glass eyes to life.

"Have you seen her, Zoe?"

"Nooooo…." came the whispered reply.

Anatolius stepped back in a panic.

From behind him came a deep, muffled laugh.

He spun around. His hand went to the blade concealed in his robes. Not that the puny weapon would have been any protection, he immediately realized. The figure filling the doorway held an upraised sword. The intruder had his free hand half buried in a bristling red beard, pressed over his mouth to stifle a laugh.

It was Thomas, who glanced back over his shoulder, trod into the room, and sat down.

Anatolius began to speak.

Thomas shook his head. "Let's not wake anyone. I'm afraid I'm in desperate trouble, Anatolius."

"That explains why you couldn't keep yourself from laughing out loud just now."

Thomas grimaced. "I couldn't help it. If you'd seen yourself, gaping at that mosaic like it was a demon come to life. Surely you've laughed on the bloody field of battle, even though it's strewn with the limbs of your dead comrades?"

"Actually, I haven't," Anatolius replied. And neither have you, he thought. He didn't believe Thomas' endless battlefield stories any more than he believed it when the Briton claimed to be a knight.

"What are you talking about?"

"John. Is he terribly angry at me?"

"He isn't here." In a furious undertone, Anatolius related all that had happened in Thomas' absence. "So John has been exiled," he concluded, "and Peter and Cornelia followed him. I expect we'll never see them again."

Thomas' face had gone as white as bone and suddenly his big shoulders shook. He drew in a great, sobbing breath, as if to steady himself before speaking.

"For one thing, John didn't kill the senator," he said. "I was at the Hippodrome and can swear an oath he's innocent."

"You were there?"

"Yes. And no, before you ask, I didn't murder the senator either."

"I don't think you're a murderer, Thomas. A naive fool, yes."

"I appreciate your confidence. I'll knock you down for the insult another day."

"What happened, Thomas?"

"I had some business at the Hippodrome. When I got there the senator was already dead, or at least it looked to be the case. I was just bending down to be certain when John appeared out of nowhere and pushed me aside. 'Go' he said. 'Run.' I took his advice and just as he raced off in the other direction, Felix and his excubitors appeared. "

"Then what?"

"As it was getting dark, I continued on to Isis' establishment and—"

"You went to work?"

Thomas shifted on his stool. "I had to, didn't I? I owe Isis money to repay that loan she gave me. And I'm trying to save as much as I can so that Europa and I can—"

"But you left John in the Hippodrome with a corpse and excubitors pouring in! How do you think it must have looked?"

"Well, you can hardly go out the door without stumbling over a dead body right now," Thomas pointed out. "Besides, John is well thought of by Justinian, so I thought he'd have no difficulty persuading the emperor that neither of us had anything to do with it."

"If you'd shown your face here after your work was over, you'd have found out a lot sooner that the situation is much graver than you could possibly think. And where have you been all day anyhow?"

"Oh, here and there."

Anatolius got up and looked out the window. The cobbled square below was deserted. Beyond the barracks at the far edge of the open space, the palace grounds spread out their eclectic collection of administrative buildings, churches, and houses set amid groves, hidden gardens, and ponds. With the coming of night windows here and there glowed like jewels under a gray sky, which further out blended with the dark waters of the Sea of Marmara.

He felt an almost uncontrollable urge to throttle Thomas, even though the fool would have no trouble killing him if he tried. "What was it that took you to the Hippodrome?"

Thomas reached into his tunic and drew out a small item he kept clasped in his fist. "It was like this, Anatolius. A business opportunity presented itself and I leapt at it quicker than a beggar after a dropped loaf. It was something to do with relics. As you know, I'm an expert on the subject—before I came here I made a living seeking the Holy Grail. I sent a message offering my services to the senator. Being a cautious man, he insisted on my dealing with an intermediary."

"Very sensible of him."

"I didn't know the person I'd be meeting, so I didn't expect to see the senator, and certainly not his cadaver. And a very fresh one at that."

Thomas opened his fist to reveal a piece of yellow enameled metal as long as his finger, formed in the shape of a T.

"This was given to me to take to the meeting. It's a cross, as you see, but the figure of the Christian god's son has been snapped off, along with the top. The fellow I was meeting was supposed to have the matching part."

Anatolius held the artifact up and squinted at it in the fitful lamplight. He could see the enamel was chipped at the top and that another chip, toward the base, marked where the feet of the crucified man would have been attached.

Thomas looked expectantly at Anatolius. "Do you think this will help find out who killed the senator?"

"It might if John were here." Anatolius handed it back to him. "Since he isn't, you'd better stay somewhere else for a while. Somewhere no one would expect to find you. If the senator was as freshly killed as you say, it's possible whoever murdered him was still nearby. If so, he might well decide to silence you in case you witnessed the crime."

"But what will Isis say when I don't show up for—"

The clatter of footsteps on the stairs interrupted them.

A figure burst into the room. Thomas dove for the doorway, smashed into the intruder, and pinned him to the wall, sword to his throat.

"By Jupiter's balls, Anatolius!" croaked Francio. "I was going to chide you for leaving the door unlocked again, but now I see why you don't bother, with guards like this."

Thomas stepped back with an oath.

"He isn't a guard, he's a friend," Anatolius said.

Francio looked dubious. "This ruffian?"

"Thomas is a member of John's household."

"Truly? There must be a fascinating story there. However, I've come to drag you away to dine. Nothing goes better with a good meal than sparkling conversation. I'll supply the meal, you supply the conversation. Bring your impolite colleague along too. Perhaps some good wine will sweeten his tongue."

"Francio, I'm sorry. I can't accept your kind invitation tonight." Anatolius paused and then smiled. "Thomas, however, is free. And you're correct. He has many fascinating stories to tell."

Francio gaped at Anatolius for a heartbeat before looking toward Thomas with an expression akin to horror.

Chapter Seven

"Master, it's the end of the world!"

John came awake at the sound of Peter's voice. It was still dark. For an instant he wondered why his bed was rocking.

Earthquake, he thought, and then remembered he had gone to sleep, as he had each night for the past week, wrapped in a cloak, huddled on the deck of the *Minotaur*.

"Hurry, master! Look!" Peter pointed at the horizon.

John climbed to his feet and squinted in the direction indicated by the servant's trembling finger. A bright glow lay along the waterline.

"The Lord's sun is behind us!" Peter cried, horror written on his face. "Another sun is rising!"

John smiled to himself. Peter's view of the world was somewhat more apocalyptic than one might expect of an elderly army cook. "That's the lighthouse in Alexandria."

Peter stared at him. "We're nearly there? The waters are treacherous? To think we've come all this way, only to run the risk of being drowned!"

"We'll be safely in the harbor before you know it."

Peter nodded, but didn't look convinced.

***

The heavenly sun had fully risen by the time the *Minotaur* came within sight of the source of its man-made twin. Peter, convinced that his prayers for their salvation from wreck had been answered, chattered excitedly to Cornelia.

"The lighthouse is impressive, mistress, but what could have possessed the builders to give it such a strange shape? A square base beneath that tier with so many sides and a cylindrical tower at the top? It looks like the Tower of Babel!"

"Perhaps the architects got into an argument about what form it should take and to satisfy everyone used all their suggestions? A compromise in stone?"

"I never expected such a sight!" Peter went on. "It may be we'll see the pyramids as well." He shaded his eyes and peered upwards. "There's a statue on the lighthouse roof! Whose could it be? How do they get fuel all the way up there? It must take a great deal to keep a fire going every night."

The nearer they drew to the harbor the faster flowed Peter's words. "I wonder if the people looking after the fire ever cook their supper on it? The master says there's an enormous bronze mirror reflects the firelight out to sea."

Cornelia laughed, then a cloud seemed to pass over her features, and she squeezed her eyes shut. When she opened them they glistened. She did not tell Peter his endless stream of questions reminded her of Europa when her daughter had been a child.

Doubtless inspired by thoughts of cooking suppers, Peter was now prattling about finding fish for their evening meal.

Cornelia watched the shore advance towards them.

It had changed little since she first visited Egypt, and how many years ago had that been? Flat, unbroken, and mostly featureless, the demarcation between land and water was obscured in a roiling heat haze. A few obelisks poked up from among nondescript rooftops. The obelisks appeared to bend and twist in the heat, as if they were being melted.

As the *Minotaur* slid past the lighthouse, between the break-waters, and into the harbor, Cornelia wondered whether she were dreaming. The bright, wavering scene reminded her of a reflection on water. If she put her hand out, it would all dissolve in ripples and she would wake.

She directed her gaze toward the crystal-clear waters of the harbor. A lion with the head of a man swam through the depths and vanished under the hull. Then she was looking down on a street lined with pink granite columns. There were monuments too. She drifted above the city like a bird. She let out a gasp of astonishment.

A startled Peter cut short his ramblings on the possibility of finding nets to catch fresh fish. "Mistress? Are you ill? It's this dreadful heat! Should you not sit down?"

The servant's voice brought her back to reality. She remembered the sunken grounds of the ancient palace, the result of the endless series of earthquakes Alexandria had suffered. She pointed this new, exotic sight out to Peter, who was almost as delighted as he had been by the lighthouse.

Within the hour, the crew was tying the *Minotaur* to a dock swarming with raucous humanity. Even then, Cornelia could not quite banish the feeling of unreality, that she had one foot in the present and the other in the past.

***

While the ship was being secured John was accosted by Nikodemos. The ship's captain was a powerfully built man with skin sunburnt so dark he resembled a bronze bust of an emperor.

"Lord Chamberlain, my instructions were to transport you to Alexandria and so my business is now complete." He gave a slight bow. "Let me add that I've never before carried a passenger by command of the emperor. It has been an honor."

"The emperor is not one to waste time when important matters are concerned."

"True, sir." Nikodemos regarded John with a keen gaze and abruptly changed the subject. "You'll find this is a fascinating country. The old ways linger and not just in heathen outposts. I've heard there are still many in Egypt who worship the sun god of old. Some have said to me that such heretics deserve nothing more than immediate execution and being left out in the open so ravens can dine on their eyes."

John was silent.

"Such vengeful talk must make the patriarch and his bishops become heaven's runners," Nikodemos pressed on, "racing to their churches to pray for the souls of both sinner and sinned against."

John noted the slight emphasis Nikodemos had placed on certain words.

Sun god. Raven. Heaven's runners.

All of them connected with his own god, Mithra, the Lord of Light whose cult was popular with military men and former military men such as John.

Cornelia had mentioned Captain Nikodemos was also one such.

"I wouldn't want to be a runner in this sun," John replied. "Rather I'd seek shelter underground."

Nikodemos looked relieved. "It's true then. You are a follower too."

"How did you know?"

"I overheard the big bear of an excubitor who escorted you on board mention Mithra."

Someone called the captain's name.

Nikodemos grunted. "Must be trouble or else they wouldn't be looking for me."

"Perhaps they need you to knot the ropes."

Nikodemos allowed himself a slight smile. "I'm sorry we can't talk longer. I ask no questions, you understand, but in any event I've given back your servant his fare and that of your wife."

"There was no—"

"Since they were required to pay their own way, I suspect you'll need the coins. Don't worry, if I see you again you can repay me. Just ask anyone at the docks for Nikodemos. I'm well known here. And please, give my best regards to your charming and talented wife."

He turned and started toward the bow, then paused. "You will find Mithra is no further from you in this land than He is in Constantinople."

John smiled wanly. If only that were true of his friends and family as well.

Chapter Eight

"No, the emperor has not answered my request for an audience," Anatolius told Hypatia. A week had passed since John's departure, and Anatolius had begun to think he might as well have been sent off to Egypt himself. "I've become remarkably unwelcome at the palace."

Hypatia had placed his frugal breakfast on the scarred wooden table in John's kitchen. Now she lingered near the brazier as if awaiting further orders, but really, Anatolius thought, to press him about his efforts on John's behalf.

He took a bite of his bread. It was stale. The cheese would not be much better. He ate the same thing every day. John's storerooms contained little else except the horrid Egyptian wine the Lord Chamberlain favored.

Hypatia spent her time tending to the sick in the hospice rather than visiting the markets Peter had frequented. Anatolius did not feel he had the authority to order her to do otherwise, even if the markets were still being held in the city. He wasn't her employer. He was uncomfortably aware he was merely a guest in the house—and an uninvited guest at that.

He wondered what sort of elaborate repasts Thomas was enjoying now he had arranged to stay temporarily with Francio.

"Couldn't you by any chance try to see Justinian again?" Hypatia persisted. "You've been his secretary for years. He knows you well, sir. Surely he would agree to give you an audience?"

"Justinian can be very congenial, Hypatia, but imagining that confers privileges can be a fatal mistake. After a request is refused, the wise man waits a while to make it again."

"What about Captain Felix?" Hypatia's jaw clenched, accentuating sculpted cheekbones in a tawny face framed by hair the color of a raven's wing. "Surely there must be someone who can help."

Anatolius sighed inwardly. Few things cut him as deeply as the disapproval of an attractive woman. "Felix agreed to look into the senator's murder when I asked him to give a hand, but I haven't heard anything yet."

Hypatia pursed her lips in annoyance. "I could make a charm, sir, one that will make the emperor agree to talk to you. Something of the sort used attract the beloved, but not exactly the same. A slightly different combination of herbs."

Anatolius smiled. "Hypatia, how can I persuade Justinian to drink a potion? And if I'm supposed to imbibe it, well, I don't think I'd care to have the emperor pining for me. Especially considering he's married to Theodora."

Hypatia filled Anatolius' wine cup and set the jug back down on the table with a loud thump, her thoughts plainly written on her face.

Anatolius resolved to caution John about treating his servants with too much familiarity, if indeed he ever saw John again.

"Have you seen Europa this morning?" he asked, changing the subject.

"She intends to remain in her room, sir, as she doesn't want to be disturbed."

"You'd think I was the one who'd sent them all away!" Anatolius blurted in exasperation.

Anatolius had glimpsed Europa only once since his arrival. She had been walking at the far end of the garden, silent as a shade, finally to vanish into the far side of the building.

"I see." He tore another chunk from his bread, chewed, and swallowed.

Thomas, he thought. Though it seemed everyone else did not wish to talk to him, Thomas would surely be happy to do so.

***

Francio's servant refilled Anatolius' cup.

"You'd think the Lord Chamberlain didn't keep a single jug of wine in his house, the way you're putting that down," Francio observed. "Feel free to have as much as you like. Perhaps it will bring you back to your senses, inspire your muse, and banish these gloomy legal pretenses."

Francio, Anatolius, and Thomas sat at one end of the polished marble table in Francio's dining room. The garden beyond seemed to extend inside through opened doors onto walls lushly decorated with coiling vines, exotic flowers, fruits, beasts, and birds, some recognizable—bears, swans, peacocks—and others whose native land lay only in the artist's imagination. They could never grace Francio's plate.

Their riot of colors was repeated in Francio's short, blue dalmatic with green trim over a long yellow tunic, the ensemble set off by green boots.

Anatolius took another gulp. "I'm trying to wash away the taste of John's fine stock."

Francio laughed. "I'd forgotten. A lover of wine might say your friend is as abstemious as Justinian. The poor stuff John prefers for his cup isn't worth drinking."

"The wines of my native land are far superior," put in Thomas.

"I didn't know there were vineyards in Bretania," said Francio with interest.

Thomas looked askance. "You haven't heard of them? I am amazed their fame has not traveled this far!"

"What splendid tales this fellow tells," Francio remarked to Anatolius. "A veritable rustic Homer! I'm considering abandoning Trimalchio's feast for a banquet based on the sort of meals eaten in this court Thomas has described to me."

He frowned. "We shouldn't be so jovial, considering the Lord Chamberlain's predicament," he went on. "However, as things stand the further away from Constantinople he is, the less danger he's in, except perhaps for running the risk of dying of boredom so far from beauty and culture."

Servants padded in and out the room so quietly and inconspicuously that the bowls they brought might have appeared before the diners by magick.

To Anatolius the salad seemed bitter. Its greens bore a suspicious resemblance to the broad-leafed weeds that proliferated in the neglected gardens near the palace administrative offices. He didn't know their names. No doubt Hypatia could identify them immediately. Perhaps he would ask her.

Francio announced the main course. "I'd hoped to serve lobster, but my supplier ran afoul of the authorities. Instead, we have a special treat. It's what I call Harbor Chicken in Poseidon's Special Sauce."

He signaled to an attendant, who removed the salad and set heaped plates before the diners.

Anatolius contemplated his meal. It resembled a coin pouch swimming in pungent sauce.

"It's boiled gull," he accused.

"Well, if you must be so crude...." Francio was hurt. "Do you know how hard it is to keep a respectable table these days?"

Indeed it was, Anatolius thought, when a self-confessed epicure offered his guests noxious weeds and seabirds drowned in garum sauce.

Thomas attacked the repast with gusto.

"You and Thomas appear to be getting along well," Anatolius ventured.

"I feel fortunate to have him as a guest. He's already given me several banquets' worth of excellent anecdotes. You know how it is at court, a good story can be more valuable than gold. My servant Vedrix is getting jealous." Francio inclined his head toward the young wine server stationed at the door and added in a whisper, "He thinks Thomas is competing with him for my affections."

Anatolius glanced at the servant. He was a dark, sturdy, sullen fellow outfitted in classical style, resembling a young man who had stepped out from the painting on an ancient Greek vase.

Thomas dropped his heavy silver knife and wiped his rust-colored beard with the back of his hand.

Anatolius decided it was time to question Thomas again. "Could we speak in confidence? Could Vedrix leave the room?"

Francio instructed the man to do so and then turned to Anatolius. "My servants are very discreet, but I always humor my guests. Well-known for it, in fact. What did you want to discuss?"

"Thomas has of course explained why he requested temporary lodgings with you?"

"Oh, yes, and it's all very exciting! However, he hasn't revealed how it came to be that he found himself in the Hippodrome at that particular time."

"That's what I'd like you to clarify, Thomas."

"It's as I told you a few days ago, Anatolius. I heard about an employment opportunity while I was guarding Isis' door."

Fidgeting like an impatient child, Thomas recounted how he had overheard a loose-tongued servant bragging to one of the girls at Isis' establishment about his master's plans to surreptitiously obtain a fabulous relic that would astound the city.

"I've never heard such braggarts as I've heard in that place," Thomas concluded.

"Who was this servant?" asked Anatolius.

"Isis won't allow the names of any of her guests to be bandied about. He was a young man, but completely bald. He and Antonina were standing in the corridor and she kept rubbing his head. For good luck, or so she said," Thomas sniggered.

"You doubtless hear a lot of fascinating stories at your work. It must be like having a vast library of human experience at your fingertips." Francio sounded wistful.

Thomas nodded. "Standing by the door all night, unless a brawl breaks out there's not much to do but listen. My ears pricked up when I heard mention of a relic. As I've told you, I'm somewhat of an expert there."

At Anatolius' prodding, and despite numerous interruptions from Francio, Thomas recounted how Antonina had finally been persuaded, although still refusing to provide a name, to identify her customer as belonging to Senator Symacchus' household. Thus had Thomas found his way to the senator's door.

Anatolius saw clearly what had subsequently happened. "So in short, you offered to sell the senator your services in obtaining this relic, not to mention keeping your mouth shut about it afterwards? From the senator's viewpoint, it was as much a threat as an offer!"

Thomas scowled. "I thought it was a very reasonable one, and so did the senator. However, as I said, he was cautious. That's why I was given a certain little item I showed you a few days ago."

"Take his word for it, Anatolius," said Francio. "The man's memory is perfect. He can describe to you every bit of armor worn by every foe he's killed."

"And probably each man's eye color as well. It's time I returned to John's house. Francio, are you taking all the precautions I advised?"

"I think I can see my house is properly guarded."

"Thomas, keep trying to remember anything that might be useful. If you recall something, Francio will get word to me. You must remain hidden for now."

"How is Europa?" Thomas asked.

"Well enough." Anatolius didn't mention he had not spoken to her. He turned to Francio. "Thanks for your assistance. I count it a great favor."

Francio spooned the remaining sauce off his plate. "As Publilius Syrus put it," he replied with a grin, "treat friends as if they may one day be enemies."

Anatolius looked surprised.

"Not you. It's what's on my spoon." Francio flourished the silver utensil. "I commissioned a set of them, to be decorated with various quotations. It's to stimulate dinner conversation, should it lag."

"Are they all taken from Publilius Syrus?" Anatolius wondered.

"Yes. Originally I engaged a court poet for the job. One Crinagoras. Do you know him? Unfortunately, to accommodate the length of his verse my guests would have been forced to eat with spears."

Anatolius chuckled. "Thank you again, my friend." He picked up his own spoon and read its lettering. "I am advised that accepting favors sells my freedom. It's all very puzzling. I suppose I should try to talk to Felix next. I feel quite lost."

Chapter Nine

Peter trudged through the network of alleyways behind the harbor in Alexandria, clutching his satchel to his chest. He had crept out of the hostelry before dawn. Now the sun beat down on his uncovered head. The sparse gray hair covering his scalp felt hot to the touch. The master and mistress would have missed him hours ago, though he had planned to accomplish his mission before they realized he was gone. Now, no doubt, they would be worrying about him.

Peter had not loosened his protective grip on his satchel all morning. The bag contained silks he had packed before their hasty departure. There had been no time to prepare properly for the journey, but silks could be folded small, were light, and, being of great value, were easily converted to coins. It had been kind of Nikodemos to return the boat fare, but judging from the cost of their first night's lodgings in Alexandria, the sum regained would not be nearly enough to cover their needs.

Unfortunately, he had not been able to find any establishments dealing in fine fabrics. Perhaps that was not surprising so close to the docks. Nonetheless he was amazed he had not, at least, run across a brothel whose employees and patrons might be interested in his wares. Or so he supposed. Now elderly as well as devout, Peter's experience of brothels and their inhabitants was some years behind him.

Aside, that is, from infrequent exchanges with John's old friend Madam Isis, who occasionally visited John to chat about former times. She, like John, had once lived in Alexandria, or so she claimed. Surely Isis would know where to find a brothel in this city even after being away from it so many years?

She might have lived near the docks, he thought, might even have purchased items from the now old men he saw everywhere, squatting beside their merchandise.

Their stock in trade was mainly edible, even if barely so in some cases—sticky dates and figs encrusted with dust, pungent onions marred by an occasional rotten patch, cucumbers displaying small fuzzy patches of gray mold, and cabbages wilting from the heat.

Peter emerged into sunlight and crossed a busy square. Brightly clad men, hawk-nosed and wavy-haired, squabbled over bunches of leeks and radishes and baskets of coriander. Half-naked children teased thin, scavenging mongrels. Swirling clouds of droning, fat, black flies hovered over everything, crawled on the face of an infant held in its mother's arms, tracked across slices of melon oozing sweet liquid. The air smelled of rotted and fermenting fruit. The scene might have been just off the Mese in Constantinople, except for the throngs of long-legged ibis strutting about, hopefully sticking their curved beaks into piles of debris littering the gutters.

Peter slumped against a brick wall and made the sign of his religion. He bent his head and closed his eyes.

"Please, Lord," he murmured under his breath. "Show me a merchant, or a brothel, or even a prostitute. Someone who will purchase these silks."

When he raised his head he found he was gazing toward a cul-de-sac leading from the opposite corner of the square.

Upon investigation he found his prayer had been answered. This particular narrow thoroughfare boasted a number of emporiums selling wares different from any he had seen thus far. Here was a candlemaker, its neighbor a silversmith.

The next establishment, little more than a cubbyhole open to the street with a counter in front and shelves lining its back walls, caught Peter's interest because of the variety of its dusty goods. Colored glass bottles, statuettes, medallions, and tiny, stoppered, clay flasks jostled for space.

The shopkeeper, a big man in a voluminous red and white striped robe, accosted Peter in Coptic.

When Peter replied in Greek, the shopkeeper responded in Greek of a sort. "Remember good. Yes?"

The man grabbed a green bottle from his stock and held it out to Peter, who saw it was engraved with a picture of the lighthouse as he had seen from the *Minotaur* the day before.

"Pharos? Yes! Remember good! Yes?" The shopkeeper grinned, showing big teeth akin to granite blocks.

Peter shook his head and tapped his satchel.

The shopkeeper displayed one of the crude clay flasks, no bigger than his thumb. "Holy oil! Yes? Remember good! Yes?"

Peter would have liked to buy a souvenir for the master, something featuring a pyramid. Under the circumstances he couldn't part with so much as a nummus. He shook his head and showed the man the silks.

When the shopkeeper understood the type of transaction Peter sought, his smile vanished. He pointed toward the end of the alley. "Pedibastet," he said and turned away.

Pedibastet's establishment was one of the most curious Peter had ever encountered. Not even in Constantinople had he seen a shop selling cat mummies.

Pedibastet sat on his haunches in front of his place of business. He was a swarthy man with an elongated face. His tunic was black, and his hair shone like ebony. On the ground before him lay his wares, feline corpses whose bodies were concealed in grubby wrappings reaching to their necks. Peter couldn't help thinking of Anubis, guarding the dead.

The purveyor of cat mummies stood up, bowed, and introduced himself. "I can tell you have journeyed from afar. I bid
you welcome. Would you care for refreshment?" His Greek was
not the best, but compared to the seller of souvenirs he might
have been an orator.

"Refreshment?" Having endured the sun beating on his head
like a hammer for hours, Peter was tempted by the prospect of
a sip of wine.

Pedibastet motioned toward his shadowy doorway. A stout
youngster, also garbed in black, darted out with a brimming cup
which he pressed into Peter's free hand before vanishing back
into the darkness.

"You will surely honor me by accepting my humble hospitality," Pedibastet smiled. "After you have drunk my poor wine may
I draw to your attention my offerings? Expensive they may be,
I admit, but few in Alexandria have such wonderful samples of
increasingly rare items, reminders of a time so ancient that not
even the oldest of the old can recall it. In short...."

A sweep of his hand took in all of Egyptian history and his
stock of recumbent felines equally. "I have for sale," he went on,
"having obtained them at great expense and not a little danger, I
may add, authentic mummies of the animal sacred to the great
goddess Bast."

Peter looked at the small, log-like bundles topped by shriveled
feline heads resembling large, whiskered raisins. Here and there
tufts of fur protruded untidily between the wrappings.

"Well...." His tone was doubtful. "I am not certain what
purpose the mummy of a cat would serve in my master's household."

The man waved his hand again. "You are obviously newly
arrived in Egypt, my friend. Have you never heard of the luck
of Bast? Your master is wealthy?"

Peter agreed that was the case. He didn't mention that the
only wealth currently at his master's disposal was in Peter's possession.

"In that case, your master would most certainly be interested in one of my little friends. An interesting and unusual memento of his visit, and of course the ladies do love the dear little things. Think how delighted he would be to display such treasures, timeless reminders of his journey to Egypt. Why, I would even lower my price for one such as he, for I am certain he is a man of culture, of great taste. See, already the luck of Bast is working for him! Take this beauty, for example."

He picked up a bundle that looked much like the rest, Peter thought. Indeed if anything it was somewhat more soiled than the others.

Glancing around and lowering his voice as if he feared their conversation might be overheard, Pedibastet went on. "This cat came from the garden of the temple to the goddess of love. The temple lies in ruins now, but descendants of the sacred cats live there still. There are those who feed them, since not every trace of the old religions are gone. I mention this as I can see you are a man of the world, and can draw your own conclusions."

Pedibastet looked around again. "I would not tell this to anyone," he continued, "but your face is that of a man who can be trusted. I have a few temple cats living with me, so devoted am I to their welfare. Would you care to see them?"

Intrigued, Peter indicated he would.

Pedibastet gestured him inside his cavern-like shop. It was odd, Peter thought as he entered, that the man would leave his priceless stock outside unguarded for anyone to steal.

Perhaps the local populace was not interested in such antiquities.

The interior was eye-wateringly pungent and, once his eyesight had adjusted to the gloom, Peter saw it was sparsely stocked. One or two boxes turned upside down displayed small wooden statues, roughly carved and painted, and a few pottery pieces. Every item offered for sale depicted cats.

One or two live specimens were also in evidence, washing their faces. A small brown cat watched from a corner, while a portly black feline sitting by the half-open back door observed the men with disdainful eyes as they passed by on their way to the garden behind the shop. The green and shady place Peter had expected to see turned out to be little more than a walled expanse of dirt where more cats slept or sunned themselves.

Within a few steps, Peter discovered that while a garden of plain dirt was not aesthetically pleasing it was, however, very convenient for the relief of cats.

"I thank you for your hospitality," Peter said after glancing around. "However, I have something I would like to sell you. The merchant down the street seemed to think you might be interested."

Pedibastet's mask of affability dropped as swiftly as a eagle plummeting down on its prey. "You are not here to buy one of my wonderful mummies?"

Peter apologized. "I regret I seem to have misled you."

Pedibastet gazed thoughtfully at Peter's satchel. "But your master is rich?"

"He is, sir."

"Then why would he want to sell me anything?"

"He doesn't know. If he did, he would be displeased."

Pedibastet did not seem deterred by the admission. "Do you think he might be interested in my humble offerings?"

"My master is interested in many strange matters."

Pedibastet pondered briefly and then smiled. "I'm a little short of funds today. People speak ill of Egyptian bankers, and…well, I'm certain you don't want the details. Suffice it to say, doing business in Alexandria is different than doing it in other great cities. As a gesture of good will, however, which you can repay by bringing your master to my shop tomorrow, I will purchase your wares for a small sum, provided you add a service to them."

"A service?"

"You will need to be nimble. Can you run very fast? But no…." Pedibastet paused for a heartbeat. "At least you could try. My assistant broke his leg and the boy Rameses is busy wrapping one or two new arrivals more securely."

"How do you expect me to obtain more silks? And what does being nimble have to do with it?"

"Silks?" Pedibastet's long face dropped.

Peter opened his satchel to reveal its contents.

"Not a cat?"

Peter looked at the seller of cat mummies in horror. "You thought I was trying to sell you the master's cat? That's what you expected me to catch? Cats? But why? You have so many already. Surely you don't mean—"

"I breed cats." Pedibastet's tone was soothing. "What did you think? There are many cat lovers in Egypt. Now, as to your master's visit—"

"Are you certain your real business is not ransoming cats?"

Pedibastet looked dumbfounded. The idea had never occurred to him although, he admitted to himself, it was definitely one to be pursued as soon as possible.

"There must be no one but fools left in Constantinople for anyone to have hired you as a servant!" he replied in exasperation. "My business is manufacturing cat mummies to sell to foreign visitors. Please leave immediately. You've wasted enough of my time!"

Peter crept out of the shop past the preserved remains of Pedibastet's pathetic victims. As he crossed the bustling square again, he noticed another promising alleyway.

He would try once more before returning to the hostelry, he decided.

The elderly servant was distraught. In retrospect it was obvious enough what the rogue's trade involved, but what Peter's reason told him, his good nature often didn't want to believe.

The narrow way he entered was populated only by a couple of strolling ibis. Peter navigated carefully around them. He heard the footsteps behind him too late, began to turn, and then the world went black.

Chapter Ten

The captain of the excubitors could not see him.

The clerk relayed the information to Anatolius with a knowing smirk. The message was the same one he'd delivered five days running, but the smirk had grown more pronounced every day.

"I insist I must speak to Captain Felix. It's an important matter and I am the emperor's secretary."

"You mean you were his secretary. The captain is not here. You can try again tomorrow, if you wish."

Anatolius left. The smirk followed him out into the corridor.

Why was Felix being so uncooperative?

He thought back to his last meeting with his friend. He'd asked him how he was faring in the search for Senator Symacchus' murderer.

Felix had appeared uneasy, and finally admitted no official investigation was being undertaken. "Why not? Because Justinian hasn't ordered one. And why should he? John was caught red-handed."

As Anatolius questioned Felix further, it had become apparent John had not told the excubitor captain about Thomas' involvement. If the Lord Chamberlain had chosen to withhold that information, it wasn't for Anatolius to reveal it.

Had Felix somehow sensed Anatolius was not being entirely forthright? Was that why he refused to see him?

Anatolius decided he might be able to catch Felix at home.

He took a shortcut through the palace grounds. As he came around the corner of a pavilion, he was startled to see the man he sought walking swiftly ahead. Although several neglected flower beds and overgrown ornamental shrubs separated the two men, the burly, bearded figure was unmistakable.

Anatolius followed his friend at a distance. Felix did not turn toward the administrative complex where he had his office or down the path that would have taken him home. Instead he went out past the great bronze doors of the Chalke and strode along the Mese, moving rapidly further into the city.

Anatolius hurried along behind. Ordinarily he would have simply hailed Felix, but today he was angry about his friend's seeming avoidance of him as well as curious about the man's destination.

Had Felix been abroad on official business, he would certainly have been accompanied by a couple of his excubitors.

Even more intriguing, however, Felix was wearing a nondescript tunic over the leather leggings of an off-duty soldier, essentially disguising his rank.

Felix turned down a narrow street and vanished inside a tavern. It was a seedy establishment, opposite a public lavatory. The main attraction of the former appeared to be that it was open.

The plague had cured many a drinking problem and put more than a few taverns out of business.

There was no colonnade here. A row of shops opened directly onto the narrow street. All were closed, their wares protected by metal grates pulled down and locked to iron rings in the cobbles. The amount of debris that had accumulated around and behind the grates testified how long the businesses had been shut.

Anatolius eyed the tavern. Beside its door hung a wooden sign cut in the shape of an amphora, but so irregularly made it could well have been created by a carpenter who had imbibed the entire contents of his model.

Feeling foolish, he stuck his head around the tavern door and peered in.

The cramped room was dim. Felix was talking to someone whose back Anatolius did not recognize at a table set against the rear wall.

Why shouldn't Felix meet a friend for a cup of wine?

Even so, given Felix's recent odd behavior, Anatolius was prepared to think the worst. He crossed the street and went under the marble archway into the lavatory. From inside, framed by the arch's bas-reliefs of Greek gods, he could observe the tavern without being noticed.

Or so he hoped.

The smell made him gag. A glance at the state of the floor showed the facility hadn't been cleaned recently—not to mention that he would have to burn his footwear when he returned to John's house. Public services were vanishing even faster than the public. He wasn't surprised the long, communal marble bench boasted only a single customer, seated at the far end. The man, slumped forward, ignored him.

Anatolius fixed his gaze on the tavern and its peeling plaster exterior. Flies droned. Time passed. More flies appeared, adding their complaints to the others clustering around the malodorous facility. He began to think if Zeus turned an ear toward the earth, all that god would hear from the capital would be a buzzing akin to that of a gigantic insect.

The man at the far end of the bench still hadn't moved a muscle. Anatolius now realized he was dead. The morbid notion came to him that urchins had found a corpse in the street and sat it there as a macabre jest.

He almost missed Felix's companion emerging from the tavern. All he could make out was the man's retreating back.

He briefly considered following from sheer curiosity, but it was the captain of excubitors to whom he needed to talk. Thankful to be able to leave his temporary shelter, he went into the murky tavern, and sat down next to Felix who looked up, startled, from his wine cup.

"Something smells…." Felix's gaze moved to Anatolius' feet.

"I plan on burning my boots, Felix, but something else will still offend my nostrils. What have you been doing about helping John? Why have you been avoiding me?"

"You must have followed me here. Is that what a friend does?" Felix sounded hurt. His words were slurred. Anatolius realized his companion was intoxicated.

The portly owner of the establishment waddled toward them. Anatolius put him to flight with a baleful glare that conveyed the clear message: "Observe my elaborate robes. I am from the palace and that means trouble if you interfere!"

"Are you in some sort of difficulty, Felix?"

The captain stared over Anatolius' shoulder for a short time as if considering the question, then slammed his cup down, splashing wine on the scantily clad women dancing lewdly in the fresco beside them.

"That's it, Anatolius!" he roared. "I know what you're going to complain about. You're going to complain that I've taken up gambling again even though it's my business, not yours! Not to mention just a small wager now and then doesn't hurt anyone…."

"I was going to say you're intoxicated—"

"Now there you're totally wrong! Totally! Totally, totally wrong…."

Anatolius decided Felix could not possibly have got so inebriated in the short time he'd been inside the tavern. He must have begun drinking not long after he rolled out of bed.

"Who was that man who just left? Someone you've been placing bets with, I'll wager!"

A huge grin parted Felix's unkempt beard. "You'll wager? You criticize me for betting, but you'll wager?" He started to laugh.

"Proprietor!" he yelled. "Listen to this jest! The gentleman here questions my wagering yet he bets himself! Did you ever hear anything more comical?"

"Yes, I have," replied the man from the other end of the tavern. "Mostly concerning the empress!"

Anatolius waited for the captain's mirth to subside. "Felix, you can't become involved in wagering again. You know you swore you were finished with that years ago."

Felix grunted. "Shows what you know. The man I was speaking to isn't a gambler. He's a horse trainer. How could I wager with the races cancelled thanks to this pestilence? But I am keeping informed. I am an informed man. Very, very informed."

He took another gulp of what remained of his wine. "I know the Greens lost their best horses last week. I wager you didn't know that! That's how informed I am. The owner sold them, you see. Race horses are worth more to butchers than bettors these days."

Anatolius suddenly felt queasy. He couldn't help wondering whether Francio, the universal gourmet, might not have taken the opportunity to sample the flesh of a Hippodrome champion.

"More than one person has remarked to me that fewer people seem to be dying," he replied. "The emperor and empress have returned to the palace, as you know well enough. Would they put themselves in danger if it were not true?"

"Fewer people are dying because there's hardly anyone left to die," Felix pointed out.

It was possibly true, Anatolius thought uneasily. The plague seemed determined to linger until Constantinople was deserted.

"Felix, I know there is no official investigation, but have you found anything out about the murder of Senator Symacchus? Anything to free John of suspicion?"

Felix tugged at his beard. "No. Not a thing. What could there be? John was there when we arrived. I saw him myself. He was standing over the body."

"But he denied killing the senator."

"He didn't deny it when we arrived at the Hippodrome. Took one look at us and ran. It's not like John at all. What in Mithra's name does it all mean? That's what I want to know. It's a puzzle. A puzzling puzzle."

Felix attempted to pick up his partly filled cup and knocked it over. The proprietor lumbered over with a rag almost before the rosy stream hit the straw on the floor. Anatolius' glare forced him away again.

"And why did you happen to be at the Hippodrome with so many men at that specific time, Felix?"

"I've explained already."

"You haven't."

"I haven't?" Felix frowned. He looked genuinely perplexed. "But why was that?"

"Felix, I can't tell you why you didn't tell me. Just tell me now, would you? Why were you there?"

"A fellow came and told me," Felix explained. "Said a senator was being murdered in the Hippodrome."

"A fellow?"

"A man. A stranger. Came into my office. And he was right. I raced over with my men, but Symacchus was already dead."

"Wasn't that a bit unusual?"

"I wouldn't say so. Once the cord was around his neck he didn't have a chance."

"I meant wasn't it unusual for someone to go to your office to report an impending murder? Most people would rush to the nearest barracks, don't you think? Or stop a guard on the street?"

"Perhaps he worked at the palace and naturally thought of the excubitors first?"

Anatolius nodded eagerly. "Good! Now we're on the track of something useful. What makes you say that? Think? Was it the way he dressed? Was the face familiar because you'd passed by him in a hallway or seen him on the palace grounds?"

Felix shook his big head like a petulant child. "I can't say how he was dressed. What do you take me for, one of Theodora's ladies-in-waiting? An expert on sartorial elegance? Yet sometimes I wonder at that, considering the type of tasks Justinian orders me to carry out."

Anatolius stood. It was obvious he wouldn't get anything useful out of Felix in his current state. His immediate problem now was seeing the captain home in one piece. "Come on, Felix."

The dim room darkened further. He noticed the proprietor had blocked the doorway with his considerable girth. He flipped him a coin and the man moved aside.

Felix remained seated. "You go ahead. I need another cup of wine. Or two. Or even more."

Anatolius sighed. Trying to shift the big excubitor from his chair would be like trying to move a boulder with a twig.

"Here's something you'll like, Felix," he said with a grin. "I'll wager you can't get from here to your house without falling into the gutter."

Chapter Eleven

"The next thing I knew I was lying in the alley and...." Peter's voice cracked as he forced the words out. "...The last few coins were gone, master."

The servant hid his anguished face in his hands.

Peter, Cornelia, and John sat in a wide doorway on a street not far from the hostelry where they had spent the night.

The sun had passed its zenith, but heat still lay honey-like upon Alexandria. The city seemed quiet, John thought. Had they already become accustomed to its raucous patchwork of sounds—the rattle of carts, the cries of hawkers, the screams of dusty children who wore amulet necklaces and little else?

John looked at Peter appraisingly. "You're not hurt?"

Peter picked a flat, oval seed from his scanty hair and tossed it into a rut nearby. "Fortunately I fell into a heap of rotten melons."

A brown bird dropped from nowhere and flew off with the discarded seed.

"It was better than I deserved for my carelessness," Peter went on. "I don't think the thief meant to harm me, and he left my satchel. Except...." His voice trailed off again.

"Never mind, Peter. It was an excellent idea to bring silks to sell. Let's see them," Cornelia told him.

With obvious reluctance Peter pulled the satchel open.

The shriveled head of a mummified cat glowered out.

"The thief took them, mistress, and left this as payment. I was going to throw the nasty thing away, but somehow the way it seemed to look at me...."

Cornelia chuckled. "It's adorable, Peter. I won't let you abandon the poor thing. What should I call him? How about Cheops?"

"It's clear who's responsible," John said. "Show me this emporium, Peter. I will resolve the matter with Pedibastet quickly enough."

John began to stand. Cornelia placed a hand on his arm. "This isn't Constantinople, John. You have no authority here."

"I'm certain I can do a good enough impersonation of a high official to frighten Pedibastet into returning Peter's coins!"

"Dressed in those rags?"

John looked down at his threadbare, stained tunic. "You're right. It's a pity I don't have one of my ceremonial robes."

"If you did, we could sell it for more than enough for our boat fare to Mehenopolis," Cornelia said.

The trio fell silent for a time.

"But master, why would the emperor order you to a place on imperial business with no means of getting there?" Peter finally asked.

"A good question," John replied with a thin smile. He did not care to mention that Theodora was responsible for their lack of funds. The change in arrangements ordered by Justinian worried him. It would worry Peter and Cornelia even more.

Cornelia soon spoke sharply. "It seems to me Justinian does not care how you arrive at Mehenopolis. In fact, it's entirely possible he didn't want you to arrive at all."

It was true. Theodora's interference in John's exile had been peculiar. Was it possible she had acted with Justinian's blessing?

John put the thought out of his mind. "More importantly, at this point we have to find our fare to get to Mehenopolis. They always need workers to load wheat on the docks. I can do that."

"Master!" Peter burst out. "The Lord Chamberlain should not be carrying sacks about like a common laborer! I would be—"

"By the Goddess!" Cornelia interrupted. "John, don't you remember how we earned our keep the last time we were in this land?"

"I haven't forgotten. You were part of a bull-leaping act and I helped guard the troupe."

"Not just bull-leaping. Remember there was also a magician called Baba? An engaging rogue, but always a crowd pleaser."

"We don't have a magician with us, mistress," Peter timidly pointed out.

"Baba taught some of his knowledge to the other performers," Cornelia replied. "He said a magick trick is like a coin in the hand. You'd never go hungry with something of the kind to entertain and astonish people. I could teach you and Peter one or two of them."

Peter looked alarmed. "My apologies, mistress, but I am not certain such an act would be a Christian thing for me to do."

"We don't have time to learn magick," John added.

"That's so," Cornelia admitted. "What about a bit of play-acting? We sometimes did that, you'll recall, and you could easily—"

John raised his hand imperiously. "Cornelia, I'm not a performer."

"How can you say that? You take part in all those elaborate processionals to the Great Church and the Hippodrome and other such tedious ceremonies without looking bored. Of course you can act!"

***

"I am Empress Theodora, and I demand you fetch the Lord Chamberlain immediately! There is an extremely delicate problem of great urgency that requires his immediate attention!"

The visibly trembling old man thus addressed bowed obsequiously and scuttled off.

The imperial speaker peered up toward the tip of the obelisk beside which she stood, and slowly stroked the monument's warm sandstone. "I'm glad to see Egypt, and it seems Egypt is glad to see me."

A few onlookers guffawed. Cornelia adjusted her crown, which John had cut from a dried melon rind. Although she spoke Coptic nearly as fluently as John, she had chosen to speak in Greek, realizing that in this part of Alexandria, so near to the docks, most passersby would speak that language.

"Now that I've traveled all the way from Constantinople," she continued, "what would my loyal subjects like to hear about? My charitable works on behalf of former prostitutes? Or would you prefer I relate my theological discussions with the Patriarch?"

"Tell us about the chickens and the grain," someone yelled.

Peter, playing the empress' aged servant, had returned and now held his hand up to the side of his mouth and addressed the growing audience in a loud whisper. "Don't insult the empress by mentioning her past indiscretions! She's a good Christian now, you know."

Then, his orthodoxy offended by the line he had spoken, he added, "Even if she does believe the monophysite heresy that Christ has not two natures, but only one, and that fully divine."

"We all agree with the empress here, old man," retorted one of the now considerably larger crowd.

"And knowing Theodora, if He really had two natures she'd bed them both," offered another.

A flurry of other remarks followed.

"How many bishops has she got hidden in the Hormisdas Palace now?"

"At least she claims they're bishops...."

"I wonder what kind of services they offer her?"

Peter covered his ears in horror.

The shouted demand came again. "Tell us about the chickens and the grain, empress!"

Cornelia stamped her foot. "It's always that wretched matter! Do you really believe that in my youth I would strip off my garments, lie on the ground, and allow chickens to peck grain from my private parts? I don't know what you're talking about!"

Peter stood silently by, until he noticed Cornelia glaring at him. "Ah…" he muttered, "…er…Highness, I just heard the chickens…ah…talking."

"Talking chickens?" Cornelia clapped her hands. "This is truly a miracle! And what did these remarkable fowl say?"

"Dinner's on the empress!"

This brought forth coarse laughs and applause.

"Highness, here is the Lord Chamberlain!"

The crowd began to titter as a tall, thin figure in a tattered tunic approached with obvious reluctance from behind the obelisk.

A few wits continued to add their comments to the performance.

"If that's a Lord Chamberlain I'm a pharaoh."

"What cave did you drag him out of?"

"In Constantinople they starve their Lord Chamberlains and dress them in rags, didn't you know?"

"What is this most urgent problem, highness?" asked John.

"A most intimate matter, Lord Chamberlain. It concerns the emperor's heir. I wish you to arrange for the child to be presented to the court with appropriate ceremony."

"Heir? But surely everyone knows there can be no heir?"

Cornelia gave John an exaggerated scowl. "I do not understand your meaning. Make yourself clearer immediately."

"Highness, everyone knows the emperor is not a man, but a faceless demon and therefore incapable of siring children in the usual fashion."

"True," Cornelia purred, giving the obelisk a tickle, "but I am an unusual woman. Servant, bring the imperial infant here at once."

Peter bowed and presented his satchel to Cornelia. She pulled out a diminutive figure wrapped in what might have been swaddling clothes, but when she held it aloft the withered, whiskered face of Cheops the mummified cat glared reproachfully at the audience.

The first coins landed beside John's boots.

Chapter Twelve

Anatolius stopped halfway up the steep incline. He bent over and stood, staring down at his boots and catching his breath. His destination, the house of Senator Symacchus, sat atop the ridge overlooking the Golden Horn. It was all but invisible from below, hidden by apartment buildings, warehouses, workshops, and bakeries piled in a jumble of brick and mortar along the hillside.

After his heart stopped pounding, Anatolius took a deep inhalation and continued the climb. He cut from one precipitous street to another, navigating by the only part of the senator's dwelling he could see—the monumental rooftop cross that towered above everything else.

Except for this ostentatious declaration of religious belief, the late senator's home turned out to be as modest as many of its neighbors. The unremarkable brick facade offered no clue to the high status of its departed owner.

At Anatolius' rap, the sturdy door opened a crack.

"Can I help you, sir?" A wan face peeped out.

"I've come from the palace on a matter of business."

There was movement behind the narrow gap, a chain rattled, and the door swung open. "If you have an appointment with the senator, I fear he will not be able to see you." The deep voice didn't match the young man's slight frame.

"I'm aware of your master's tragic passing. I'm investigating the matter."

The young man gestured Anatolius into a long, dim vestibule and shut the door. "From the palace, sir? For a heartbeat I was afraid…but never mind. One has to be very careful these days, and of course with the senator so recently departed…."

The servant's boyish face was exceptionally pale and framed by long fair curls. He looked familiar but Anatolius couldn't recall any previous meeting.

"I will be reporting to the captain of the excubitors," Anatolius said, truthfully. "I wish to ask the servants a few questions, in case they can shed light on this recent tragedy. And you are…?"

"My name is Diomedes. As to whether I can help, I will try, but I was merely the senator's reader."

Diomedes led the way into the atrium. The spotless black and white floor echoed similar tiles lining the ornamental pool gracing the airy space. A cross hung on a whitewashed wall, while an alabaster statuette of a crocodile displayed on a pedestal looked strangely at odds with the general impression of stark Christianity.

Light spilled down from the compluvium and through the open entrance to an inner garden, visible beyond an austere office.

The light accentuated the heavy powder on the young man's face. Anatolius now remembered where he'd seen the servant before. It was in the halls of the Great Palace a few years earlier, among the band of similarly made-up and ubiquitous court pages.

Now, however, Diomedes was too old to serve as a decorative object.

"First, I wish to talk to the senator's head servant," Anatolius said.

"Achilles? I fear he is not here."

A faint smell of herbs and flowers filtered into the atrium.

"Then we shall talk in the garden."

Anatolius selected a bench shaded by a stunted fig tree. The location had the benefit of keeping their conversation private as well as allowing it to be conducted out of sight of most of the crosses sprouting from flower beds set around the edge of the green, quiet space.

He indicated they should both sit. "My understanding is that the senator lived alone, apart from his servants?"

Diomedes confirmed this had been the case. "His wife died many years ago. She was Egyptian, and distantly related to the Apions. You may have noticed the household still reflects her influence."

He directed Anatolius' attention to a statue of the jackal-headed god Anubis which squatted in a patch of herbs.

"That explains the crocodile in the atrium," Anatolius observed. "And so the senator had connections by his marriage to a very influential family?"

"Indeed, sir. The master also had extensive holdings here and in Egypt."

"In view of his death, presumably you will be looking for other employment and lodgings?"

"Oh, I shouldn't think so! The senator had no children, but he had an estranged brother, not to mention a half-brother, and a number of more distant relatives. More than a few of them live in Egypt, and doubtless they'll all journey to Constantinople to pay their respects now that he's gone. The Quaestor's office is overseeing the estate until everything is straightened out. They're moving as fast as the law allows. Since the senator's family will be staying here while they visit, and many visits may be necessary, I might well grow gray here."

He brushed a stray curl out of his face. "Not that I care to go gray."

"What was it you read for the senator? Religious works? I understand he was widely known as a devout man."

"He was of the opinion it was one's duty to read the scriptures oneself, sir. To commune directly with the Word, as he described it. No, I read the classics for him. He loved Homer especially, and especially the way I read it. He used to say my voice could bring the dead back to life. If only it were true...."

Anatolius wondered whether master and servant sometimes sat together on this bench for such readings. Sheltered from all sight of the symbol of their faith, it would have been easier to hear the voices of those writers who believed in the old gods. "Can you think of anyone who might have wanted to kill your master? Had he lately quarreled with anyone, for example?"

"Not a soul, sir. For all his wealth and power my master was as upstanding a Christian as any desert hermit. Everyone knew of his charitable works, although he forbade any of us to speak about them. It was not just a question of monetary donations, either. For instance, he often took in court pages who had outgrown their usefulness."

"You were once a page yourself, I believe," Anatolius said.

"Yes, sir, I was. The senator gave many of us work and shelter. Otherwise we would have been on the street when we were turned out after becoming men. He was much-loved."

Anatolius asked the servant for a description of the household.

"I'm the wrong person to ask, sir. While I was his reader, I also helped here and there on occasion, doing weeding or occasional cleaning, that sort of thing. Mostly, however, I spent my time in my room up on the third floor. We readers must constantly practice our orating to gain the full effect when declaiming texts, you see. So I can't tell you much about what went on in the household. Achilles, now, he could have told you everything about everyone."

"When do you expect him back?"

"He won't be returning."

"He's left the city?"

Diomedes made the Christian sign. "No, sir. The truth of the matter is, well, Achilles has been dragged down into the underworld. Yes, demons came and took him away!"

The servant cast a frightened look over his shoulder as if he expected to see fiends lurking in the laurel or sunning themselves in a flower bed.

Dropping his voice to a whisper, he continued. "It was about a week ago now, on the very night the master was murdered. My room is at the front of the house, so it overlooks the street. It was a few hours after sunset, and glancing out I noticed three or four men—or so I thought them—were just leaving the house. I couldn't see who they were since they were moving away so briskly and by then of course it was quite dark. Nothing about them struck me as familiar, but Achilles was with them."

"You are certain of it?"

"I cannot be mistaken, sir. I know him well and could identify him easily. He is bowlegged, you see, and quite bald. I was puzzled but not alarmed until just as the last man was about to go around the corner after the rest, he turned and seemed to look straight at me!"

Again Diomedes made the Christian sign. "It was no man, sir. It was a demon from the pits of hell! And nobody has seen Achilles since!"

Chapter Thirteen

The crocodile nosed its way along a channel that sliced through the towering reeds stretching stiff fingers up from Lake Mareotis.

The boat for which the carved reptile served as a prow slid along behind. As the vessel glided through the water, it moved in and out of patches of shadow where smaller paths had been cleared for the benefit of those who lived on the lake's islands.

The maze of passages reminded John of the hallways of the palace's administrative buildings.

A startled heron flapped into the air.

Down a narrow corridor where the sky was a blue sliver glimpsed above marching ranks of reeds growing so thickly a wider boat than theirs could not have passed between them, John glimpsed a fisherman emptying a net filled with wriggling silver into his small craft.

Fortuna had smiled, John thought. He had found a captain willing to take Cornelia, Peter, and himself up river for the amount they had earned from a single, excruciating performance, and on a boat embarking within the hour.

The captain carried a full cargo of wine amphorae as well as a quantity of timber lashed to the deck Anything extra by way of payment from the half dozen or so passengers he was transporting was a gift from the gods, the more so since it would not need to be reported to the boat owner.

Soon the vessel left marshes and reeds behind and entered a network of canals that would eventually take them to the Nile. John and Cornelia sat on deck and watched men working the fields, laden donkeys plodding patiently along, and nut-brown children waving from muddy banks. Compared to the heat and noise of Alexandria, the boat was an oasis of calm.

After a while Peter approached. He was beaming.

"What an interesting country this is, master! It's one thing to pour the wine, but quite another to see the grapes used to make it, being grown in such odd ways."

He waved a hand at the vineyard past which they were sailing. Workers watering the vines waved back. "That one has vines growing up poles, but the one we saw after we left the lake had vines on a sort of trellis."

"What a keen eye for detail you have, Peter," Cornelia said.

"Thorikos pointed it out to me, mistress. He's the stout fellow in brown robes."

Cornelia nodded. "With the embroidered stripes down the sides." She turned to John. "He has a rubicund face, or at least a rosy nose. His shape reminds me somewhat of a pear."

"He was a deacon in Cilicia," Peter put in, "and he kept a wine-importing business on the side. He's very comfortably off. We got into a conversation about his travels. Since he's getting on in years and has no family, he decided to spend his savings to see the world. He says that although he misses the comforts of home, so far it has been most interesting."

"There are endless wonders to be seen in Egypt," John said.

"That's exactly what I said, master! Thorikos has never been to Constantinople either. I ventured to suggest he should make it his next destination, once the plague has gone. Lord willing that be soon."

Peter waved his hands again. "And then Porphyrios chimed in and said he was of the same opinion—a traveler hasn't seen a great city until he'd visited Constantinople. So of course I told them all about the palace and the court. I may say they were impressed."

John exchanged concerned glances with Cornelia. Peter's garrulous nature might turn out to be a cause for concern. It was part of the reason he did not care to reveal everything he knew concerning his mission. Not everyone had trained their tongue as well as he had. Still, it was always wise to know with whom they were travelling, especially when night fell.

"Who is Porphyrios?" John asked.

"A charioteer. He's raced at the Hippodrome. A fascinating fellow. He said that dogs always run along the bank when they drink from the Nile, to avoid being dragged in by crocodiles! We must be careful, master!"

"I hope you aren't developing a fear of those creatures before you ever see one," Cornelia said. "What other stories was this character telling you?"

"He mentioned that auburn hair is considered ill-omened in Egypt. Thorikos was horrified and said he was glad his had long ago turned gray. Though he regretted that as it was also thinning, it did not protect his scalp from the glare of the sun very well."

"Porphyrios sounds like quite the teller of tales," John observed.

Peter nodded enthusiastically. "Indeed, master. He also told me the Blue racing team are superstitious about anything green."

"I suppose that's not surprising given their bitter rivalry with the Green faction," Cornelia said. "What's Porphyrios doing in Egypt?"

"It's another remarkable story, mistress. It seems he's been exiled."

"Did he say why?" Cornelia asked.

Peter shook his head. "No, and he looks the sort of man who wouldn't appreciate being pressed for details. Besides, no sooner had he told us than he launched into a detailed account of every race he's been in, and what's more, insisted on showing off that odd-looking belt of his. He had it woven from the team's reins after his last winning race, hoping it will bring him good fortune."

"What about that little man who's as black as a Nubian? The beekeeper?" Cornelia wondered. "I notice he rarely leaves his hives unattended."

"He was the first person I talked to after we came aboard. He speaks quite passable Greek. I didn't realize those clay cylinders were hives until he told me. I asked him why he was traveling with his bees, and he said he followed the spring flowers every year. He sells a fair bit of honey. It's used for everything from curing headaches to dressing wounds."

"I expect he does a brisk trade," Cornelia replied.

"He told me some terrible tales about crocodiles too, mistress. They leap up and drag people off the river bank or even boats and devour them before anyone realizes a companion has gone!"

"What's this beekeeper's name, Peter?" John asked, glancing toward the stern where, he noted, the disgraced charioteer and the itinerant beekeeper were now in deep conversation.

"Apollo."

"The ancient sun god!" Cornelia said. "What an appropriate name for a beekeeper, when sunlight is so vital to the flowers from which bees take their sustenance."

The unwelcome, unspoken thought came to John. To the ancients bees represented souls.

He hoped it was not a bad omen.

Chapter Fourteen

Felix pounded up the stairs. "Anatolius! I've just heard one of my men's found a body in the water. It might be that missing servant you told me about. It appears the man was murdered."

Anatolius, paused, caught by surprise midway between the kitchen and John's study, holding a wine jug.

Hypatia stood beside the open house door, looking bemused, as Felix urged Anatolius downstairs and across the atrium.

"But Felix, what about Hypatia and Europa—"

"They'll be perfectly safe behind locked doors," Felix growled.

Anatolius hastily pushed the jug into Hypatia's hands. Then he and Felix were marching across the cobbles.

"When you told me the man Achilles vanished the same night Symacchus was murdered, I didn't expect he'd ever turn up again," Felix said. "Even though we've got a city full of dead bodies, I told my men to keep their eyes open and gave them your description of the man. I've sent for the senator's reader, of course, and perhaps he can identify the body."

They went out through the Chalke and quickly turned off onto a side street. Before long they were crossing a square scantily populated with passersby.

As they approached the sea wall, a bundle of black rags lying in a warehouse doorway sprang to life and staggered toward them, coughing like a sick crow.

"Sirs! Sirs! If I may introduce myself? My name is Tarquin. My services are much in demand at the palace. I know what gentlemen of refinement prefer." The ragged young man simpered and pushed greasy hair away from his pallid face. The motion revealed the swellings on his neck.

"He doesn't realize he's a dead man," muttered Felix. "Or doesn't care."

Anatolius tossed a coin. "Off with you, now."

Felix spat on the cobbles. "You might as well throw your money in the sewer, Anatolius. He'll be taking the ferry with Charon soon."

"Well, at least he can afford a little wine now to ease the journey." Anatolius stepped through a gap in the waist-high sea wall that opened onto a steep stairway. Its steps were slick with sea spray and bird droppings.

When they reached the bottom, and Anatolius dared look up from his boots, he saw an excubitor and a crowd of gawkers on the dock gathered around what might have been a sodden sack of wheat.

It was the corpse, bloated into an inhuman shape.

The lantern-jawed excubitor with a gourd-like nose noticed Anatolius staring. "Don't be thinking about prodding it, sir," the man advised him. "He'll burst like an overfilled wineskin."

"He's been in the water several days," Felix remarked, "so he could very well have gone in the night Symacchus was murdered."

Beyond the dock, a humid miasma clung to the calm waters of the Golden Horn. Flies buzzed around their newly found feast.

The corpse stank. Anatolius tried to breathe through his mouth.

"It's definitely murder, captain," the excubitor reported. "Observe the cord he's wearing around his neck."

Felix bent to get a closer look at the swollen and discolored flesh, sending up a swarm of flies. "Criminals all think the same, Anatolius. Need to get rid of bloodstained cloaks or inconvenient bodies? Toss them in the water."

"And water's never far away in this city," observed a bystander.

The captain uttered an oath and stood abruptly. "This could well be the man who came to my office to warn me about the senator's murder."

"How can you tell?" To Anatolius the livid face retained no hint of individual features.

"For one thing, our friend here was young and yet bald. Even though the fellow dashed in and out, that stuck in my mind. He was too young to have lost all his hair. Once you've seen a few bodies fished out, you can begin to visualize what they probably looked like before they went in. This definitely was not an old man."

Diomedes made his way through the crowd of onlookers, and after a hasty glance at the body turned to Felix.

"Yes," he said, "that's Achilles, or at least those are the clothes he was wearing last time I saw him. May I leave now?"

"I'm afraid I'll need some further information. Wait here."

Felix took Anatolius by the elbow and led him to a spot behind a pallet of marble blocks, out of view and earshot of everyone.

"This is getting complicated. I see the senator's so-called reader wears a lot of powder."

"So-called? You suspect Diomedes' duties extended beyond reading?"

"You told me he was a former court page. He's far too old now for that sort of work, but then some of these aristocrats like their duck hung longer than others."

"You're thinking Diomedes had something to do with the murder because of some relationship with the senator?"

"Murders, Anatolius. Jealousy has killed many a man."

"Yes. Murders. It is getting complicated. It's possible, I suppose, but I must say I'm dubious about the idea."

"One thing seems certain at least. Whoever killed Symacchus also killed Achilles. It is too much of a coincidence that two men from the same household were strangled within hours of each other. Anatolius, I owe you a favor for getting me home safely from that tavern the other day, but if Justinian discovers how many excubitors I've had searching for a servant supposedly carried off by demons...."

"John told you he didn't murder the senator, and how could he be responsible for this murder when he was arrested immediately?"

Felix scowled. "As far as everyone else is concerned, since Justinian has said he's responsible for Symacchus' death, naturally makes it so, or at least for all practical purposes."

The captain ran an agitated hand through his beard. "But you're missing the main point, Anatolius. Don't you see? It was Achilles who came to tell me what was happening in the Hippodrome. Someone wanted Senator Symacchus dead, and further for some reason wished the senator's body found exactly when we did. Obviously, this person intended to ensure the messenger sent to bring us to the Hippodrome wouldn't be able to identify him later and took appropriate action. He's certainly thorough, I'll give him that."

"Nevertheless, whatever it takes to untangle this mystery, I think you'll agree we must see justice done. I've been wondering if Justinian sent John off to Egypt for his own protection. But if so, why?"

"I'd suggest Theodora's involved," Felix replied. "We all know she's hated John for years. In fact, according to rumor he's no safer on his way to Egypt than he is at the palace."

"What are you talking about?"

Felix paused. "You don't know? Of course not, since you haven't been spending time at the palace lately. It's being whispered that an assassin's been sent after John."

Anatolius' fists clenched. "Why didn't you tell me before now?"

"It's just a rumor, although a plausible one, I admit. More than one man's been sent away in disgrace so the messy business could be accomplished out of sight of the capital."

From where they stood, Anatolius could make out the mouth of the Golden Horn. A solitary ship was entering it, haze boiling around its outline. He wondered if the vessel had come from Egypt.

"Even if it's true, Felix, John's been gone several days. He should have reached his destination by now."

Chapter Fifteen

How strange, thought Peter. Every passenger was disembarking at the same place.

He had risen early, before coils of mist swirling over the river had dispersed as the sun strengthened. Now the acrid smell of cooking smoke drifted from a settlement strung out beside the landing place.

Already shadufs rose and fell. On the journey up the Nile, they had become a familiar sight, buckets at the end of sapling arms dipping into the river and rising, dripping, to empty their precious cargo into channels watering narrow patches of cultivated land.

Peter was not the only early riser aboard.

First he had run into the rosy-faced traveler Thorikos, arranging his small mountain of baggage on deck. Then Porphyrios the charioteer had appeared and commenced pacing up and down, flexing his muscles—limbering up for the land journey, as he put it. Finally, Apollo had begun to laboriously roll beehives to the ship's rail nearest shore.

They had been on the Nile for days, the north wind at their back a stronger force than the lazy, southern current. Peter soon lost track of the number of villages they had sailed past, each a nondescript straggle of mud huts clustered beside the river whose annual inundation brought them life each year. Beyond, beginning at their back walls, a vast emptiness stretched as far as the eye could see.

The river was busy and their passing boat caused little notice, other than an occasional hail from a child running along the steep bank paralleling their vessel, hoping for a coin or a piece of bread to be tossed ashore.

Reed boats of an ancient pattern bobbed here and there on the slow-moving water as fishermen cast their nets in the broiling heat, but most of the shipping was commercial. For a while they had journeyed behind a boat hauling a cargo of large blocks of sandstone, doubtless destined for an imperial monument, church, or other official edifice.

At sunset the boat had tied up in the shallows. Like his master, Peter slept with a blade close to hand. He had been ashore only once since they left Alexandria, accompanying John to a small riverside market where they purchased several portions of smoked fish, a small sack of raisins, and a handful of shriveled figs to augment the meager fare provided on board.

"Are you going to Mehenopolis too, Peter?" asked Apollo, pausing in his work. He was dressed like the laboring peasants Peter had seen everywhere on their journey, being clad in nothing more than a loincloth.

"I stay there for a time every year," the beekeeper continued. "See that smudge over on the horizon to the right? That's the rock marking the oasis."

Peter peered in the direction indicated. "A rock? In the middle of the desert?"

"There's a lot of them. More importantly, there's water there."

Peter asked if their destination was large.

"It's not a big settlement, but it's popular with pilgrims."

"Pilgrims?"

"Surely you've heard about the snake oracle? That's why that outcropping I pointed out to you is called Tpetra Mphof. It means Rock of the Snake. I thought your master and mistress were on their way to see it, like Thorikos."

"No, the master is traveling for business reasons."

"I'm here on business too. As I told you, it's one of the settlements I visit every year. I graze my bees there. The headman, Melios, is very fond of honey. I suppose he could hardly avoid that, with a name meaning sweet." Apollo laughed. "Melios runs the settlement, or tries to at least. He's the largest landowner there. Talk has come down the river he's offended someone who wishes him ill, someone who's using magick against him."

Peter gazed at his companion with astonishment. "It can't be possible to harm anyone that way, can it?"

"Then how else could it be his are the only sheep who have beheaded themselves?"

There was a splash. Apollo pointed in the direction of the sound. "Did you see the size of that crocodile? They're attracted by the prow of our boat. Remember what Porphyrios said about them, Peter! Be careful!"

Keeping his distance from the dangerous side of the vessel, Peter left the beekeeper, who resumed his task. At the stern, John and Cornelia waited to disembark. The boat had approached as near to land as was prudent. Now several smaller craft bobbed toward them.

"That looks most unsafe to me, master." Peter eyed the low craft that arrived first, steered by a weathered ancient whose long white garment was soaked to the waist after he waded into the river to launch his vessel. "I should imagine a crocodile would have no trouble at all leaping into it. Or it might even capsize!"

"Never mind, Peter," Cornelia put in quickly. "Even if it does, we're close enough to shore to be able to get safely to land."

Peter nodded absently, staring at a large dog standing on the bank, eagerly lapping up water.

"You're all disembarking here?" asked a booming voice.

The charioteer was as enormous as his voice. The big, deeply lined face evidenced middle age, but the muscles in his arms resembled thick ropes. "I'll wager you're bound for Mehenopolis as well," he went on. "You can't get anywhere else from here, except further into the desert! It looks as if we'll have quite a caravan!"

***

In fact, the anticipated caravan turned out to consist of a single donkey cart.

The travelers sat well back from the hives, giving Apollo plenty of room to lean against the loudly buzzing stack of cylinders he had piled at the front of their conveyance.

The beekeeper batted indolently at the occasional escaping insect. "I'll find most of them waiting for their friends when we arrive in Mehenopolis," he observed. "Melios has a well planted garden, and there's little else to suit my beauties' dainty appetites around here."

It was true. The dunes began a short distance from the river settlement. There was no sign of road or track. However, the rock outcropping marking the location of Mehenopolis rose from the horizon, like Constantinople rising from the sea, and served to point their way.

John noticed Porphyrios insisted on sitting as far from the front of the cart as possible. From his nervous backward glances it was apparent the charioteer had not positioned himself there to leave more room for his fellow passengers, as he claimed. John thought there was something sad but faintly comical about such a large and powerful man being so afraid of tiny bees.

The cart driver, the same ancient who had ferried them to shore, sang to himself about his love waiting for him on the opposite side of the river. It seemed to be the only song he knew. Again and again he sang of braving treacherous waters to reach her. A hundred times, his love gave him the strength to evade reptilian jaws.

"I wish just once that would end differently," Cornelia finally remarked to John. "Couldn't his strength fail him? Then the poor crocodiles could have a good meal, and we'd all have some peace."

"Even the squeak of these cart wheels, if they were without that voice accompanying them, would sound nearly as sweet as a work by Romanos Melodos," agreed Thorikos.

"I suspect the lover on the other side of the river could use a rest as well," the charioteer commented with a grin.

Thorikos chuckled, despite previous complaints about the damage the jolting of the cart might be doing to his aging bones, not to mention that the glare of the sun hurt his eyes and was giving him a headache.

It was nearly sunset by the time the cart drew near to their destination. The first sign of approaching civilization was a weathered man with straw-like hair sitting on a crude wooden sled. A donkey tethered to a nearby palm tree chewed contentedly at a tuft of brown weeds.

"Greetings, good pilgrims!" the man called out. "Please help an unfortunate who was lamed falling from a scaffold while helping to repair a holy place."

Thorikos tossed a coin over the side of the cart. "Clever fellow," he said. "I'll wager he's stationed himself out here to relieve pilgrims' purses before the beggars in Mehenopolis get the chance."

Beyond the tree shading donkey and beggar, the desert sloped into a shallow bowl filled with greenery. A thick growth of palms formed a dark, dusty sea which lapped at the base of the outcropping. Silver threads marked drainage ditches criss-crossing the area. Mud brick huts could be glimpsed here and there as the travelers rode further toward Mehenopolis, and before long a high wall came into view.

"That's Melios' estate, where my buzzing friends and I stay every year," Apollo said. "The pilgrims stay in the tent camp at the foot of the Rock of the Snake. The rock is where the maze is situated."

Declining help on the grounds his bees did not care for unfamiliar people to handle their homes, he and the cart driver began unloading the hives, piling them by the estate gate.

Peter leaned over the side of the cart. "The maze?" he asked with interest.

"That's something else pilgrims come to see as well as the oracle I was telling you about," Apollo replied, wiping his brow.

Thorikos broke in. "That's why I've traveled so far myself, Peter. I heard fascinating stories about this maze, and the oracle sounds most curious and well worth a visit too."

The fast sinking sun, although wrapping Mehenopolis in a purplish twilight, still imparted a golden-red tint to the upper part of the outcropping and the low, crumbling wall that encircled its flat top. A semi-ruined building with a high, dark doorway facing east was just visible through a wide gap in the wall.

"That's the building you enter to get into the maze," Apollo informed his fellow travelers.

A maze, John thought. How appropriate. He had begun to feel he was already deep inside a labyrinth, without a torch to light his way out.

However, now that he had at last reached his destination, he could at least get to work.

Chapter Sixteen

"Please sit down, Batzas."

Anatolius remained standing in front of the window of John's study. His visitor, a younger man with the broad, unmarked face of an overgrown boy, placed himself on the nearest stool. "Did you bring the documents I requested?"

Batzas' hands tightened on his bundle of papers. "Yes, sir, but—"

"I hear you're doing well with your temporary new responsibilities. Justinian has not yet named my successor?"

"The emperor is hoping you will reconsider and return."

"I don't think I shall. I'll put in a good word for you. The work you've done for me has always been excellent."

"Thank you, sir."

"Now to business. You composed the letter of introduction given to the Lord Chamberlain, I believe?"

Batzas confirmed this had been the case. Like every first-time visitor to John's study, Batzas kept glancing uneasily to the girl in the wall mosaic. Anatolius was surprised John did not bring people there to be interrogated, considering the assistance Zoe's discomfiting gaze would give him.

"Sir, I have those old drafts you were working on, but Justinian ordered the one for the Lord Chamberlain's introduction be destroyed."

"That is the usual procedure."

"I was thinking, on the way over, pardon me, sir, but I can't reveal anything—"

"I wouldn't expect it, Batzas. As secretary to the emperor you must cultivate discretion as diligently as a gardener tends her herbs. If anyone had approached me with suspicious inquiries about imperial correspondence, I would have reported the fact to Justinian immediately."

"That's exactly what I would do in the same circumstances."

"You are an astute young man. However, you are also aware that the emperor intensely dislikes being disturbed with trivial matters?"

"Understandably."

"You'll appreciate then why I asked you to bring me all the documents I left in my office. As I mentioned then, although I am no longer his official secretary, Justinian has ordered me to draft further correspondence regarding the Lord Chamberlain. There is a detail that has unfortunately escaped me. Naturally, I don't want to impose on the emperor."

He took the bundle Batzas had brought and rifled through it. "What miserable luck! I was certain I'd made a note of it."

"Of what, sir?"

"The Lord Chamberlain's destination."

Batzas stiffened. "Sir, I am not permitted—"

"It's just that I can't recall how the place was spelled. Those Egyptian names are always so difficult, and I was hoping you could recall the spelling."

"Oh. Well, if that's all it is. I can probably remember it." Batzas looked at the ceiling for a brief time, resembling a schoolboy who was being quizzed. "It's M-e-h-e-n-o-p-o-l-i-s."

Anatolius accompanied the young clerk to the door. It irked him to serve as a doorkeeper, but it was quicker than calling for Hypatia, who for once was spending the day there rather than in the hospice. He wondered if she was still at work in the garden.

How could a Lord Chamberlain employ only two servants? There were clerks at the palace who employed more.

As he saw Batzas out, a small brown bird flew into the atrium. They were always getting into his own house too, probably because they nested under the peristyle. He'd even seen them come straight down through the compluvium to bathe in the atrium's impluvium.

He didn't want the avian intruder to get upstairs, where there would be no escape and its panic would foul the floors. It was already perched halfway up the stairway, so Anatolius trotted forward, waving his hands. The bird took flight in a small explosion of pinfeathers, but fortunately fled into the garden.

Anatolius followed. Looking up, he saw the bird dwindle and vanish into the deep blue rectangle of sky framed by the roof of the peristyle.

Hypatia was working in one of the herb beds. Her hands were black with dirt and her tawny face, sheened with perspiration, glittered like polished marble.

At his greeting, she brushed a strand of hair away from her forehead, carefully using the back of her hand. Nevertheless, the gesture left a streak of grime. "I'm almost finished here, sir, and as soon as I get cleaned up I'll see what I can find for the evening meal."

"Don't worry. You're overworked, Hypatia. What have you been pruning?"

"It's fennel and dill, sir. The fennel's got into the dill and if it's left there it will weaken the stock. Dill needs the light in the center of the garden, so I've been digging up the fennel plants to move them further away."

"That sounds like an excellent solution." He was trying to think of something else to say when she gathered her tools and went into the house.

Anatolius strolled around the garden for a time and then returned upstairs.

He decided to put away the will he'd been working on and go to see Thomas again.

When he entered the study he saw someone bent over the desk, studying the documents scattered there.

The figure straightened and turned, revealing a scarred ruin of a face whose skin resembled that of a fowl left on the spit too long.

"Hektor!"

"What are you doing, Anatolius, creeping around the Lord Chamberlain's former residence? You startled me!"

"I'm staying here in his absence."

"Indeed? And so it's true this is your new line of business?" Hektor plucked a document up by a corner as if it were something distasteful. It was the will.

Hektor let it drop. "You've gone from being Justinian's secretary to sweating in the employ of bakers. Such a pity."

The former court page was dressed in spotless white garments decorated with embroidered squares depicting Christ on the cross and the risen Christ.

Unfortunately there was no finery in the empire that would draw attention away from the disfigured face.

"You have no right to be here, Hektor," Anatolius snapped.

"I expected the house to be abandoned after the Lord Chamberlain's enforced departure, and the carelessly unlocked house door gave me no reason to think otherwise."

"It's still occupied, as you see."

"You're not doing a very good job, are you? What if I were a common criminal?"

"Instead of an uncommon one? Well, if you haven't come to scavenge whatever you can steal like some carrion-eater then why are you here?"

"I intend to take possession immediately." Hektor glanced around the room. His gaze lingered on the wall mosaic. "It's a most desirable property and could be furnished attractively. The Lord Chamberlain's notion of comfort is not mine."

Anatolius observed that John was a man of simple tastes.

"Then he'll be much happier in a hovel in Egypt."

Anatolius heard a step in the hallway and glimpsed Hypatia, who vanished in the direction of the kitchen.

Had she been listening?

"Leave, Hektor. You're not welcome here."

"What's the hurry? John won't be coming back. Our dear empress was correct all along. He was a cunning villain and now he's been unmasked. Yet who would have guessed he'd go so far as to murder a senator? Whatever could he have been trying to conceal?" Hektor made the Christian sign. "I shall pray for his soul, sinner that he is."

"Do I have to throw you out?" Anatolius grabbed Hektor's arm.

Hektor jerked away. "Beware, Anatolius. If I appeal to the emperor—"

"You don't appeal to anyone now, I'm afraid. Since I was the emperor's secretary until recently, he knows me well, and I doubt he'd take much notice of whining complaints about me from a prancing fool like you."

"You mistake me for the person I once was, Anatolius. The terrible accident I suffered was a gift from heaven. The veils of sin were lifted from my eyes and I saw the vanity of earthly things. However, we must also be practical. Even those who serve the Lord must have a place to live."

"Why don't you find a vacant pillar to crawl up and take up being a stylite instead of causing trouble for everyone?"

Hektor glared. "Your friend John will not be needing this house again."

"He'll be back before too long. How can you possibly doubt it?"

"Being in the confidence of those who are highly placed, I've been entrusted with more than a few secrets," the other replied.

"You mean you're a keyhole specialist."

Hektor raised his gaze to the ceiling. "Lord," he muttered, "please help this deluded paga—"

With a quick movement Anatolius struck Hektor square on the chest, sending him sprawling to the floor.

"I'm impressed! Your prayer's been answered already! I've neglected the gymnasium lately and needed help getting exercise. Shall we continue?"

Hektor scrambled to his feet, fists clenched. "I'll be back to take possession of this house when your protector is dead, Anatolius!"

His voice was a low snarl. "Until then, I wouldn't make myself too comfortable here if I were you," he went on. "It won't be long until the Lord Chamberlain is on his way to whatever part of hell is reserved for pagans. Indeed, he may be writhing in the flames right now if the assassin has already caught up to him!"

Chapter Seventeen

Melios barely looked at John's introduction. He broke the seal, unrolled the scroll, glanced down, and then up again. "You are John, Lord Chamberlain to Emperor Justinian? I am honored, excellency, deeply honored."

John's host had the leathery skin of a desert ascetic stretched over the plump body of one born to privilege. A helmet-like wig of traditional cut framed the headman's face and thin lines of kohl drew attention to brown eyes, one clouded by that affliction Egyptians called a rising of water. However, the spotless white linen he wore might have been stolen from the back of an ancient Greek sculpture.

To John, Melios appeared to be a man with his feet planted, unsteadily, in two cultures.

"As you see, the emperor has sent me here to look into the matter of your sheep," John said.

"Why would the emperor be interested in my flock? It was declared and taxed accordingly last year. Is there an accounting problem, some difficulty of that kind?"

"Nothing of that nature." John wished the knot he had to untie was as mundane as correcting tax rolls. "What interests Justinian is the strange way they've died. It should be explained in my introduction."

Melios unrolled the scroll again and peered at it. "The writing is minuscule. I fear I do not see so well in this light. To think that my poor beasts, scratching out an existence almost beyond the very border of the empire, would be discussed in the Great Palace. They are such humble animals compared to the tigers and peacocks gracing the beautiful mosaics lining imperial corridors! I suppose I should not be surprised. There must be little that escapes Justinian's attention."

"Where did these deaths occur?"

"There was only one, excellency, but that was quite enough for me. Furthermore, it cut its own throat rather than decapitating itself, but these reports do gain in the telling and retelling, don't they? In any event, the unfortunate animal killed itself in its pen."

"I wish to examine where it happened."

"Certainly. I'll show you the gardens on the way."

John followed Melios outside and around the back of the house. Moonlight silvered the path.

"My servants must labor ceaselessly to maintain these gardens," Melios said. "As Horace put it, you may force out nature, yet she'll insist on running back."

He indicated a curved planting of cornflowers. "I realize this garden is as dust compared to the palace grounds, but I flatter myself that here I have created an inferior mirror of the lush greenery which our exalted and blessed rulers traverse in the coolness of evening, despite the constant problems we face here in maintaining sufficient irrigation."

The identification of plants was a skill which eluded John, although he could see the array was well tended. "In Egypt water is wealth, and here it is obvious you have spent it wisely."

Melios smiled. The palms bordering their path gave way to shaggy trees with thick, gnarled trunks.

"Sycamore figs," explained Melios. "And those bushes with the big red blossoms are Paion's flowers, named after the physician who used them to cure the gods of their wounds. You will know that, being a man of learning. I had them imported to protect my livestock, having heard they have that power. I regret to report the blooms do not glow in the dark as common gossip has it, although if they did we could set tubs of them indoors and save a great deal of the money spent on lamp oil." He chuckled. "But then I am a Christian, so perhaps the plants refuse to work their pagan magick for me."

"I suspect you would enjoy talking to my gardener, Hypatia. She has a vast knowledge of herbs."

"Is that so? My head gardener is just the same. For example, see that bed of squill over there? He concocted a mixture from them for a persistent cough one of my house staff had last winter, and it cleared it up right away. He's currently treating my rheumatic knees with the same useful plant, although so far all it's done is make patches of my skin raw. Still, I shall persist. If it should become too painful, he can make poppy potions to alleviate my misery."

They came to an open area graced with a small pond, around which were scattered an assortment of outbuildings. A hobbled donkey lay near a stack of straw, not far from a long, low barn built of mud bricks. John noted light wavering from the building's narrow windows, which were hardly a hand wide and set high in the walls.

The barn was guarded by a man who wore no armor and was protected only by a loincloth. However, the spear he carried announced both his authority and intent.

"That's where the sheep are penned at night," Melios said. "I keep all my livestock in this part of the estate."

He motioned the guard to slide back the barn door's iron bolt. "The building is secured after nightfall and watched over until dawn."

Melios' voice trailed off as he stepped into the barn and picked up the clay lamp sitting on a shelf beside the door.

"I see you have taken every precaution to prevent unauthorized persons entering," John said.

Melios swung the lamp around. Its diffused light flowed across lines of low-walled pens filled with sheep. There were a few bleats of protest.

He walked to the far end of the barn and tapped the wooden gate of a small enclosure. "This is where we found the animal that died, excellency."

John noted the pen was empty.

"We don't use it any longer," Melios explained. "There is talk among the servants it is accursed. I have no opinion either way."

"I will need to examine this barn in daylight."

"Of course you are welcome to search any part of my estate or any of its buildings at any time you choose, excellency."

They returned to Melios' house, a building whose walls featured foundations of red sandstone with the rest of the structure constructed of the omnipresent mud bricks.

Melios showed John into the reception room. "I realize you will want to join your family in my guest house, but first, if you would not mind remaining a little longer…."

He indicated a well-cushioned chair crouching low to the floor on carved lion paws. John accepted the seat and a cup of wine.

"I regret the liquid essence of our dusty vines cannot match the wine you are accustomed to imbibe, excellency." Melios poured himself a generous libation.

"The wines of Egypt are my favorites, although I regret few appear to believe it," John replied with a smile.

Melios beamed, took a few hasty gulps, and adjusted his heavy wig with a pudgy hand.

John glanced around. The room was sparsely furnished with a few stools and unpadded chairs. His was the only cushioned seating. Other than that, the room contained an alabaster chest and another with polished wooden panels. An unlit bronze, three-legged brazier stood in the corner, reminding him Egyptian nights could be surprisingly cold.

The walls, by contrast, were crowded with frescoes depicting scenes in Alexandria and Constantinople.

Melios saw the direction of his gaze. "You must go past the Great Church every day, excellency. You may be surprised to hear I have seen it myself. I once visited Constantinople, like my father before me. It is a wonderful city."

"When was this journey?"

"A year or so ago, before the accursed plague struck. I had to travel there on business. Such a huge place! The noise! And the crowds! I've never seen so many people in one place at once. No, not even in Alexandria! It seemed to me there were enough people in the Hippodrome alone to fill all of Egypt."

Melios looked with obvious fondness at a misshapen representation of the Hippodrome, whose fresher appearance suggested it had been more recently painted than the rest of the fresco of Constantinople. "I'll wager the sight of the Hippodrome in such an unexpected place must have brought back pleasant memories?"

"Vivid memories at least," John admitted.

"I was even fortunate enough to see the imperial couple in a procession," Melios went on. "What a marvelous sight! All those silks and jewels and the emperor so handsome and the empress exceedingly beautiful, although I must admit it was difficult to see them very well with the excubitors surrounding them, and all those palace officials and courtiers hovering about like butterflies. I have penned many verses about that glorious day."

He leaned forward. "And even more surprising than that, I have met Justinian. Yes! Few can say that, eh, Lord Chamberlain? I was ushered into his august presence!"

John nodded. "The emperor mentioned that meeting to me when I last had an audience with him."

Melios was thunderstruck. "He mentioned me?" He chuckled with delight. Then his expression became serious. "That explains how he knows about my misfortune. He has had his eye on this humble settlement ever since our meeting."

"That I cannot say, Melios. I know he is interested in learning how a sheep might kill itself while locked in a barn. You have no explanation?"

"I think…." Melios began to speak, but stopped.

For a heartbeat John was convinced he would be offered a hint or an indication of a way to a solution, but his host instead concluded: "…If I may say so, Lord Chamberlain, the animal cannot be brought back to life and so I believe the event is best forgotten as soon as possible."

Chapter Eighteen

From somewhere above Francio's dining room came a booming oath followed by the heavy thump of running feet. Alarmed, Anatolius looked up into the painted vines on the ceiling. A few flecks of paint floated down like tiny leaves.

"That's just Thomas chasing the intruder." Francio plucked another poppy cake from the silver platter on the table. "Don't get excited. The enemy is smaller than a mouse. It's black-haired and moves fast. It got in from the garden. How it arrived in the garden in the first place I can't say."

He brushed away crumbs which had become trapped in the elaborate tracery of stitching that decorated the front of his robe. "I'm certain Thomas can handle such an adversary, especially considering how deftly he's dealt with all the pirates and thieves and murderous mercenaries who've had the misfortune to cross his path."

"He's still entertaining you with his farfetched stories, I gather?"

"Indeed he is. He's as well traveled as Odysseus. I must admit, however, since our small visitor has been racing about for a day or two and he still hasn't caught it, I'm not surprised the Holy Grail slipped through his fingers."

Anatolius grunted. "And what happens if Thomas catches the little intruder? Don't tell me it's bound for the cooking pot?"

Francio wrinkled his nose. "What? Dine on something resembling a stunted rat's cousin? Come now, my friend, what do you take me for? And yet, you have a point. Perhaps I should sample just the tiniest morsel, cooked to perfection with a delicious sauce, just to say I'd dined upon it, hmmm?"

"Why don't you keep a list of your culinary triumphs? You can engage an artist to add the poor creatures to the fresco on your dining room wall."

"What a splendid idea! Your creative genius is wasted on the law, Anatolius."

"I haven't had much time to waste on the law or anything else the past couple of weeks."

Francio started to pick up another poppy cake, then put it down. "I can see from the cloud that just passed over your face you're about to broach this murderous business again. Before you ask, no, Thomas hasn't left the premises since he arrived nor has he remembered anything useful to you. Nothing suspicious has happened either."

"I see. Well, I'm also here for another reason. I'm looking for information. Do you happen to know the former court page Hektor?"

Francio puckered his lips as if he'd bitten into a bad olive. "Yes, I know that odious little monster!"

Anatolius described Hektor's visit to John's house.

"Since Hektor's regrettable accident—I say regrettable since it didn't kill him—he at least now looks exactly what he is," he went on. "Since he can't make a living from his pretty face any longer, he's making one from his and others' souls."

"You may well be right, Anatolius. I've heard he's been shuttling back and forth between the Patriarch and those heretics Theodora has lodging in the Hormisdas. It seems Hektor is trying to help find some common theological ground between them. What a task!"

"What does Hektor know about theology? He was a court page. You might as well take religious advice from one of Madame Isis' girls. It's absurd!"

Francio chuckled. "You're a fine one to begrudge a man the right to change his profession! However, as I told you, I am well informed, and I gather the idea is he brings a fresh eye to the situation, one that's untainted by years of blind faith. What's more, he's a man who was specially chosen by the Lord for the task, as evidenced by his miraculous salvation!"

"I wouldn't call it a miracle. He was mistaken for dead, but, unfortunately, wasn't."

"If Theodora thinks it was a miracle, so do the rest of us. I understand she's given him a corner to live in at the Hormisdas, and—"

There was a crash, as if furniture had been knocked over at the far end of the house.

"It sounds as if Thomas may be doing more damage to your house than your strange intruder," Anatolius observed. "How do you find out all this interesting information?"

"It's quite simple. I'm fascinated by whatever it is people have to tell me. Genuine interest can loosen tongues better than wine."

"An interesting theory! Do you know anything about Senator Symacchus?"

"Symacchus? You are more knowledgeable than you pretend, Anatolius."

"I don't understand."

"You're going to ask about his employing Hektor, are you not?"

Anatolius shook his head. "I had no idea he had."

"Oh? Admittedly it was a few years ago. Hektor did some reading for the senator. They didn't get along, needless to say, Symacchus being a devout man and Hektor being…well…what he was then and now claims not to be."

"Was there any communication between them more recently?"

"I shouldn't think so. Did you know the senator has been employed for a long time by Justinian to lecture Theodora's tame heretics on orthodoxy?"

"Strange, that a man like Symacchus would have engaged Hektor," mused Anatolius.

"Not really. Symacchus liked to employ court pages who'd become too old for their particular line of work. It was one of his charitable gestures."

"Yes, that's right. That's what his latest reader told me. But Hektor…?"

Francio pondered for a time. "The senator's only vice, if you'd call it that, was a weakness for classical literature. Especially Homer. He named all his servants after characters in the Iliad. How could he have resisted employing a boy whose name really was Hektor? Unfortunately, once you get to know our Hektor you realize how richly he deserves to be dragged around the walls of the city."

Anatolius let his gaze wander to the ceiling. The sounds of the pursuit upstairs had receded. Achilles had been the senator's servant and Diomedes his reader. He should have made the literary connection immediately, he chided himself.

"The senator's reader told me Symacchus was connected with the Apion family through his late wife."

"Yes, he was. He made quite a show of the connection. He always seemed to have some guest or other from Egypt lodging in his house, even after his wife died."

There was an outburst of frenzied squeaks from overhead, followed by quick footsteps, first directly above and then on the stairs. A tiny black shape rolled across the dining room and out into the garden as if it ran on wheels rather than legs.

A panting Thomas appeared in the doorway. "That cursed creature's possessed by demons," he gasped. "I'll pursue it to the ends of the earth if I have to, but I'll get it before too long, you'll see." He leaned against the door frame as he wheezed and gulped down air.

"You'd better sit down and catch your breath," Anatolius told him. "You're going to need it. I've learned from no less a person than that vile Hektor that an assassin has been sent after John. You're going to Egypt to warn him."

Chapter Nineteen

Cornelia slipped out of the guest house shortly after dawn. Their temporary lodging was one of several mud brick dwellings in a tightly packed row near the edge of the estate. The facilities consisted of a reception room from which a narrow corridor led back to a pair of cramped bedrooms. At the end of the corridor a steep flight of wooden stairs led to a trapdoor opening on to a flat roof. The ceilings were low and the floors composed of packed dirt. The cooking and bathing facilities were behind the house, as was the custom.

Though sparsely furnished, it was more comfortable than the tents and inns where she'd lodged with the troupe. To Cornelia, who had led a life of constant travel, home was whatever village or city she happened to find herself for a day or a week. She had discovered that the best way of learning about each new place was to explore the area and speak with anyone inclined to talk.

Which is what she intended to do.

She soon realized this might prove more difficult than she anticipated. The few women carrying baskets and several vendors setting out produce for sale eyed her warily. Could it be because she was so obviously not Egyptian, and furthermore apparently had nothing to do first thing in the morning except stroll around?

Bees droned sleepily as she made her way along the path. She wondered if any were Apollo's charges.

She had left Melios' estate by way of the gate near the guest house. Before long Mehenopolis itself came into view. It was not large, and its disorderly clusters of small houses straggled out to the boundaries of cultivated land.

At the edge of the settlement she came to a tumbled pile of smoke-blackened rubble. Nearby, shaded by the ubiquitous palm trees, was a wide-mouthed well surrounded by a low parapet. A short spiral staircase clinging to the well's inner wall led down to its dark pool of water.

Next to the well a man in a rumpled, undyed robe sat half-asleep on a stone bench, waving his hand now and then to disperse insects buzzing around his head.

As Cornelia approached, he called her a greeting, his voice strong and mellifluous.

"Salutations!" Cornelia returned.

When the man stood briefly to offer a hint of a courtly bow, she saw he was tall. He had deep-set eyes, a nose jutting like an escarpment, and black hair that flowed down to broad shoulders.

"I am Zebulon. Welcome to Mehenopolis."

As Cornelia drew closer she saw that Zebulon was older than he had first appeared. Gray streaked the dark hair, and his enormous hands were veined and gnarled and trembled slightly.

She introduced herself and accepted his invitation to sit down, noting the stone bench had been formed from a broken block of red sandstone, its intact surfaces carved with hieroglyphs.

"It's not often I see a female pilgrim," Zebulon told her with a smile, "and beyond that, one bold enough to talk to a stranger." There was the hint of a Syriac accent in the man's Greek. "If you have time to spare, would you care to engage in a board game?"

Cornelia couldn't conceal her surprise. She had received many propositions during her years with the troupe, but never to play that particular sort of game.

Zebulon laughed. "I see you are wondering what I mean." He leaned sideways and groped behind the bench, finally producing an alabaster board and a cedar box, which he laid on the sandstone between them.

Cornelia examined the heavily incised circular board curiously. If this was a popular local form of entertainment, it wouldn't hurt to know something about it.

"How is it played? I see it looks like a snake coiled on itself with its head in the middle, and that there's segments marked off from the tip of its tail to its head. Is the idea to win by being first to move from tail to head?"

Zebulon nodded. "It's called Mehen and you have described it perfectly."

He opened the box and set two ivory pieces, one a recumbent lion and the other a crouching lioness, on the tip of the serpent's tail.

"We toss a coin to see how many segments we move. I'll explain the formula as we go along. Now, I believe I have a nummus. Yes, I do. If you would like to take the first turn?"

Soon their leonine markers were racing along the snake's tail, first one getting ahead a few spaces and then the other.

"Do you see many pilgrims here?" Cornelia asked. She grinned as her lioness leapt forward two segments. "And if I may ask, how did that building behind us burn down?"

Her opponent picked up the coin. "That was once my little church. One night a few months ago it caught fire, but unfortunately it could not be saved. I wasn't here at the time, having been called out to administer spiritual comfort to a sick pilgrim, and by the time I arrived back, well…."

He flipped the nummus with a practiced air. "Ah, I see heaven favors me, for I now draw ahead!"

Handing Cornelia the coin he resumed his narration. "I hope to have the church rebuilt in due time, although it seems that day draws ever further away. Until it's risen again I spend most of my time playing Mehen. Melios houses and feeds my old bones from charity and I perform occasional duties of a religious nature for his household and for others who need them."

Cornelia, catching the sad note in his voice, looked up from the board, hand poised over her lioness.

"No doubt the pilgrims keep you busy?"

"Would that it was so, Cornelia, but the majority are more interested in the maze. Then too, a fair number of them also come to see Dedi's magick tricks."

Cornelia moved her piece and handed the coin back.

"I've heard the maze mentioned, but nothing about a magician called Dedi."

Zebulon fingered his board piece. The tremor in his hand seemed more pronounced. "So you are not here to visit the maze or to consult Dedi?"

Cornelia shook her head, saying nothing.

Zebulon settled back, the game temporarily forgotten. "The maze is carved out under the old temple you can see up on the rock. Mehenopolis was once the center of a snake cult. Of course, that was long before the empire became officially Christian."

He swatted a fly away and continued. "Mehen was the snake god of the ancients, a healing god said to perform many wonders for his followers, provided they could find him in the center of the maze. That's why this settlement is named Mehenopolis."

"And pilgrims still come here to worship this snake god?"

"Worship? Not exactly, no. They mostly visit because of superstition or from desperation. Some attempt to tread the maze, for it is said the sick will be cured if they can reach its heart unaided."

Cornelia observed that did not seem such a difficult task.

"You think not? The maze is enormous and being hewn out of solid rock it's impossible to see one's way since pilgrims are not allowed to take torches. They must make the journey on faith alone. Inevitably one of the local residents has to go in and rescue them. I myself have never seen anyone healed in all the years I've lived here. Not that that discourages anyone, it seems."

He leaned forward, a fierce light in his eyes. "Yes, the sick believe if they can reach the central chamber guided by faith alone they will emerge into daylight healed. But faith in what, Cornelia? A blasphemous snake god, or Dedi, who oversees the maze, not to mention claiming to be one who can work magick and a healer himself to boot? Better to put their trust in heaven, I tell them, not that many listen. This is a battle I have been fighting ever since I was exiled here over twenty years ago."

"Exiled? How very odd! I recently met a man, a charioteer, who's just been exiled here as well."

Zebulon smiled benignly. "It may not be as odd as it seems. Consider. If the emperor orders someone to be exiled, wouldn't he send them to such an obscure place that even its name will soon pass from the memories of the exile's friends and supporters? Then too, if Justinian decides to send the next person away to the same place, it's possible he's already forgotten where the previous unfortunate is now living, and which of his courtiers would be brave enough to remind him? Not that one necessarily needs an imperial order to choose exile."

He tossed the coin lightly into the air and clapped his hands with delight when he saw how it fell. "Ah! Speaking of Justinian, I see the emperor is uppermost, so that means my piece is due three times your last move, that will be, let me see, six, yes, and…." His hand rapidly tapped the miniature lion around the remaining segments to land triumphantly on the snake's head. "…This time I win!"

Cornelia would not have expected a religious man to sound quite so gleeful about his victory.

Zebulon noticed her expression. "Forgive me. It's just that no matter who I play, I always seem to lose. I shall mention this victory to Dedi next time we speak. He may take it as a sign the church is still powerful and then perhaps I can use it to persuade him to give up his pretence of being able to work magick for the ignorant."

Cornelia lost the snake game to an effusively appreciative Zebulon twice more before she managed to extricate herself from its coils to return to the guest house.

Peter would soon be preparing the midday meal and if it went uneaten it would upset him, for the elderly servant had been doing everything in his power to maintain the usual routine of John's household.

***

As she hurried along, Cornelia wondered just how skilled a magician Dedi might be. Preoccupied with her thoughts, it was a little while before she realized the big, dark-robed man approaching along the road was staring at her. Usually she sensed the interest of strangers immediately.

She was also able to tell, as she could now, when they intended to accost her. There was something in their posture that alerted her before they spoke. It was a skill she had soon developed as a woman who performed in public and thereby often drew unwanted attention.

She picked up her pace, meaning to pass the man quickly, but he stepped forward and blocked her path.

"Aren't you the woman traveling with the Lord Chamberlain?"

The man was wide-shouldered and had the battered face of a pugilist. A scar bisected one cheek. His heavily embroidered garments would have been suitable at the court in Constantinople.

"Let me pass," Cornelia ordered.

"My apologies," he replied. "I should have introduced myself. I am Scrofa, one of the emperor's tax assessors." He bowed.

Cornelia realized the man's profession explained the grand clothing. "Is there a tax on exile now?" she asked.

"Certainly not."

"Then what do you want?"

"An audience with the Lord Chamberlain. I believe you are staying on Melios' estate?"

"Anyone in the settlement can answer that question. No doubt John will be happy to talk to you if you request it."

"I wish everyone were as happy to talk to me. Being a tax assessor is quite a challenge. To think of such ingratitude, when the emperor asks so little for the beneficence he returns."

"His beneficence is hardly in evidence in Mehenopolis," Cornelia observed. "There's a church that was burnt down a while ago, for example, and it's still—"

Scrofa scowled. "Pardon me, but if it was not for the grace of Justinian and the presence of imperial troops within a few days' travel, Melios would be up to his neck in trouble dealing with raids and attacks on the pilgrims coming here."

"By the sound of it, am I to understand that Melios did not give you much of a welcome?"

Scrofa sighed again. "It is ever the lot of the tax assessor to be treated with scorn, if not worse, and Melios was most impertinent. However, since the Lord Chamberlain is a powerful man, and one who moreover is close to the emperor, if he were to give instructions to Melios, I am certain there would be less obstruction to my carrying out my duties."

Cornelia stared at the assessor. She felt heat rising in her face. When she spoke her voice was cold. "I fear John is far removed from the emperor right now. Further removed even than you, in fact. You might better seek to have a word with your imperial master on John's behalf."

Scrofa made no attempt to follow when she strode away.

***

Melios frowned. "You wish to know about Dedi? Where did you hear the name of that rogue? I fear I can find little good to say about him, Lord Chamberlain."

John briefly outlined what Cornelia had related about her conversation with Zebulon.

They sat in Melios' reception room. From John's perspective, the fresco of the Great Church looming over his host's shoulder was an unpleasant reminder of all he had left behind, undone. The headman had eschewed his wig this morning, revealing a glistening scalp that boasted a few unruly patches of hair.

"It appears Dedi is someone few praise," John observed.

Melios chewed unhappily on a handful of almonds before answering. He was obviously choosing his words with care, but his feelings were evident in the tone he used.

"Dedi is the cause of my being in a difficult situation, excellency. He arrived from who knows where several years ago. At the time I had been headman for over ten years, and I'd always carried out my duties in a fair and just manner. Oh, you might hear the occasional complaint. That's just human nature."

"Even the emperor has his critics," John observed.

"Yes, that's it exactly! Anyway, before Dedi appeared we did not have as many pilgrims as we see these days. One or two travelers would make their way here every so often to visit the ruins, which have some interest to those who study antiquities, but that was about the extent of it. Now it's sometimes difficult to feed all our visitors, not to mention there's definitely been a rise in thefts and assaults."

John sympathized, mentioning the latter problem was akin to those experienced in Constantinople as the capital's population had grown.

"It is evident you understand my position completely," Melios replied. "This sort of thing will always become a problem as residents increase in number. However, in Constantinople the pilgrims come to worship at the Great Church or to pray before sacred relics. Here, however, we have been saddled with a man who claims to perform magick and one who, furthermore, attracts crowds which are dangerously close to worshipping a snake god."

John, a follower of a god Melios would have regarded as equally blasphemous, took an almond from the bowl. "On the other hand, I imagine the local inhabitants do gain some financial advantage by selling food and lodgings to visitors?"

"Indeed! Yet even this extra wealth brings problems. More houses, more goods, and more livestock. These additional possessions naturally add up to more taxes. Confronted by the current rates, I do think that our glorious emperor would surely agree with Tiberius Caesar, that it is the duty of a good shepherd to shear his sheep, not to skin them. This is why I took my case to Justinian himself. How can he be certain what his officials are getting up to so far away? I suspect many of them regularly inflate the taxes due and keep the overpaid amounts."

"There are very severe penalties for such actions," John pointed out.

"Yes, indeed. Even so, as you know, I traveled to the capital and there I presented a petition at the palace, requesting relief. However, while I am content to patiently await the emperor's benevolent action on my behalf, Dedi has put it abroad he has some plan whereby he can arrange for Mehenopolis not to be taxed at all. I do not believe such a thing is possible, but naturally this has led to talk of late about his becoming headman."

John noted it would take a very great magician to avoid the emperor's taxes entirely. "Dedi presumably is quite wealthy himself?"

"Definitely. There again, perhaps heaven smiles, excellency, for a day or so ago, even as Dedi boasted of this plan of his, the imperial tax assessor arrived for his annual visit rather earlier than usual. I fear those who live here will be shocked when they find out the sums they will have to pay into the emperor's coffers. I know that I was! Even though I have but a modest estate and few animals, according to the assessor's demand you would think I owned half the Great Palace!"

"The fuller our coffers the more burdensome the taxes," John offered. "It is something all of us have in common, at least."

"You grasp my predicament, but of course you would, being such a close advisor to Justinian. As you are also aware, not everyone pays his fair share, thereby placing a bigger burden on the honest. Dedi, for example, always pleads poverty in public, especially when tax assessors are within earshot."

An indignant note entered Melios' voice. "He is also not above spreading vicious slanders for his own ends either. Why, it has come to my ears he's lately been claiming I was killing my sheep in order to avoid paying taxes on them! It's absolutely untrue, excellency! As I told you, it was only the one that died, and it cut its own throat. And consider this. Dedi had warned me the sheep would kill itself. How did he know if he didn't have a hand in it?"

"You hadn't mentioned a warning before," John replied.

Melios ran his hand through what remained of his hair. "Didn't I? Well, excellency, you know how these magicians are, always claiming they predicted this or that after the fact, or else predicting everything under the sun beforehand so that whatever happens they can take the credit for foreseeing it. I didn't think it was worth mentioning."

He glanced at his glossy fingers before wiping them on his garment. "It's a mixture of rosemary oil and crocodile fat," he explained. "My head gardener makes it for me. It's said to encourage the hair to keep sprouting. As Martial tells us, there is nothing more contemptible than a bald man who pretends to have hair."

He paused. "If I may say so, I wouldn't concern myself with Dedi, excellency. He's just a fraud, taking advantage of the gullible in any way he can."

Chapter Twenty

Anatolius dipped his kalamos into the ink and continued to write. "Further, let my son Titus be disinherited…."

He was seated at the desk in John's study, but his thoughts kept straying from the will he'd been commissioned to compose.

How was John faring in Egypt? Would Thomas be able to find him before the mysterious assassin? Then there was the urgent problem of uncovering the identity of the murderer of Symacchus and his servant, not to mention Hektor's threats and his attempt to take John's house.

Anatolius forced himself to concentrate on his task. Wasn't there another provision that had to be included? Oh, yes. The kalamos moved across the parchment again.

"…and also my grandson or granddaughter by Titus."

Would that adequately cover the situation?

He didn't want to begin his legal career by garnering a reputation for unreliable advice.

The testator, his first client, owned several bakeries and gloried in the appellation of Little Nero. He'd been sent around by a friend of Anatolius' late father.

"A coarse fellow," the friend had confided. "However, he changes heirs more often than his clothes, so you can rely on a bit of steady income from him."

No doubt Little Nero would change lawyers as quickly as heirs if displeased, and explain loudly to anyone who would listen why he'd done so.

Zoe seemed to be staring at Anatolius. Her large, dark eyes appeared wider than usual, their gaze more penetrating.

Nonsense, Anatolius chided himself. How could that be? Each eye was nothing more than chips of glass.

Why aren't you looking for the murderer? she scolded him in return. That's what John would be doing.

Anatolius smacked his kalamos down. "Be quiet!"

"Sir?"

Hypatia stood in the doorway. She carried a large basket suspended from a rope handle.

Anatolius reddened. "My apologies, Hypatia. I was talking to myself. Going to the market?"

Hypatia shifted her feet. "I've come to tell you I'm leaving."

"You're off to the hospice again?"

"No. I won't be back, sir."

Anatolius stood. "Have I offended you in some way?" He wondered if he'd been too familiar with the pretty servant. "If I've said anything, inadvertently…."

"No, sir. With the master and mistress gone and Peter and Thomas as well, there's no place here for me."

"That's not true. I'm not your employer, but surely you'd prefer to stay here until John returns?"

"It's best I leave."

"You aren't part of the furnishings, I realize that, but still—"

"There are many who might think I am part of the furnishings and can be used like them, even though I am a free woman."

"You heard what Hektor was telling me, didn't you? Are you afraid Hektor will get the house and turn us all out?"

Hypatia looked at the floor. She made no reply.

"Don't worry. I won't let it happen. You don't need to fear Hektor. He holds no animosity towards you. It's John he hates."

"Mistress Europa told me the same thing, sir, but I don't see—"

"Hektor serves Theodora. She loathes John because he has Justinian's ear and his advice to the emperor often destroys the webs she spins. Naturally, Theodora's creature would take it on himself to hate John on her behalf."

"I believe it is also because the Lord Chamberlain owns a house, sir."

Anatolius asked her what she meant.

"When I worked in the palace gardens I got to know several court pages," she replied. "They were always trampling the flower beds and uprooting bushes or destroying plantings. It may be they behaved that way because their own lives are so precarious. Once they're too old to serve as ornaments they're turned out on the street to fend for themselves, and most of them will never have a home again."

"That's true, Hypatia. I never thought of it that way."

Hypatia dabbed at a tear. "I must go now, sir."

"What will you do? You're not leaving the city, are you?"

"I'm staying with a friend. I'm hoping I can get my old job back. The palace gardens are as large as ever, but there aren't nearly as many hands to tend them."

Anatolius made a last appeal. "How will Europa and I manage without you?"

"She has already given permission for me to leave, sir," was the dignified reply.

"At least let me give you a few coins."

"Thank you, but there's no need, sir. Mistress Europa has paid me my wages. However, I have something I hope you will accept."

Hypatia reached into her basket and pulled out a strange creature crudely formed of clay. She set it down beside the doorway. Anatolius saw it had pincers on its front legs and a long, curved, and pointed tail.

"I've left others around the house. In Egypt they're much favored for warding off evil."

Just what I need for protection, Anatolius thought. Clay scorpions.

Chapter Twenty-one

"This morning I went to clean my master's boots and there was a scorpion on one of them!"

Peter surveyed the lush greenery of Melios' estate as he addressed the owner's head gardener. "I've got it trapped in a empty jar for now. It's fortunate I was a military man. When we were in camp, we soon got used to checking our boots before putting them on."

The man he addressed, who had introduced himself as Hapymen, bent to pinch a large spike of white flowers rising from what appeared to be an oversized onion. He wore nothing but a skirt of unbleached cloth that fell halfway to his knees. His sunken chest displayed every rib, while sunlight gleamed on the smoothly shaven dome of his skull.

"Very wise of you, Peter. Don't forget to shake your clothing vigorously as well."

He hadn't done so, Peter recalled in alarm. Immediately his garments were infested with crawling scorpions. He could feel their stingers tickling his sides.

No, he realized with relief, that was only sweat.

"Is it true what the gossips say about Melios' unfortunate sheep, Hapymen?"

"It is. The master donated the dead animal to the pilgrim camp. Being a cautious man, he refused to serve it to the household in case it had also been poisoned. Happily all those who partook of it survived!"

Hapymen spoke with a thick Coptic accent. When they first met, Peter had thought there was something strange about the man's eyes. They held a look of perpetual surprise. Now, he realized, there was nothing unusual about them. Hapymen's eyebrows had been shaved off along with his hair, giving him a startled look.

"Could you tell me where I might buy vegetables in Mehenopolis?" Peter asked. "I've wasted half the morning searching the market. There was nothing suitable to be had."

"There's no need to do that, Peter. If his guests do not dine with him, Melios doesn't expect them to purchase food, not with a flourishing garden on the estate. Besides which, the very idea would be an insult to his hospitality. No, indeed, he would be very upset to hear of such a thing. Feel free to take whatever you need, but stay away from the beehives. If you disturb the beekeeper's precious bees you'll find Apollo has a nasty sting."

"Do you think he would part with any honey?"

"Yes, he will. You know, his bees seem never to sting him. It's remarkable. And since we're on the subject, I would advise you not to mention mutton within Melios' hearing."

"Of course. I can see he would not care to be reminded of the, er, incident. Don't worry, Hapymen. Servants soon learn to practice discretion at the Great Palace."

He paused. "One more thing. At the market I heard there's a fellow here who calls himself a magician, and he and Melios are involved in some sort of dispute. I suppose I shouldn't mention him either?"

"That would be best, Peter. I don't know why Melios and Dedi cannot get along. It would make things so much easier for everyone. As it is, we all have to tiptoe around them as if they were a couple of sleeping crocodiles. Yet look at me. I serve these same two masters. Do I not look as calm and serene as a sleeping cat?"

A remarkably skinny cat and one with no fur, Peter thought, but simply nodded agreement. "I have seen your fine handiwork here. What tasks do you perform for Dedi?"

"I help with his magickal performances from time to time. I'm also his cook, which goes hand in hand with gardening, does it not?"

"That's true." Peter wistfully recalled Hypatia, whose plantings in the Lord Chamberlain's garden provided a constant supply of excellent herbs for his kitchen and who furthermore was Egyptian-born.

"Mehenopolis is fortunate, Peter. There's plenty of money to be made from the pilgrims," Hapymen was saying. "For many of us, the extra income we earn from supplying them carries us through leaner times, such as when the tax assessor comes calling. Which unfortunately happens every year, as regularly as the Nile rises."

"I hope you don't take undue advantage of your visitors!"

His companion grinned. "Many in the cities charge a great deal more than we do for food and shelter and other necessaries. My real trade is as a potter and I have done well selling pilgrim flasks. They're a fine memento of anyone's visit."

"I saw some in Alexandria," Peter remarked, "but there weren't any to be seen in the market this morning."

"I'll bring you one tomorrow as a small gift I hope you will honor me by accepting. My work makes up in piety what it lacks in beauty, as I would be the first to admit! However, I fear my loyalties are divided this afternoon. I must be off now to Dedi's kitchen."

Peter accompanied Hapymen along the path leading toward the main gate of the estate. His companion gestured at the vegetable beds between which they were passing. "If you see anything you need, don't forget you may help yourself."

Peter stopped to examine a thick planting of what he guessed was a type of lettuce, although the tightly wrapped leaves formed tall spikes. He reached between two to uproot a choice specimen and his hand encountered something hard.

Stooping, he looked closer.

Staring up from the lettuce was a bearded man no taller than Peter's knees, clothed in mummy-like wrappings and painted black. The effigy's hands were below his waist, holding the base of the enormous protuberance Peter had grasped.

Peter released his grip with a cry of disgust.

Hapymen laughed. "That's just a statue of Min. He's our ancient god of fertility, as you can clearly see. He's standing among the lettuce because it can inflame the passions, if such aid is needed. I doubt your master wants anything like that, though, since I've caught a glimpse or two of his wife!"

***

John drew his hand back from a pale thigh.

When there was no response from inside the dwelling, he rapped at the peculiar door frame again.

It was constructed from pieces of broken statuary. A knee served as a corner while an irregularity along one side turned out to be the curve of a back.

Dedi's house stood at the base of the Rock of the Snake, at the end of a path twisting through a grove of palm trees. The long, uneven structure poking out of the rubble at the bottom of the outcropping was a weird agglomeration of rock, mud brick, and pieces of sculpted marble.

Dedi finally materialized out of the dim interior. The magician was unnaturally short, not much taller than one of Theodora's dancing dwarves. Bristles, rather than a proper beard, covered his sallow jaw. He had a mouth like a carp, filled with teeth which protruded from his gums at every conceivable angle.

"Lord Chamberlain! I was expecting you to call! I've set out refreshments, if you would care to step inside?"

John smiled, unimpressed by the magician's pretended pre-science. He couldn't place the man's accent. Persian, or some Arabic tongue, possibly an obscure African tribal dialect, or just the result of the crooked teeth.

"Don't think I'm a prophet, excellency," Dedi said, vanishing back inside. "The whole oasis is abuzz with news of your arrival. Flies on a dung heap are as nothing compared to it!"

John had to bend to avoid the shapely calf forming the lintel. It was cool inside. Breezes wandered in through open windows, stirring air redolent with the delicate scents of dried herbs and the more piquant odors of onions and garlic. The interior proceeded back, the front room opening directly into another and that, so far as John could tell, into yet another.

Dedi offered John a stool and presented him with wine and a plate of dates before pouring himself a libation.

"I am supposing you wish to talk to me about my work here, excellency?"

Clothed in a dusty brown robe, Dedi did not give the impression of being a wonder worker. He looked as if he would be at home behind a plow.

"I wish to complete my inquiries as soon as I can."

Dedi beamed. "Then I shall be brief and try not to waste too much of your time. I can guess what it is you wish to talk about, for you have no doubt heard of my magickal powers?"

"I'm told you've made such claims."

Dedi looked disappointed. "Claims? Excellency, please let me speak plainly. Although I do my little performances purely for entertainment, it does not mean they are nothing more than tricks or illusions."

"Aren't you treading on dangerous ground? Magicians tend to be frowned on by the authorities."

"Do you mean because I might be seen as irreligious? I believe magick is the best argument for the reality of miracles. If I can work magick then why not a relic of the church? Miraculous cures connected with them are not unknown. And as far as oracles go, there has always been one in Mehenopolis. I didn't carry it here on my back! If we respect the Delphic oracle without condemning those who visit and study it, why should the same forbearance not be extended to the oracle of Mehen?"

"All very reasonable, Dedi, except that officials are often not logicians. You must be aware of your personal danger if the authorities misunderstand your performances. However, I have not been sent to remonstrate with you over that. My interest is in the matter of Melios' sheep. He seems to think you had something to do with its strange demise."

Dedi chewed thoughtfully on a date plucked from the pottery plate. "I'm flattered that news of my magick has reached such exalted ears, the more so as Melios insists on denying its power."

His face darkened in anger. "In confidence, excellency, the headman has been trying to claim ownership of Tpetra Mphof, the shrine, and its maze for years. We've had endless arguments about who owns the property. My land stretches around most of the base of the outcropping, and Melios inherited the remaining plot. That's where the pilgrims' camp is located. He charges them shameful fees for the privilege of staying there."

"The demands of commerce often clash with sentiment, religious or otherwise."

"I fear so, but after being waylaid and beaten within an inch of my life more than once, but unable to prove who had ordered it—although I know full well it was Melios—I have been forced to take matters into my own hands. No doubt you are already aware of this, so I will not deny it. I told Melios if he did not immediately stop his attempts to intimidate me and take my land I would be forced to show what I could do in retaliation. He laughed in my face!"

Dedi's tone grew more indignant and his mouth worked like that of a fish thrown up on shore. "I informed him it was unwise to force me to demonstrate my magickal powers. He said he did not believe in them, that it was all pap for the ignorant, and challenged me to prove otherwise. I proceeded to do exactly that."

"You're claiming that Melios' sheep didn't kill itself. You're admitting it was you who killed it? By magick?"

Dedi nodded and popped another date into his mouth.

John stared at the magician. He had journeyed halfway across the civilized world to find...what?

A murderer who confessed to a crime that was an impossibility.

Chapter Twenty-two

On his way to John's storeroom, Anatolius decided to explore the house further.

There had never been any need for him to venture beyond the study, garden, or kitchen, since Peter had always been close at hand, ready to fetch wine or provide a meal for John's few guests.

Besides which, he was bored. The baker's unfinished will, still waiting on the desk in the study, only added to the attraction of a walk around the house.

He was surprised to discover that a corridor, beyond a doorway at the far corner of the garden peristyle, led to a series of deserted and nearly empty rooms. Dim light filtered in from the garden. The floors were covered in veils of dust which showed the passage of small creatures, while Anatolius' boots left larger tracks of bright mosaic.

One room held a number of wooden boxes. Upon investigation he found they were filled with scrolls. Lifting a tag attached to one, he saw it was a ledger belonging to the tax collector who had owned the house before John, but who, having fallen from imperial favor, had subsequently lost his head.

The scrolls should be in possession of the imperial treasury, Anatolius thought.

There was a rumble. At first he mistook it for the sound of a cart passing by. When it came again he recognized thunder. The dim light was fading.

There was another sound. A scraping.

A startled mouse scuttling away?

Anatolius looked through the archway to the next room and saw movement in the gathering shadows.

A pale shape.

He stepped through the archway warily.

The other gave a low, startled cry.

"Europa!"

The young woman's plain white robes hung loosely. Anatolius could make out the points of her shoulders. Her face was gaunt.

"I'm sorry if I surprised you, Europa," Anatolius said. "I thought I'd do a little exploring."

"I was looking around myself. Why does father own such a large place when he spends all his time in the kitchen or the study?"

She was right, Anatolius realized; John was usually either beside his brazier, like a peasant farmer, or reading and communing with Zoe in his study like a philosopher.

"The Lord Chamberlain is required to have a large house," he said.

"Is that one of Justinian's laws?"

"Well, no, I was jesting."

"I hear you've taken up the law."

"Yes, I am no longer the feckless poet who showed you around the city so many years ago."

"I had forgotten that." Her tone was suddenly icy.

Still, thought Anatolius, her delicate features were perfection and her eyes dark pools.

"I'm sorry. I didn't express myself well, Europa. I didn't mean…that is, I realize you're a married woman, and, well, I admit I was attracted when we first met…."

The sudden clatter of torrential rain overhead broke the ensuing silence.

Europa sighed. "I spoke too sharply. I was thinking about Thomas, and worrying about my parents."

"I understand. I don't want you to feel uncomfortable here now that Hypatia's gone. I seem to be making everyone uncomfortable these days."

She gave him an appraising look. "I'd like to show you something I discovered."

She led him to the end of the corridor, and opened the door there. "Look at this!"

Anatolius found himself staring into a luxurious bath. It was obvious it had not been used for years.

Rain poured through a circular opening in the domed ceiling, dimpling the leaf-strewn greenish water of the round marble pool which occupied most of the room. A voluptuous and much larger than life statue of Aphrodite stood beside the bath. She leaned forward, one knee bent, to gaze into an oval marble mirror which the sculptor had thoughtfully made horizontal, providing a useful shelf for perfume bottles or cups of wine.

During all the time Anatolius had known him, John had patronized the Baths of Zeuxippos. Many preferred the camaraderie of the baths, but for John it meant not company but exposing to the public the wounds about which he never spoke. The more Anatolius learnt of his friend the less he seemed to know him.

The rain hissing into the bath chilled the air.

Europa gestured toward the walls. "Look at the mosaics. If Peter peeked in here those angels of his would need to carry him off immediately."

As Anatolius' eyes became more accustomed to the gloom he began to discern details. He felt his face flush. The subject of the mosaics indicated they had been created by the same artist who had created the wall mosaic in John's study. In that rural scene he had tilted many of the tesserae in an ingenious manner so when night fell and they caught the lamplight, viewers might almost imagine they could see debauched, pagan gods cavorting in the clouds. Here, nothing had been left to the imagination. Madam Isis could have sent her girls to view them for amorous lessons.

"I wouldn't be surprised if the wife of the previous owner of this house declared that since Theodora had a private bath, then she would have one too," Europa remarked as she pulled the door shut. "At least Thomas will be back soon. He said he'd be gone no more than a few weeks."

Anatolius looked away, hoping she hadn't caught his sudden scowl. It pained him to think the lascivious mosaics had turned her thoughts to the uncouth barbarian. Why were women invariably attracted to men of the coarsest sort?

"Try to be patient," he advised her. "These things often take longer than might be expected."

Europa's mouth drew into a thin line. The expression reminded Anatolius of her father. "These things? What things? Thomas isn't one to go into details about his work. What exactly is this business that took him away so suddenly?"

"I'm not entirely certain, Europa."

A peal of thunder overhead shook the floor.

If Anatolius had not been trying to suppress his poetic instincts, he would have taken it as an admonition from the gods.

Chapter Twenty-three

From high above the footpath zigzagging up the precipitous face of the Rock of the Snake there came a dull, reverberating boom.

John, Cornelia, and Peter looked upwards.

They had almost completed the arduous climb. In some spots the path was little more than a narrow rut. In others, crude stairs had been carved from the rock face. The party had started out just after sunset, their way illuminated by lamps set along the path.

Below, John could make out the lights of the settlement and Melios' estate, piles of embers glowing in the blackness. Beyond Mehenopolis stretched an ocean of darkness, except to the east where the distant Nile, illuminated by the torches of boats and barges and the fires of villages lining the banks, hung like a fiery necklace in the void. The sky was clear and stars shone more brilliantly and steadily than they ever did over Constantinople.

Again they heard the resounding boom.

"Is that thunder, master?" Peter asked.

"I should think not," answered Thorikos, toiling along behind them. "It's just Dedi's gong announcing a performance is about to begin. Magicians and soothsayers do so love their gongs!"

They had encountered Thorikos resting at a bend where the path widened for a short length. The portly traveler struggled to keep up with them, panted continually and wiped his perspiring forehead, but beamed with excitement all the same.

"Porphyrios told me it doesn't rain in this land for entire generations," Thorikos went on, with more enthusiasm than breath. "And just as well, said I, since everything's built out of dried mud, not to mention I would hate to catch a fever after being up here on a wet night."

From the base of the outcropping, the ruins on its top, a victim of some ancient downpour, resembled a mound of jagged, broken pots discarded by a lost race of giants. By the time John and his party arrived at the plateau and passed through the gap in its partially eroded wall, darkness had shrouded the building. A fire in the space before them cast flickering shadows against a facade constructed of blocks of red sandstone incised with hieroglyphs, interrupted by a high, dark doorway framed with wooden beams.

"That's the entrance to the maze," said Thorikos. In the fire-light the traveler's round face appeared scarlet from the exertion of the climb. "Not very impressive, is it? I hope I haven't come all this way for nothing."

Looking around, John noticed the flat area in which they were standing was scattered with rubble. The doorway before them must have once been inside a larger structure from which building material had been scavenged over the years. Part of it might well have found its way into the wall of Melios' house, quite possibly having made several stops between leaving the temple and arriving at his estate.

The crowd in the clearing resembled one that might fill a marketplace near the docks in Alexandria, all ages and all manner of dress, similar only in that very few were Egyptian. Thorikos greeted several people by name.

"I'm staying at the pilgrim camp," he explained to Cornelia. "Just think of me sleeping in a tent in the desert! It's terribly cold and uncomfortable, of course, and my friends at home will never believe it! I gather this is a popular destination because it isn't really famous yet. Naturally, everybody wants to visit the wonder no one knows about!"

"Do you intend to venture into the maze?" Cornelia asked.

"I considered it, as I have been feeling a little unwell, but decided not to. What if I got lost and couldn't be found again? I suppose whatever ailment I have doesn't require a miracle to cure it. Or not yet, at least."

Once again the gong was struck. The sound issued from the temple's dark doorway, the interior space amplifying the note and creating an eerie confusion of echoes.

Two men strode past carrying a pallet and placed it next to the fire. The weathered man they carried looked familiar.

"That's the beggar we saw on our way into Mehenopolis," said Thorikos. "I saw him again in the pilgrim camp. He told me he'd collected enough from the charitable for the offering he wanted to make in order to enter the maze. He's hoping to be healed."

Thorikos paused and wrinkled his brow. "Please don't imagine I believe such blasphemy but it'll make a fine cautionary tale when I return home."

The chattering crowd began to congregate around the fire.

"I'm going closer," Thorikos said. "I've come this far, so I might as well take a few more steps and get the best view." He bustled away.

Hapymen emerged from the ruined temple carrying a table and a sack. He arranged items from the sack on the table and vanished again.

"That's the gardener I was telling you about," Peter said to John.

John noticed how Peter's gaze kept moving toward the fire. "Go closer if you want, Peter. I'm content to stay here."

"Thank you, master." The servant made his way forward, sat down beside the man on the pallet, and was soon deep in conversation with the sufferer.

Cornelia remained at John's shoulder. "I'll be interested to see if Dedi uses any of Baba's old tricks," she remarked.

John scanned the crowd. A few were dressed in rags barely suitable for a desert hermit, while others wore garments far too fine for climbing outcroppings.

Hapymen returned with a large, lidded basket which he set beside the fire. When he had departed again, the gong sounded once more. A cloud of thick, luminescent smoke billowed from the ruin's doorway, roiled outwards, and dissipated, revealing the diminutive figure of Dedi.

The healer and worker of magick held up his arms. "Welcome!" he shouted. "Shortly the favored among you will be permitted to consult the oracle. Before that, however, I must address certain important matters of which I have become aware."

Assuming a severe expression, Dedi looked around the crowd until his gaze fell on John. "I know there are those among you who doubt my abilities. For them, I will demonstrate the powers which I claim are genuinely mine."

"What powers are those?" someone called out. "Would you care to wager on how genuine they are?"

Dedi's crooked-toothed mouth puckered into a smile. He picked up two items from the table. "Certainly I'll wager with you, my friend. As you see, I am holding one coin in each hand."

The coins flashed in the semi-darkness as he held them up to catch the firelight. He stretched his arms straight out on each side at shoulder height, so that his hands were as far apart as possible. "Shall we wager you will pay me twice their value if I cannot cause one coin to join the other without bending my arms? Yes? We are agreed? Very well!"

Dedi shouted a few unidentifiable words, and then, keeping his arms stiffly extended, swiveled to one side, bent slightly at the knees, and dropped the coin from his left hand on the table. Then he swiveled the other way, and picked up the coin with the hand of his still rigid right arm.

A roar of laughter rose into the night sky as the unlucky wagerer picked his way forward and tossed Dedi a few pieces of copper, giving the magician a rueful grin.

The magician bowed and strutted in front of the flames, a tiny figure attached to an enormous shadow. When the merriment had subsided, Hapymen reappeared bearing a pottery bowl which he set on the table. He remained standing beside Dedi. Dedi tapped the bowl. "Here is an attractive vessel made by my assistant, Hapymen. I may say that he is an excellent potter, whose wares are of a finer quality than many of you can obtain in your native lands. What's more, he needs your business. His wife is always complaining that coins seem to leap out of his hands as if by magick!"

Several in the audience guffawed loudly.

Dedi nodded his head knowingly. "I can tell some of you face similar domestic situations. But then, it doesn't take a seer to guess that. If you would be inclined to assist Hapymen with his household expenses, and I trust you are, he also offers fine pilgrim flasks such as are sold in Alexandria."

Dedi leaned forward, glanced around, and went on in a conspiratorial tone. "Things are getting so difficult, my friends, poor Hapymen may be reduced to begging. He won't be able to make a living at it, I fear."

The magician shook his head in exaggerated sorrow. "No, you see, there is a problem with the begging bowl. Coins may be thrown in," he said, suiting action to words by tossing one of the coins he held into the bowl. "But they leap right out!"

As he spoke, the coin in the bowl flipped upwards, and landed on the table. Hapymen grabbed the coin, bowed, and departed speedily, waving his prize in triumph, pursued by surprised gasps and delighted laughter.

John noted that Peter was smiling as he watched Dedi intently. It would be instructive to see if the servant, being closer, had seen through the trick.

"He's good at manipulating the crowd," Cornelia observed. "A little humor puts them off guard, and working by firelight is convenient for concealing sleight of hand. What do you suppose he'd say if you wished to ask the oracle the puzzle on Melios' estate?"

Scarcely had she spoken when Dedi, having astonished a man of bucolic aspect by producing three small stone scarabs from the latter's ear, assumed a grave expression.

"Now that I have shown that I can indeed do all I claim, we will see if the oracle will favor us with a pronouncement."

There was an excited murmur as he removed the lid from the basket beside the table, knelt down, and removed what was inside.

In the confusion of shadows and firelight, it was difficult to see what was happening. Cries of astonishment and terror began to ring out as Dedi got back to his feet.

The magician had draped a snake around his shoulders. The reptile was enormous and looked larger still compared to its diminutive handler. Though the size was startling, what was more shocking was its human face.

The crowd fell as silent as the stars overhead. The only sounds were the crackle of the fire and the crunch of Dedi's feet as he paraded back and forth, a grotesque silhouette in front of the flames.

The creature truly lived. The firelight sparkled in its scales as the massive body rippled.

Dedi grasped the beast just behind its dreadful head and held it up. The face was tiny and wizened, half concealed by a fall of lank, black hair. Baleful eyes stared out at the crowd, their gaze cold and deep as the night sky.

Some of the crowd averted their eyes. Hands flew up to cover faces. Others fell to their knees or made the Christian sign.

Finally Dedi spoke. "Who wishes to consult the oracle of Mehen?"

To John's surprise, it was Peter who climbed to his feet.

"My friend here, sir, has a request!" Peter blurted out. "He's been crippled for years. He wishes to know if he will ever find a cure."

Dedi lifted the snake higher. Firelight lapped over it. The reptile moved its head to-and-fro, then down and forward, as if fixing its gaze upon the sick man.

Peter's eyes were wide and filled with the reflection of the fire.

The snake spoke. It did so without moving its shriveled mouth. The sound was wavering and high pitched, neither entirely human nor animal. It might have been coming from a great distance, as would the voice of a god.

"He who hath faith to brave the maze shall be granted his cure by the great god Mehen."

John gave Cornelia a sidelong glance. She was smiling. Evidently, like John, she was not deceived by Dedi's skill at throwing his voice. John was particularly impressed by the man's impudence in presenting a snake with a patently false head as an oracle.

Dedi immediately dropped the reptile back into its basket. Clever, thought John. The oracle had not been on display long enough for the crowd to get over its initial shock.

The magician accepted the beggar's donation, and the pallet-bearers carried the man toward the temple entrance.

"Now we shall soon see if Mehen chooses to honor us with a demonstration of his powers," Dedi announced.

Hapymen appeared to bear away the basket. Excited conversations broke out and people moved toward the temple entrance.

Dedi mingled with his audience for a while. John noticed that more than once brief conversations were followed by donations.

After a time, Dedi strolled over to John and Cornelia. "I picked you out of the crowd, Lord Chamberlain. Height can be a disadvantage if you wish to go unnoticed."

The magician turned toward Cornelia. "I noticed your lady as well. Beauty holds a similar disadvantage. And how did you both find the performance?"

"Most impressive," John replied, "as a performance. On the other hand there are explanations for every wonder we've seen tonight."

"You are a difficult man to convince."

John offered a thin smile. "It's like the matter of Melios' sheep. Given enough close observation, every puzzle can be logically solved, even one such as that. No magick was involved, despite what Melios and others believe."

Dedi pursed his fish-like mouth. "I draw my power from Mehen, Lord Chamberlain, and Mehen's powers are beyond imagining. These powers, once unloosed, are not always fully controllable, as I have tried to explain to Melios on more than one occasion."

Shouts of amazement interrupted him as the crippled beggar who had entered the maze on a pallet shuffled out, smiling and looking down at his feet as if he'd never seen them before.

Dedi waved an arm toward the healed man. "You see, Lord Chamberlain. He walks. Compared to such a miracle, forcing an unfortunate animal to kill itself is a trifle!"

Chapter Twenty-four

You can deduce much about a man by studying his will.

The realization came to Anatolius as he labored in John's study, attempting to reduce to legacies and legal phrases the personal and business relationships in the life of Little Nero, owner of bakeries.

His thoughts had been wandering. That notion was the first useful one he had had all day. He laid down his kalamos, picked up the wax tablet he used for taking notes, and went in search of Senator Symacchus' will.

The Quaestor maintained a depository of legal records in a converted warehouse just off the Forum Constantine. Despite extensive renovations and whitewash, the building still smelled faintly of the wine that had once been stored there.

A pallid shade of a fellow by the name of Perigenes, an assistant to the Quaestor, escorted Anatolius up four flights of stairs to a cavernous space filled with shelves burdened by scrolls, codexes, boxes, and bundles of parchment.

"We keep the testamentary materials up here so they're closer to heaven," Perigenes remarked, with such a marked lack of enthusiasm Anatolius guessed he'd repeated the jest a hundred times.

Perigenes climbed on a stool and brought down a box whose contents proved to be a large number of loose sheets of parchment and several small scrolls tied together with red ribbon. Handing the box to Anatolius, he remarked there appeared to be more reading contained in it than the entire *Odyssey*.

A displaced scroll on a shelf near the floor caught Perigenes' eye. Examining the document, he saw the parchment had been badly gnawed.

"Look at that," he grumbled, unrolling its remains. "A rat's eaten some poor heir's villa. See, right there's the description and location of the bequest, but the rest of the line's gone. Even the best legal efforts are no match for a hungry rat."

He showed Anatolius to a marble table set against a wall. "You can study the documents there, but you can't take them away with you. As you know, the Quaestor's handling the administration of the senator's estate. Or, rather, I am. It's a difficult task, with so many legacies involved. I expect you're used to these matters?"

"Actually, I've just recently taken up the legal profession."

Perigenes' face brightened. "How would you like to be an assistant to the Quaestor? I'd be happy to sell you my job for ninety nomismata. It's a bargain. I could ask for one hundred. It's a privileged position."

"I'm afraid I'm not interested. I just left an administrative position."

Perigenes' expression settled back into gloom. He left, muttering about working one's whole life and all it took was a single ravenous rat to cheat half your heirs out of their inheritances.

Anatolius sat down, placed his wax tablet and stylus on the table, and spread the documents out in front of him.

He began to read.

Senator Symacchus' will was that of a man who had not been expecting death. To the original document, drawn up decades earlier, shortly after his marriage, there was appended a long succession of carelessly drafted codicils. Evidently the senator had been in the habit of bestowing legacies whenever the fancy took him, which going by the dates seemed to be every other month.

Thus his cook was given a set of pots, a favorite reader his copy of Virgil; the crosses adorning the garden were reserved for a monastery. The doctor who'd treated his fever during the last year of Justin's reign could expect a silver platter he'd admired during his visits to the ailing senator, if the doctor was still alive.

There were grants of property as well as various sums of money. As far as Anatolius could tell, Symacchus had never revoked any of the codicils. It would be a nightmare untangling the bequests, not to mention tracing beneficiaries mentioned only once, and that years before.

Anatolius read on, scratching occasional notes.

Following the death of Symacchus' wife, he had bequeathed the bulk of his estate to the church, but it appeared there would be little left by the time the legacies were distributed, meaning that litigation was sure to follow. The church would not be content to pray for what it was to have inherited.

According to what Francio had told him, the senator had surviving relatives, and doubtless in turn they would challenge the church.

It was a legal labyrinth.

What seemed like hours later he was again speaking to the glum Perigenes in his cubicle of an office on the ground floor.

"And what about this man?" Anatolius paused to consult his tablet. "Bishop Crispin. Senator Symacchus refers to him as his good friend and esteemed colleague. He left him a collection of pilgrim flasks, whatever they might be."

"I've had to search out as many as I could find of those listed in the will. Such a vexatious task! I recall the bishop, of course. He resides in the Hormisdas."

"A monophysite?"

"I suppose he must be, if he's living there. Everyone knows Senator Symacchus was among those sent by Justinian to preach orthodoxy to Theodora's crowd. Don't be surprised that the senator left something to a heretic. I believe he left a bequest to every soul in Constantinople."

"Except for yourself?"

"Not at all. To me he left the hellish task of administering his damnably generous will! Do you know, he left a jeweled cross to a one-legged beggar with a residence whose address is given as somewhere along the Mese not far from the Augustaion?"

Perigenes sounded on the verge of tears.

"I can help you out with one task at least," Anatolius said.

"Do you think so? Then I'll lower the cost of my position to eighty-five nomismata. You won't find a better legal job, not at that price."

"I can't accept your offer, but I'd be happy to deliver the pilgrim flasks to Bishop Crispin."

Perigenes drooped. "I suppose at least that would be one less thing to worry about. I'll draw up the appropriate authorization to obtain them from his servants. Do you know where to find the senator's house?"

Before Anatolius could reply, a ruddy-faced young man strolled into the office.

"Working early, Perigenes? I just got in myself. I'm afraid Bacchus kicked me in the head again last night. Have you heard the dreadful news? It's all over the—" Noticing Anatolius, the newcomer stopped abruptly.

"Never mind him, he's just a lawyer," said Perigenes. "What dreadful news?"

"Oh, well, if you say so. It's dreadfully dreadful. You know Francio and his recreation of Trimalchio's feast? The one everybody's been invited to?"

"I wasn't!" Perigenes sounded hurt.

"Never mind. You won't be missing anything. No one will be missing anything, except poor Francio, that is."

"What do you mean? What will Francio be missing?"

"No, no. I meant we'll all be missing Francio, but now that you mention it, Francio will be missing everything too."

"What are you talking about?" Anatolius demanded. His tone was sharp. "What's happened?"

The visitor looked startled. "Then you have not heard? Francio's been murdered! Strangled with an eel!"

***

"Soup?" said Anatolius.

"That's right, eel soup. If you spill a bowl, don't step in it. It's slippery stuff, especially after you've had a cup or three of wine."

Francio gingerly patted the bandages swathing his head. He sat on his bed, propped up on huge cushions embroidered with pictures of the geese whose feathers filled them. Compared to his usual finery, his plain, pale green tunic made him appear more naked than he did at the baths.

Felix stood beside the bed. He had been at the house to question Francio when Anatolius arrived. The servant Vedrix lurked at the doorway, looking distraught.

Anatolius explained he had been given to expect much worse.

Francio laughed, then grimaced in pain. "Amazing how these rumors grow, isn't it? You fall down in your dining room and by the time three people have passed the story on, it's become a wonder. By tomorrow I shall have risen from the dead."

He tapped his squashed nose. "Alas, if I'd fallen on this it might have fixed it."

"You can jest now, but you're lucky to be here," Felix told him. "And I don't mean because you were attacked by a bowl of eel soup."

Turning to Anatolius, Felix explained. "In the middle of the night, two ruffians got in. Fortunately Vedrix there has sharp hearing, woke up, and sounded the alarm. They departed in great haste."

"That would've been the end of it," Francio said, "but after all the excitement I felt more hungry than tired. Vedrix brought me the soup and you know the rest. I've never had any trouble with intruders before. Do you think they were looking for—"

"Valuables? Yes! What else?" Anatolius interrupted hurriedly, at the same time warning Francio with a glare he hoped Felix didn't notice. He had made it clear to Francio it would be wise not to tell anyone Thomas had stayed with him. Was it some slip of the tongue by Francio or his servants that had brought the intruders to his house?

"I'll drop in again tomorrow," Anatolius said. "Meantime, make certain the doors are kept locked."

Anatolius accompanied Felix into the atrium. He resolved to say nothing about Thomas to the excubitor captain. Keeping secrets from a friend made him uneasy, yet John must have had good reasons for not telling Felix about Thomas' presence at the Hippodrome on the night of the murder.

"The city's gone mad since the plague arrived," Felix remarked. "Thieves are getting used to finding houses unoccupied. When they discover someone's at home they go ahead with their business anyway."

"Have you made any progress in your investigations?" Anatolius asked abruptly.

Felix shook his head. "It's a complicated affair, Anatolius. Look at it from my position. John was exiled by Justinian. There are hints all is not as it seems. Theodora is involved in this in some way and I'll tell you why. She ordered me to withhold the funds Justinian intended to provide John when he was sent away."

"So she forced you to disobey Justinian's orders? Well, if you've done it once—"

Felix gave an exasperated sigh. "You don't see the point, do you? John can fend for himself. I couldn't afford to make myself a target for the wrath of the empress."

"I'm not surprised she interfered," Anatolius replied. "I told you about my little discussion with Hektor, and wherever he is, Theodora's shadow isn't far away."

Felix laughed. "True enough. She's had him running her errands since he was knee-high and she heard about him mutilating a dead chicken for the edification of the other pages. I hope I don't have to remind you to be careful, Anatolius. You never know what to expect with Hektor. However, since you asked, I'll try to make further inquiries without attracting the attention of the imperial couple."

Anatolius smiled. "Thank you, my friend. Now, I've discovered something you might find useful. The senator had connections to the Apion family, and he also hosted a stream of guests from Egypt. Some were relatives and others apparently came to the city for business reasons. It might be helpful to learn more about as many of these people as possible."

Felix tugged his beard. "I take it you imagine the senator's guest list might have something to do with his murder?"

"Well, after all, the country played such a large role in his life, why not in his death as well? Then too, consider that of all the places he could have been exiled, John was sent to Egypt. There could well be a connection, and he may already have found it."

Chapter Twenty-five

John finished his walk around the barn where Melios' sheep had died. The sun beat down with such ferocity even the shadows seemed to have taken cover.

He examined the structure's heavy wooden door, noting its strong, iron bolt. The barn's window slits were too narrow to admit a person. On the other hand, the roof consisted of a mat of branches. Could they have been moved aside to allow an intruder to gain entrance?

"It wouldn't have been possible, excellency. There were guards posted all night and the area was well lit to boot. Any intruder would have been seen immediately."

Huya, the man who addressed John, was lean and dark. Like the guard on duty the night before, he was clothed only in a scrap of cloth, the working attire for so many in this land—a far cry from the robes men wore to work in the great palace.

"And the door remained locked all night, according to Melios. Is it possible someone might have heard a suspicious sound from inside and decided to peek in? Or perhaps it was suggested that the door be relocked, just to make sure it was secure?"

"No, excellency."

John entered the barn. The interior consisted entirely of a corridor flanked by rows of identical low-walled pens. He looked into the nearest, then scanned the rest of the building. So far as he could tell, each enclosure had a shallow stone trough. Aside from that, they were featureless boxes.

The sheep nearest the door began to bleat plaintively. Its neighbor joined in. Soon the whole place was in an uproar.

John questioned Huya further.

It was from him that he learnt Melios had not related the complete story.

Dedi, it seemed, had not only predicted the death but had also issued a challenge. He would demonstrate his power by forcing the animal to kill itself, despite any precautions Melios undertook to protect it.

"Apart from the guards," Huya said, "the master ordered charms hung in the pen as well as a protective garland for the animal. Zebulon also blessed it before it entered the barn."

"And how did it manage to slit its throat? I see nothing here sharp enough."

"Dedi brought a sword wedged in a split post. It was tied to the gate of the pen."

"Who put it there?"

"He did, but he was escorted in and out by two guards. Nobody else went inside before the building was locked. We had been on watch for a while and then suddenly we heard a terrible sound. We rushed in but we were too late. The sheep lay dying, blood gushing from its neck and staining the sword blade."

"Is there something else, Huya?" John asked. "You're obviously uneasy. What is it?"

"Excellency, it's Dedi. There are evil powers abroad in the world, and his magick is stronger than iron bolts. What if he finds out I have been speaking with you?"

John assured the guard there was a reasonable explanation, one that in time would be revealed.

The solution would doubtless shed light on matters more vital to the empire than a lost animal.

However, he felt disappointed. He had half-hoped the extraordinary story related by Justinian might, upon investigation, prove to be nothing more than common trickery on the part of Melios. Yet what reason could there be for the headman's actions, if such was shown to be the case?

On the other hand, demonstrating Melios' untrustworthiness could well have been vital in discovering the plot Justinian feared.

It was time to interview people other than those directly involved in events on the estate.

***

John found Apollo in the garden near the edge of the estate, keeping watch over his temporary apiarium. The cylindrical clay beehives were lined up in horizontal piles of six along the boundary wall next to a bed filled with exotic flowers. Bees buzzed in and out of the small holes at the front of their homes, and looped intricate paths among the showy blossoms nearby.

The dark-skinned beekeeper was dressed, like Huya, in nothing more than a scrap of cloth around his loins. It occurred to John that were he in charge of bees he would have preferred to keep more of himself covered.

"That's right, my beauties, make haste to gather your harvest," Apollo admonished his bees. "Lord Chamberlain, salutations! And the same from my charges here. I know many find it comical that I talk to them, but they are just showing their ignorance. Quite a few people tell their bees of all household happenings, good or bad."

"I've heard of the custom. However, I'm hoping you can tell me about certain matters relating to imperial business."

Apollo gave a low bow. "I would be honored to assist in any way I can."

"You journey with your beehives to Mehenopolis each year?"

"Yes, excellency. I travel along the Nile so my bees can enjoy the spring flowers as they come into bloom. Melios allows me to stay on his estate, as you see. I've been coming here for at least ten years. He charges no rental, but I always give him a gift of honey before I leave."

John studied the profusion of colorful flowers. Alive with bees, the flowers bobbed and swayed as if stirred by a brisk wind. "I'm partial to honey cakes myself," he admitted with a slight smile.

"My beauties' gold has medicinal use too," Apollo boasted. "In fact, Melios is treating that cloudy eye of his with a concoction of honey and tortoise brains. Last year I suggested he keep bees himself. He agreed it would be a fine plan were it not for the fact he's terrified of them. That's why my hives are set as far from his house as possible."

John asked the beekeeper if he had been on the estate the night of the incident in the barn.

"No, excellency. I wasn't. In fact this is the first time I've been here since it happened."

He paused. "I have noticed one thing that's different this year. Melios seems to be afraid of Dedi. The last time I was here he was just angry with him. However, I'm not surprised he should fear the magician, after that strange business. Next time it might be Melios' neck. I advised him to obtain a protective charm for himself. Some dismiss them as superstitious folly, but what I say is if their use brings comfort to the troubled, can it be so very bad?"

John recalled the children he had seen in Alexandria who wore little except amulets. "The people here still put great store by magick, it seems. Zebulon must consider such beliefs as distressing as Melios finds Dedi."

Apollo snapped off a large, globular, red blossom and held it out on his upturned palm. Almost immediately a bee alighted on the flower.

The beekeeper peered at his charge fondly as it busied itself. "Zebulon has labored here for years and as diligently as my little friends, but he finds his efforts fall on stony ground. As I'm sure you've learned, Zebulon fled from Antioch many years ago. The orthodox can unfortunately be most intolerant. Here Zebulon has food and lodging and a ready audience for his sermons, although I believe Melios recently had to speak severely to him about wasting the servants' time with that strange game of his."

The bee flew away and Apollo dropped the red blossom as he glanced over John's shoulder and along the path.

Peter approached, carrying a rush basket brimming with greenery.

"Master, I've just harvested some fine vegetables for the evening meal, and I was hoping Apollo could spare some honey."

"Certainly," Apollo replied. "However, I'll need your help, with your master's permission."

John agreed. He'd intended to question Apollo further about the denizens of Mehenopolis. Often someone who visited a place only occasionally could see it more clearly than a permanent resident. However, that could wait.

Apollo picked up a torch lying beside the stacked hives. At the touch of a striker it produced a billowing plume of smoke.

He handed the torch to Peter. "Hold that to the rear of the hive when I remove the back. As soon as the smoke gets in, the bees will retreat through their front entrance, and then I can reach inside and steal their wealth."

At close quarters, the piled hives emitted an almost palpable humming. Peter leaned as far away from the chosen cylinder as he could and extended the smoking torch.

"Don't worry," Apollo assured him. "Bees know nothing of leisure. Unlike the faithful, who are instructed to work only six days for their gold, my beauties labor every day. In fact, their sole joy is work. They'll happily replace what we take. Just think, if we were bees, the emperor's tax assessors would bring us immeasurable pleasure." He deftly detached the back of the hive as he spoke.

Several bees emerged and flew towards Peter.

The servant stumbled back a step, lost his balance, and fell against the stack of hives behind him.

Dislodged, the topmost rolled down and hit the ground an arm's length from Peter. On impact its back popped off.

Peter's eyes widened in horror.

John leapt forward to pull him away from the angry swarm of bees.

Except none appeared.

Nothing spilled from the opened hive except a bundle of dirty rags.

John bent and picked it up.

A yellowing bone fell out.

He yanked at the string tied around the bundle. A medallion hung from it.

John glared at Apollo. "That's an ecclesiastical seal. What are you doing with a hive full of relics?"

Apollo looked astonished. "Excellency, I have no idea. Someone has taken advantage of me. Alas! What did the villains do to the poor bees that were in there? For all I know my beauties are wandering Alexandria, homeless!"

***

Since Apollo continued to profess ignorance about the surprising contents of his hive, John decided to ask Melios how much he knew about the itinerant beekeeper who took advantage of his hospitality every year.

As he reached the row of palms shading the side of the headman's house he heard his name spoken.

There was an argument going on inside the building.

On further listening, it seemed he was mistaken since the subject under heated discussion did not involve him.

"As for your assessments, Scrofa, I have declared everything!"

The voice belonged to Melios. It came through an unshuttered window a few paces away.

"Anyone who claims I have hidden anything can be brought here to accuse me to my face!" Melios went on. "In fact, I insist upon it! People better have proof of their outrageous claims! Hidden assets indeed! I wish I had assets to hide! I told your predecessor the same thing last year when Dedi, that miserable charlatan, tried to get me into difficulties with the authorities."

"Yes, so I heard. In fact, I was instructed to closely examine this Dedi," came the reply in quiet Greek. "However, I always begin my work of assessment with the headman of a settlement. After all, isn't he the most important person in the area?"

"Certainly!" Melios sounded mollified by the tactful reply. "I shall be happy to open my accounts for your inspection first thing tomorrow morning if that would suit you. I'd have had them available immediately had you not arrived early this year."

"That will be acceptable, Melios."

The scrape of a stool and closing of a door announced the tax assessor was leaving.

Egypt was a simple country as well as a superstitious one, John thought. In Constantinople wise men did not conduct personal business beside open windows.

He lingered outside, looking after the departing man before entering the house. Though many who toiled in the imperial administration tended to be thin of frame, Scrofa was broad-shouldered and well-muscled. He was obviously a man in excellent physical condition, one who would be difficult to intimidate and doubtless chosen specially for the job when the time came around to undertake the highly unpopular task of yearly tax assessments.

Melios was in the reception hall where he had entertained John before. He appeared agitated, but he greeted his unexpected visitor warmly enough. "Lord Chamberlain, I was going to seek you out. What brings you to my door?"

"I wish to question you about the beekeeper."

"Apollo? He's been visiting me for some time now. He supplies me with honey in return for allowing him to keep his bees here for a few weeks every year. It's a simple arrangement, one with which we are both happy."

"A few pots of honey are not much of a fee for the privilege of staying here," John pointed out. "Given the tax problems you've mentioned, I'd expect you to charge more."

Melios' womanish mouth tightened. "Well, I don't. May I ask you the reason for your interest?"

"I have just discovered that Apollo appears to be smuggling religious relics in his hives."

Melios did not seem either shocked or offended. "Is he? It's nothing to do with me, excellency! For all I know he's decided to start selling them to Dedi's pilgrims. After all, my own head gardener sells flasks of sacred oil to visitors. That sort of transaction is commonplace here and in many other places, Lord Chamberlain."

Melios paused. His gaze turned to the depictions of Constantinople scenes adorning the walls. "You are a cosmopolitan man, Lord Chamberlain. I am deeply honored you and your party are my guests. Such men as yourself are always welcome in my household, but I see so few of them. We two are men of culture and learning, students of philosophy, and lovers of the arts, isn't that true?"

"You flatter me, Melios."

"I only speak the truth. I mentioned I had been about to seek you out. I wished to inform you of a small gathering I've planned in your honor. At least we can put this nasty business of the sheep behind us for an evening."

Chapter Twenty-six

Anatolius felt uneasy as he labored up the steep street toward the monumental cross marking Senator Symacchus' house. He was not being entirely truthful with either Felix or Europa. What would they think when they found out?

Could they be of more assistance if he shared his knowledge? John's life was at stake, as well as the lives of Cornelia and Peter.

Assassins left no witnesses.

He had his doubts about Thomas.

Except for the fact that Europa remained in Constantinople, Anatolius would not have been surprised if Thomas took to his heels rather than travel to Egypt to warn John. On the other hand, Thomas had lingered in the city after talking to Anatolius after John's departure.

That proved he did not intend to flee.

Didn't it?

Anatolius tried to put his misgivings aside. He couldn't help thinking how vulnerable John would be in Egypt. The wise man was always wary at the palace. In Egypt, John would have no reason to be alert for the stealthy footstep, the sidelong glance, the shadowy figure moving around the corner. In a place where everything was unfamiliar, would John be able to sense the subtle disturbance of the normal that signaled danger?

Surely John would not let down his guard?

A stray dog loped toward him, blunt nails clicking on the street. The animal's ribs were visible. It wrinkled its muzzle and growled. Anatolius shouted a lurid curse and the dog turned tail and ran.

If only all problems could be so easily solved.

Anatolius' rap on the senator's door was again answered by the slim, deep-voiced servant Diomedes.

"I'm assisting the Quaestor with the senator's estate," Anatolius explained. "I've come to retrieve certain items to deliver to a legatee." He presented Diomedes with the authorization Perigenes had provided. It had been an unwise move, Anatolius felt, because there would surely be claims on the estate that would cause numerous administrative difficulties. It would be as well for Perigenes if he found a buyer for his position as soon as possible.

Diomedes led Anatolius down a hallway adorned with crosses and pedestals bearing basalt sculptures of Egyptian deities. They arrived at a room piled high with chests and sacks. Diomedes rummaged around and eventually handed Anatolius a sandalwood box of a size suitable for storing jewelry. Inside, Anatolius found a dozen stoppered, cylindrical clay bottles, none longer than his forefinger.

"That's the master's collection of pilgrim flasks, sir."

Anatolius examined one. It sported a tiny handle on each side and bore an incised picture of a figure in a tunic standing between two camels. *St. Menas* was written above the scene in barely legible Greek letters. "How unusual! Do you know where he purchased these?"

"They were gifts from his guests. Everyone who took advantage of the senator's hospitality presented him with a token of their appreciation. I don't suppose these crude little things cost much." His tone conveyed his opinion of the generosity of the senator's guests.

"What is their purpose?"

"Miracles, sir. Each of these flasks is filled with oil from a lamp in a martyr's tomb, or water from a spring near the spot where a miracle occurred. It's said these mementos possess holy powers from being in close proximity to such holy sites."

Anatolius examined the collection. Several flasks bore the same inscription and scene as the first. One or two were incised with simple crosses, while another featured both a cross and a broad, wavy line. It was a crude but effective attempt to render the sea and so doubtless most appealing to pious mariners, he thought.

"Did Senator Symacchus ever mention Bishop Crispin?"

"No, sir, not to me, but perhaps his bequest will serve to lessen the bishop's disappointment that the master failed to obtain the Egyptian relic he had promised him."

"And you know this because…?"

Diomedes reddened. "Achilles told me, sir. One of the senator's guests, a fellow called Melios, talked about it constantly and Achilles overheard. He was always gossiping about the master's business. I warned him more than once it would lead to trouble, but he took no notice."

"Indeed. Tell me, were you in the senator's employment when the former page Hektor worked here?"

"No, sir. Hektor was a reader, like myself. Servants who've been here longer than I recall him well."

Anatolius did not reply. His gaze wandered over the contents of the room. From a shallow basket he plucked one of a number of enameled metal crosses.

"I'll take this with me as well, Diomedes. I'll notify the Quaestor's office I have it. The bishop's legacy only mentions pilgrim flasks, but I am certain he will appreciate this small item too."

Chapter Twenty-seven

Cornelia persuaded John to take a walk after sunset brought a welcome coolness to the air.

Behind them the buildings on the estate subsided into dark shapes dotted with stray will-o'-the-wisps of lamplight. Starlight glimmered on irrigation ditches. A sickle moon rode hungrily low on the horizon.

After a lengthy silence, Cornelia laid her hand on John's arm. "My thoughts often turn to those we left behind in Constantinople."

John looked down at her. "I understand how you feel, Cornelia. I think of them often too."

"And when my thoughts aren't in Constantinople, they're here, but in the past. Being together again, in this land, feels almost as it did then."

John's hand rested for an instant on hers. "Tell me, why did you never marry?"

The question took Cornelia by surprise. "I never thought of marrying. When you didn't return, I kept hoping...."

"I was an impetuous young man. I could have decided I didn't want to be tied down."

"You might have decided to leave me, John, but you would have told me so. You would never have crept away in the night."

John nodded. "Even so, many years passed before we met again."

"It didn't seem so long, especially with a daughter to raise. So I waited for your return, and meantime kept hoping I might see you in the audience in some dusty town square." She laughed softly. "I never realized you had risen to such high office, that it would be necessary for the troupe to perform in the Hippodrome in order to find you again."

"If I had thought our lives could be the way they were before, I'd have sought you out, no matter where you were. I would have been content to remain with you, no matter how small or dusty the village. But, of course, it cannot be that way."

"Why did you suppose it cannot be, John?"

Before John could answer, light flared in the sky.

"Look!" Cornelia pointed to a fiery ball that soared above Mehenopolis' thick canopy and mounted swiftly past the sickle moon into the heavens above the Rock of the Snake.

Suddenly the air was filled an unearthly screeching, as if someone had cracked open the door to the Christian hell to allow the sound of souls screaming in endless agony to emerge.

Shouts echoed from the direction of the estate.

John and Cornelia ran toward it.

Above, the fireball wheeled and looped, throwing off showers of sparks. Long shadows spun wildly over the path and gardens along their way.

Then the flying thing fell like a burning rock.

The terrible screeching ended abruptly.

Red light danced in the open space in front of Melios' barn. The stack of straw was ablaze. Men ran up, shouting and gesticulating, shaking their fists at the now empty sky. A child toddled past unattended, sucking its thumb and whimpering.

"It's Hecate come to kill everyone!" an indistinct figure cried. "Only Dedi can save us!"

"No, it's an angel sent to punish us for listening to Dedi, that blaspheming bastard!" another shadow answered.

Words were exchanged that Cornelia couldn't make out. Then, deciding to reinforce his theological position, one of the debaters shoved the other, whose quick refutation consisted of a fist to his opponent's jaw. Several onlookers stepped forward to join the incipient fray.

Cornelia noticed the tall, stooped figure of the old cleric, Zebulon. He strode toward the melee and without hesitation grabbed one of the fighters by the shoulder.

"Stop it! Do you think heaven would reveal itself with a cheap display such as this? If the Lord wanted to deliver a message He'd do more than send an angel to set fire to a pile of straw."

The fighters looked abashed. Grumbling darkly, they turned away from each other.

Zebulon glanced around, shook his head, saw the unattended toddler, and contented himself with taking the child's hand. "Come along, little one. We'll find your mother."

Cornelia and John made their way through the crowd toward the fire.

Sheep bleated frantically and servants cursed as they ran back and forth between the pond and the blaze, throwing ineffectual buckets of water at the conflagration.

Melios stood a short distance off, clasping and unclasping his hands. His milky eye shone like that of a wild animal.

"You need a bucket line," John told him.

The headman stared as if he'd been struck dumb.

"Organize a bucket line before you lose your barn!" John said.

"Have you seen Apollo?" The headman's gaze darted to the air, then side to side, as if he expected another flaming apparition to come flying at him any instant. "His bees don't like smoke. I don't want swarms of angry insects everywhere."

John proceeded to organize the frantic servants himself. Some he grabbed by their arms and he yelled and gestured at others, cursing profusely.

"I'm surprised to hear the Lord Chamberlain has the regrettable vocabulary of a dock worker," said a voice at Cornelia's shoulder.

Zebulon had returned.

"He's in the habit of cursing in Coptic because so few in Constantinople understand it," Cornelia explained. "I suppose he's forgotten here he's using the native tongue."

"And using it extremely colorfully, if deplorably, though I will say most effectively."

Already the men had formed a chain and begun to pass brimming buckets of water along it in rapid succession.

"The flying demon will make a good subject for a homily," Zebulon remarked, "although I had been thinking I could base a meditation on a more prosaic horror recently visited upon us."

He inclined his head in the direction of Melios' house, toward which a burly figure strode.

"I mean of course the tax assessor," he went on. "No doubt Scrofa is worried assessable property might go up in flames. However, I notice he doesn't seem anxious to help prevent any losses."

Recalling her brief conversation with the assessor, Cornelia suspected Scrofa was just as likely to be taking advantage of the commotion to search the house to establish if Melios was hiding undeclared property. "Now you mention it, where has Melios gone?"

"Perhaps he doesn't have a quotation from the classics appropriate to this occasion? In any event, the Lord Chamberlain seems to have taken the situation in hand. Don't forget, Cornelia, I am always ready for a game of Mehen."

A big man appeared on the scene.

"You need some muscle here," he shouted at John.

It was the charioteer, Porphyrios. He took his place at the end of the line, flexed his sinewy arms, grabbed hold of the next bucket as if it were a wine pitcher, and tossed the water in a long coruscating arc.

A few dark fragments of ash, ringed in bright orange, floated upwards, rotating slowly, and drifted away.

There was a sudden bray of anguish.

Startled, Porphyrios looked around.

The donkey tethered near the barn was trying to back away from a large patch of dried weeds the flying sparks had set afire.

Porphyrios dropped his bucket.

John picked it up. "Untie the donkey, Porphyrios. Quick!" he ordered.

"Me?"

"Yes, you!"

Porphyrios grimaced. "Ah…what about the next bucket…."

Seeing the charioteer's confusion, Cornelia sprinted over to the distressed animal and set it loose. As it galloped off across the flower beds, Porphyrios doused the smaller fire.

For a little while Cornelia stood and watched John. He worked quickly and efficiently, issuing occasional orders, working alongside the servants, his manner decisive.

Since the fire was soon brought under control, she decided to return to their temporary lodgings. Turning to leave, she saw Thorikos running toward her. Even in the dying firelight she could see he was breathless with exertion and excitement.

"Isn't this a wonder?" the rotund traveler gasped. "The entire settlement must have seen that flaming demon! What tales I'll have to tell! Who would've thought a dull fellow like me would ever witness such sights?"

Not pausing for a reply he hurried on toward what remained of the night's drama.

Cornelia decided to take a short cut back rather than following the path. As she moved away from the remains of the blaze, the night closed around her. The sliver of a moon faintly silvered the ground before her.

The hubbub of voices faded. Now she could hear the buzz and chirp of insects.

Walking slowly, she kept her gaze on the ground.

Before long she bent down and picked up what she'd expected to find.

A feather.

***

"Master, is that you?" Peter stuck his head out of his room and peered down the hallway.

There was no answer. The only illumination came from a terra-cotta lantern hanging at the end of the corridor.

He was certain he had heard a footstep.

"Mistress? Have you returned?"

Hadn't he lit the lamp in the front room?

How long could it have been since he had dozed off?

He made the sign of his religion, picked up the lidded clay jar by his door, and crept out into the hallway.

Yes, there was the sound again, a barely distinguishable indication of movement.

The other door off the hallway opened into the room the master and mistress were using. He glanced in. Dim lantern light spilling in from the hallway slanted across the bottom of the pallet, leaving the rest of the room dark.

Peter edged slowly inside.

There was something on the bed. At first glance it might have been a small reclining figure.

Peter raised the jar, then stopped.

He had made out glassy eyes and a withered snarl.

It was only Cheops the cat mummy.

The light flickered, as if the flame in the lantern had been disturbed by a breeze.

Or by someone passing by behind him. Peter pivoted slowly. The hallway was empty.

He was certain there was someone else in the house. He could feel the other's presence.

The master and mistress might return at any time. They wouldn't be expecting someone to be waiting for them.

Waiting with evil intent.

Peter offered a silent prayer, clutched the pot tighter, and moved cautiously toward the darkened front room. As he stepped into it, he spotted a glint of light.

Was it a hungry blade?

He hurled the jar.

It exploded against the wall, sending fragments rattling around the room.

The intruder let out an oath. There was a crash and the house door flew open.

A gust of cool night air rushed in.

The nocturnal visitor had departed in haste.

Peter began to light the lamps. He hoped that before the master and mistress arrived back he would be able to find all the scorpions he had collected in the jar.

He sighed.

He was not certain now how many he had captured.

Chapter Twenty-eight

Anatolius sought solitude by the pool in John's garden, but found Europa pulling weeds from the herb beds.

As he approached along the graveled path, she looked up from her labor and began to giggle. "Anatolius, where are you going dressed like that?"

"I borrowed this fine clothing from Francio. Don't you like it?"

"Since you ask, I don't think those birds are suitable for a lawyer!"

His bright blue garment was embroidered with strutting peacocks, the colors of their tails repeated in the wide border edging neck, sleeves, and hem.

"Indeed. However, we must always dress appropriately for the task in hand."

"Do you have to appear disguised as a cage full of peacocks now or has Theodora engaged you to spy on her menagerie?"

"I'll explain later," Anatolius muttered, aware of how feeble his words would seem.

He had decided it would be best to disguise himself before visiting Bishop Crispin with the pilgrim flasks. He didn't want the bishop to be able to give a recognizable description of him. It would be safer if no one at court discovered he had been asking what might be termed prying questions.

"You're very mysterious all of a sudden, Anatolius. Where's the guileless young man I once knew? Is this newly-found reticence part of your new profession?"

"I wish people would stop questioning my decision to become a lawyer! None of us are in our usual humors with everything that's going on, are we? I might equally ask what you're doing tending to the garden."

"Tending to the plants gets my mind off everything. I'm really worried about Thomas. He should be back by now." She sighed. "The emperor must value father's advice. Or must have valued it, before...."

Europa looked at the water gurgling into the pool through what was had once been the mouth of some stone creature now too eroded by time and the elements to identify. She sat down on the marble bench under a nearby olive tree. "Could father have killed the senator?"

Anatolius was shocked. "It's not in his nature! Surely you cannot think so?"

"Isn't it? He was a mercenary, wasn't he? He killed men."

Anatolius paced over to the side of the pool. "Indeed. In this case, though, it just isn't possible."

"Will he be in great danger in Egypt, do you think?"

Anatolius hesitated. "Even so far away, he's still under Mithra's protection."

Europa's bleak smile showed she had given his pause more weight than his answer. "I have petitioned the Goddess to bring them all safely home. Let's hope the patriarch doesn't get wind of the Gods don't go away just because the emperor proclaims some law or other."

"True, but in public we're all Christians."

Europa wiped away tears.

"Thomas will be back soon," Anatolius told her. "Do your best not to worry."

Europa made no reply. The quiet trickle of water into the pool was the only sound in the garden.

"It's so still," Anatolius commented. "It's as if even leaves don't care to exert themselves enough to move."

"Now you sound more like yourself! You could make an excellent set of verses from that one thought alone!"

Anatolius shifted his feet. "To be illiterate is—"

"You take words too seriously, Anatolius." Her tone was suddenly so cold.

Too late, Anatolius recalled that Thomas could not read.

"There are too many words being written," Europa went on, glaring at him. "All these lawyers and poets and officials and churchmen scribbling their lives away. And what do most of those words do? Hurt someone, or hide something, or cause trouble one way or another."

"I didn't mean to offend you, Cornelia. Thomas is a bit of a wanderer, and you're—"

"A wanderer too. I've spent my entire life traveling with a troupe."

"Yes but—"

"I ride bulls and I do it half-naked, just as my mother did."

Anatolius looked at the formless form set in the pool. The hardest rock was not proof against time. "I'm sorry. You misunderstand. I didn't intend to insult your husband. I was only concerned. People will wander off from where they're safe, with no idea what they're getting into—"

Europa peered at him. "Thomas is able to take care of himself. It's Hypatia, isn't it? You're worried about Hypatia!"

"Certainly not!"

"Anatolius! You're blushing!"

He disconsolately flapped a peacock-emblazoned sleeve. "I'm just embarrassed by this garish garment."

Chapter Twenty-nine

A scorpion scuttled toward the chest.

Before it could slip out of sight, Peter swept the creature into a wine cup with the flat of his blade. John cracked open the lid of the jar and Peter dumped his venomous captive inside to join the other.

"I think that must be all of them, master."

Dry, scraping noises came from the jar as John set it into a corner.

"I should have chased the intruder, master," Peter apologized. "I might have been able to see who it was. At first I wasn't even sure it was a man."

"What else could it have been but a man?"

"There are demons even in Constantinople. Considering that blasphemous performance at the pagan shrine, I wouldn't be surprised if demons were as thick as scorpions hereabouts."

"Then let's hope they all stay away. You did well, Peter. It was a most inventive weapon."

"It was Zebulon who inspired it, master. I remarked to him this was a strange place with many dangers, and he mentioned those ancient travelers in the wilderness, beset by fiery serpents.

He said the serpents were scorpions, for in the language in which the holy books were written serpent and scorpion are rendered by the same word."

"It sounds like an interesting conversation, Peter."

"Oh yes, it was indeed. I was going to gather vegetables and met him by Melios' house. He invited me to play his strange game. Naturally I refused, but after I explained why I thought it blasphemous, we got into a most interesting theological discussion. I would have liked to have talked longer. He promised next time we met we'd continue our discussion about how the Son of Man was lifted up, just as Moses lifted up the brazen serpent in the wilderness to cure the sick. As I walked back, I began to think about serpents and snakes and scorpions, and well, that was how it came about."

"An interesting story," John said.

Peter frowned. "Even so, master, certain statements he made lead me to suspect he is less than orthodox, like many here." The distress in his voice was marked.

John agreed, then turned his thoughts back to the recent attack. Had the intruder used the commotion caused by the flying demon to hide his activities, or had he purposely created the fiery diversion in order to—what?

The door banged open and Cornelia entered. Behind her, the only evidence of the recent excitement was a column of luminously gray smoke rising against the stars.

"Look what I found, John!" She held out a handful of half-burnt feathers. "It appears the secret of the illusion is known to charlatans all over Egypt."

Peter stared at the pungent scraps.

"It's to impress the ignorant, Peter," Cornelia explained. "You'll recall in Alexandria I mentioned Baba, the magician in the company John and I traveled with years ago? Well, one of his most frightening tricks for shows taking place after dark was pretending to conjure up a flaming demon."

"However did he accomplish that, mistress?"

"Like most magick, it's simple once you know how it's done. After Baba intoned some meaningless incantation, an assistant hiding behind a house would put a torch to a hawk or some other large bird and then set it free. Do you remember, John, the time the unfortunate demon set half a village alight and we had to flee? We can be certain Dedi's responsible for tonight's blaze."

"In which case, it was probably intended to further intimidate Melios. It might have been a diversionary tactic too," John replied, and related Peter's experience earlier that evening.

Cornelia looked thoughtful. "Whoever came in here might just have intended to rob us. A fire is the perfect opportunity for theft. After all, a Lord Chamberlain, even if he's dressed in less than magnificent garments, would surely be traveling with bags of gold, wouldn't he?"

Peter nodded solemnly. "I'm sure that is the opinion of most of the people in Mehenopolis."

"What I would really like to know," John said, "is where Dedi was at the time the flying demon appeared, particularly since we first saw it rising above the Rock of the Snake."

"That reminds me," Cornelia said. "There's something I want to show you."

***

Cornelia led John along a path through a stand of palms. Their towering height reminded John of the columned cisterns that competed with dungeons for space beneath the Great Palace. He preferred not to dwell too much on thoughts of those subterranean chambers into which so many vanished and from which so few returned.

"You're quiet, John. I'm not surprised. I've found being back in Egypt after all these years disturbing. It's as if we've stepped through a doorway into the past."

"If we have, it must have been a doorway to a different past entirely. But here we are, together, and what is it that I am to see?"

Cornelia looked up at him, her face barely distinguishable in the dim light from the thick dusting of stars arching overhead.

"Do you ever wonder if we'd been able to stay together how different our lives might have been?"

"I've asked myself often and there's no answer. Which also seems to be the case with this accursed investigation. I'm beginning to feel exactly like Theseus following Ariadne's thread, only I fear I've dropped mine and am wandering about in circles. I'm not even certain what I'm seeking."

Cornelia smiled. "Where do you find yourself right now, John?"

"I've established very little. In brief, Dedi and Melios are competing for leadership of Mehenopolis and they're also arguing about ownership of a piece of land. Dedi claims to have caused a sheep to kill itself. Melios is terrified of Dedi. Then too someone, probably Apollo even though he denies it, is smuggling religious relics by hiding them in his beehives."

"Selling relics is a thriving trade and bees are excellent guardians, since it's not only Melios who's afraid of them. Remember how Porphyrios sat at the back of the cart, as far away as possible from the hives?"

John was silent for a while. "I've also been devoting some thought to Porphyrios. It's highly suspicious that more than one exile was sent here at the same time."

"Porphyrios must be grateful he was parted from Constantinople rather than from his head. And what about Zebulon, who apparently exiled himself, fleeing persecution years ago?"

"He's safe here, at least. Who would journey this far to assassinate an old cleric?"

"Let Zebulon draw the wrath of Justinian and sailing beyond the Pillars of Hercules won't save him."

"Expecting a mere mortal to escape the wrath of the emperor is akin to asking him to undertake the labors of Hercules. Speaking of which, unfortunately thus far I have not been as successful as Hercules in performing my task," John concluded.

"You may not have captured the Cretan bull like he did, John, but you certainly snared a Cretan bull-rider!"

John did not seem to hear her comment. "Cornelia, something has just occurred to me. It isn't beyond the bounds of possibility that Zebulon is involved in the sheep's mysterious death."

Cornelia expressed her doubts.

"Consider," John replied. "He serves as spiritual advisor to Melios and his household as well as to visitors and those who live in Mehenopolis. I could see Zebulon arranging it to discredit Dedi, given he knew Dedi would claim the credit. The magician is a dangerous heretic from Zebulon's point of view, but if his wild claims and vanity could be used to maneuver him into declaring his hand in something forbidden, such as magick, and then the authorities were informed of it…."

They emerged from the palm grove. The vast pearled cloak of the sky stretched overhead.

"John, I have to confess. I may have killed that sheep. Yes, I could have climbed into the rafters of the barn during the daytime, hid there until the door was bolted, and then dropped down and—"

"It's more likely you've been in the sun too long as well, Cornelia. Why do you make such a ludicrous claim?"

She assumed a theatrical pout. "I thought if I were a dispatcher of woolly animals you might pay more attention to me."

John glanced around. "What is it you wanted to show me here?"

Cornelia reached up, caught John around the back of his neck, pulled his head down, and kissed him. "I want to feel you against me again. What do you say? Cheops will look the other way!"

John looked up at the stars cascading across the horizon with a brilliance he'd not seen since his youth.

"I think he will. It's time we returned to our bed, Britomartis."

Chapter Thirty

From outside, the Church of Sergius and Bacchus was a squat, domed structure slotted uncomfortably between the Church of Peter and Paul and the architectural jumble of the Hormisdas Palace. Anatolius would never have guessed the building could contain the vast, airy space into which he stepped. From a floor of gray-veined marble, two tiers of red and green marble columns ascended to a vaulted sky filled with a glittering mosaic host of holy men and angels.

It was almost enough to make a Mithran believe in the Christian heaven.

He had, however, come to the church on secular business.

"I visited your lodgings and was directed here by your neighbor," Anatolius said to Bishop Crispin. "That's to say, the man who had taken up residence in the alcove with the statue of Diana next to your room. I expect you've noticed he's got his laundry draped all over her?"

"I believe that is more for the sake of her modesty." The monophysite ecclesiastic was a slight, narrow-faced man with a sparse black beard. He wore black robes cinched with a wide red belt. "Timothy is exceptionally learned. He spent several years meditating in a cave. Why do you wish to speak to me, young man?"

"I'm here on behalf of Senator Symacchus."

The bishop looked Anatolius over as if he were a dubious theological argument.

"You were left this legacy in his will," Anatolius went on, holding out the sandalwood box. "It's his collection of pilgrim flasks."

Crispin took the box and opened the lid. "How very kind of him to remember one with whom he so often argued!"

"I understand you held opposing religious views?"

"We sometimes win our opponents' hearts, though they disagree with us intellectually." Crispin held one of the tiny flasks up to his eyes. "Symacchus now knows which of us was right." Placing the flask back in the box, he sketched a blessing.

"Are these interesting items very valuable?"

"It would be as well to ask the same of the blessings of the saints! If you mean are they worth anything in nomismata, I doubt it. As Symacchus knew, I collect them for my own enjoyment. Most of these examples are of a common variety, although I see one or two of a type I've not seen before. Still, I am very happy to have them. Thank you."

"How did you come to take up such an interest, if I may ask?"

Crispin gently closed the box. "Perhaps you think collecting objects from far-flung places is a strange interest for one who has been a guest here at the Hormisdas for most of Justinian's reign? Let us say it's because I must make my pilgrimages vicariously. Envoys and new arrivals to our enclave contribute to my collection."

It was, Anatolius knew, well known that Theodora's monophysite guests were likewise the orthodox Justinian's prisoners. They were under the empress' protection in the Hormisdas Palace, but not allowed to stray far from it.

"You have lived in Constantinople for a long time?"

"I arrived here more than a decade ago. I was with a delegation trying to fashion a compromise with those of the emperor's religious persuasion. It transpired it was not the Lord's will for that effort to succeed. I was content to remain. The local authorities in Antioch have long persecuted those with whom they disagree. You see what's inscribed on the entablature?"

Lifting his gaze to the white marble frieze carried atop colored columns, Anatolius read a portion of the chiseled verse indicated. "...Pious and heaven-crowned Theodora...."

"The empress ordered this magnificent church constructed for us. And, to be honest, to house the thumb of Saint Sergius as well."

Crispin tapped the box lid. "When even the oil from a lamp burning near a tomb is imbued by some essence of the saint interred there, contemplate how much more powerful is the smallest scrap of the saint's earthly husk."

"If the thumb of a Roman soldier is worthy of such a church, there must be relics worth an empire," Anatolius observed.

"Were you a friend of the senator?"

"I fear I didn't know him well."

"He spoke most eloquently on behalf of the orthodox point of view," Crispin said. "Justinian cannot reproach him for failing to persuade me that I am in error. True belief withstands any amount of reasoning."

Crispin looked Anatolius up and down again, more critically than earlier. "It occurs to me that I do not know your name. Again, thank you for bringing the senator's gift. Now I must attend to my devotions."

As Crispin began to turn away, Anatolius drew forth the cross he had taken from the senator's storeroom. He had chipped its enamel and snapped off the top so that it now resembled the broken artifact Thomas had been given to identify himself to the person he was to meet at the Hippodrome.

Crispin stared with ill-concealed surprise at the cross Anatolius was holding. "Where did you get that?"

"From an acquaintance of the senator's. A man who told me of the offer he made to Symacchus, one he would like to convey to you, now that the senator is dead."

Crispin's suspicious gaze remained fixed on the broken cross. "Are you certain this man you mention knew the senator? I believe you have been sorely misled, whoever you are."

"What do you mean?"

A faint smile flickered across Crispin's narrow face. "The senator told me about a certain clumsy fellow who made a pretense of knowing things he clearly could not know, of having knowledge he did not possess. At one point, statements very akin to threats were made to the senator by this oaf. You say you bring the same message. The senator was recently murdered."

Crispin paused. "Therefore in the circumstances I have no choice but to report our conversation to the authorities, my gaudy peacock friend," he went on. "I shall pray your life is spared, but my petition is much more likely to be granted if you are far away from Constantinople."

Chapter Thirty-one

John strode toward the ruins of the church over which Zebulon had once presided. The rising sun reddened smoke hanging over Mehenopolis, evidence of meals being cooked before the settlement began its day's work. Fog steamed off the still surface of an irrigation ditch.

The bleakness of John's humor did not match the perpetual sunlight of this strange country.

What could the night's events have been intended to accomplish? Had the visitation by the supposed demon been a warning? If so, to whom? Was Dedi again demonstrating his supposed powers to Melios, or was someone else warning of the consequences to those of the settlement who had been displaying allegiance to a magician?

John could not envision Zebulon setting fire to a bird, although the cleric would have more reason than anyone to try to dissuade Mehenopolis' residents to depart from what he considered blasphemous practices—not to mention his church had been burnt down.

John had not formed any conclusions by the time he came upon Zebulon seated on his accustomed bench, between the well and the ruined church.

The cleric had already captured a visitor. He was sharing a loaf of bread and a jug of water with the charioteer Porphyrios.

"Salutations, Lord Chamberlain!" Zebulon bowed without rising. "Would you care to share our humble repast?"

The big charioteer sitting beside him had left just enough space on the carved sandstone seat for John's lean frame.

"An exciting night, wasn't it, excellency?" remarked Porphyrios through a mouthful of bread.

Zebulon turned his face toward the sun. His profile, with its great beak of a nose and long flowing hair, was impressive, John thought. He would not have looked out of place clothed in sumptuous ecclesiastical garments, officiating in one of the capital's great churches.

"A wonder so easily explained, Lord Chamberlain, and yet there seems no way to convince the ignorant of the truth," Zebulon said. "I fear Dedi has provided many with food for thought." He looked at the crust in his hand. "But is it poisoned or wholesome fare?"

"Do you believe Dedi was responsible for the flying demon?" John said.

"Isn't it obvious, Lord Chamberlain? I can't tell you how the trick was done, but I'm positive he's the culprit."

"On the other hand, if it was a genuine omen, a sign of ill to come, don't you think Melios ought to be worried?" Porphyrios put in.

"Why do you suppose the warning was directed at Melios?" John asked.

"Because it was his property that was set on fire."

"I regret to say Melios has a strong tendency to superstition," Zebulon said. "He may well believe the demon was a personal message to him."

Porphyrios shrugged. "Aren't we all superstitious, if we're honest about it? Even if we don't agree with those who wear amulets to avert the evil eye, we all believe something."

"Doubtless the same applies to charioteers?"

"True, excellency. I once worked for a team owner who immediately dismissed anyone found to have had anything to do with the color green. This was when I raced for the Blues. Our most experienced man lost his job for eating lettuce at the wrong time. He only ate it for his indigestion. We lost all our races that day and that only confirmed the owner's belief that green was to be avoided."

John had to lean forward slightly to direct a question to the cleric. "Would you say superstition is stronger in Mehenopolis than religious convictions? I'm thinking of Dedi's magick against Melios' beliefs."

"The Lord will give us the answer soon enough," Zebulon replied.

"You and Melios are both monophysites?"

"That's right. We wouldn't be popular in Constantinople. Why are you interested?"

"What about Melios' problems with imperial taxes? Could it be these ruinous rates he complains of are a form of persecution, because of his religion?" Porphyrios suggested.

"I'd hardly call taxes persecution," Zebulon replied. "If they are, we're all martyrs. I would have been happy enough to pay higher taxes if I had been able to remain where I was. Besides which, the emperor tolerates us in Egypt. The empire needs Egypt's wheat. If you're a heretic or considered to be one, I say find yourself a far-off field of wheat to occupy, as in effect I did."

A naked, sun-browned boy, his legs white with dust up to the knees, came running up the road, vanished down the spiral staircase clinging to the inside of the well, reappeared, and ran back in the direction from which he'd arrived, water sloshing from his large earthenware pot.

"You've been here a long time, Zebulon, in fact since before Dedi arrived. I imagine you and Melios have become united against his influence," John said.

"Not so, excellency. Our discussions are confined to spiritual affairs and matters relating to his estate."

"And the snake game?"

"I fear not, Lord Chamberlain."

"Your host has avoided sitting down at that board with you all these years?"

"He did play it once but he insisted on placing a substantial wager to make it more interesting, as he put it. I didn't care for the idea, but he shelters and feeds me so I agreed. Unfortunately he lost. He's refused to play ever since. It's a pity, since I can't seem to better anyone else, except for your good lady. I'm hoping she'll visit me again today."

John suppressed a sigh. Zebulon was always voluble on the subject of his game, if nothing else.

"I was told you blessed the sheep before it was placed in the pen?"

"Yes, at Melios' request. I was uneasy about it but as you'll appreciate felt I could hardly refuse since he's given me shelter all these years. Dedi heard about it and ever since he's been proclaiming the animal's death proves Mehen is more powerful than the Lord. What he conveniently doesn't mention is that Melios took all sorts of other precautions. Protective garlands, charms, that kind of thing. The sheep even shared its pen with a clay scorpion."

Zebulon absently traced a hieroglyph incised on his bench, where sprightly quail chicks, reed baskets, sinuous snakes, zig-zagging lines, and seated scribes formed undecipherable messages. "Every day I sit on a bench carved from a block of stone that was once part of the temple up there on the Rock of the Snake. Much of its material has been used to build houses in the settlement. No wonder the people cling to strange beliefs, despite all my efforts."

John seized his opportunity to mention pilgrim flasks and from there, recalling the bones hidden in Apollo's beehive, moved on to the subject of trading in relics.

Porphyrios grunted. "There's plenty of money to be made that way. Sorry, Zebulon, but you must admit while those departed holy men may have been poor, their bones and such have since made a lot of men wealthy."

Zebulon laughed. "True enough. Well, excellency, I suppose I can't persuade you to engage me in a game? What about you, Porphyrios?"

The charioteer got to his feet. "I'm always ready for a strenuous contest, but unfortunately I have urgent business."

"I fear I must decline too," John said. "Doubtless someone willing to play will come along soon."

Zebulon smiled. "Send your servant some time if you can spare him, Lord Chamberlain. I enjoyed talking to him. He's a born theologian."

John followed Porphyrios, who marched energetically away. He soon caught up and matched the charioteer's stride.

"I have the impression you want to speak to me in private, Lord Chamberlain. I can't fathom why. I've only just arrived here myself, so I have no idea what's been going on. Thinking about the relic trade, it strikes me a fellow in the sort of financial straits Melios claims to be in would find it a useful source of income."

They were passing along the bank of a wide ditch. Bees droned, reminding John of Apollo's charges.

After an initial hesitation, Porphyrios continued. "I thought it best not to say anything in front of Zebulon, but mention of taxes reminded me about something. The assessor has been asking Melios questions about you."

"How do you know this?"

"I happened to be at Melios' house when Scrofa arrived. He requested a private interview so I retired to another room. Their talk became somewhat heated, so much so I could hardly avoid overhearing what was being said. He pressed Melios for details about your movements and the real reason you were here. Not that Melios could supply any information beyond what everyone in Mehenopolis knew. Scrofa had hardly departed when you arrived, so I decided to leave and return later in the day since it was obvious Melios would probably not be available again for some time."

So John had in fact heard his name spoken as he approached Melios' house. "I intend to interview Scrofa later this morning. Doubtless he can shed light on his interest in my movements."

Porphyrios shook his head. "I'm afraid he'll not be easily found, excellency. According to Zebulon all the tax assessors who visit Mehenopolis take bribes. Just imagine Scrofa's consternation when he arrived, ready to put his hand out as usual, only to find one of the highest officials of the empire in residence. He must be terrified you'll discover what's he's been doing and report him to the authorities."

Porphyrios came to a halt and stared thoughtfully at the ditch. Sunlight ran across its water like liquid fire. "Lord Chamberlain, I may as well confess I've been lying to you," he went on. "I'm not an exile. Now that we're alone, I can reveal the real reason for my visit."

He scowled. "I was losing one race after another. Finally I discovered someone had buried a curse tablet behind our stables. You've probably seen them? Little bits of rolled lead with vindictive magickal imprecations written on them. I threw it into the Marmara. However, since I didn't know who was responsible—there are many who are jealous of my prowess—I feared he would obtain another and I wouldn't find it."

"It's been some time since races were held in the capital, thanks to the plague."

"And that gave me the chance to come to Egypt, since I made inquiries and learned the best charms come from this land. My intent is to purchase a protective amulet and thereby change my fortunes once racing resumes. When I heard rumors about a powerful magician in Mehenopolis, I came here."

"Dedi deals in such things?"

"Right now he's considering the matter."

"You're haggling over the price, you mean."

"Well…yes…but now you have my story. It isn't the sort of tale I'd care to have spread around, so you can understand my bending the truth a little."

***

Peter had almost finished chopping vegetables for the evening meal when Hapymen arrived.

"Your master keeps you busy," his visitor observed. Sweat ran down his brown chest in rivulets.

Peter half wished he could shed his clothing for the clout of cloth which was all Hapymen wore. It would be much cooler although a lot less dignified.

"It's the master's right, but I'm not as busy as I should be." Peter wiped the blade of his knife on his tunic. "I still haven't obtained everything I need to make honey cakes. He dines on so little and most of the time doesn't seem to take notice of what he's eating. That's a dangerous practice at the palace."

"I suppose all that rich food upsets the humors at times?"

Peter's head bobbed below the table as he bent to rummage in his basket of garden produce.

"That's true enough." He reappeared with what he had sought. "As you see, as part of the evening meal I'm preparing onions. The master likes them chopped and boiled. He doesn't care for elaborate fare. Just between us, I suspect the palace banquets he's required to attend are a terrible penance to one with such simple tastes."

"I don't know that I would care to be present at one either, Peter. Judging by what you've said, I wonder if it's safe to break bread with the emperor."

"I have myself heard gossip, after a sudden death supposedly caused by tainted fish, that it was not as spoilt as it was claimed to be. Garum sauce covers many sins." Peter nodded knowingly and resumed chopping.

"But surely you're not suggesting poison?"

"You must make up your own mind on that, Hapymen, but remember, life at court is not always quite the way it appears."

"After Melios visited the capital, he requested his cook to recreate some of the fine meals he had had there," Hapymen remarked. "The attempt wasn't too successful, although I'm certain that in one case the master confused the ingredients for two separate dishes and thought they were for one."

"Oh?"

"As I recall, it involved a mixture of eggs and cheese and swordfish, which sounds bad enough, but then the cook was instructed to add cabbage and garlic as well." Hapymen gave a dramatic shudder. "Quite a few servants were in my vegetable beds that night, picking lettuce to quell their stomachs!"

"Many in Constantinople enjoy that particular meal. Monokythron, it's called, because it's all cooked together in one pot. Not that I care for it myself. It's far too rich for an old army cook like me."

His visitor laughed. "Speaking of which, it's as well I stopped by, Peter. You need better onions for your master's meal. That one's well past its best. When they grow that large, the flavor becomes far too strong."

Peter looked dubious. "Yes, well, it's rather bigger than most as you say. I haven't been paying as much attention this morning to my duties as I should. Last night was extremely upsetting."

Hapymen nodded sympathetically. "We're all out of humor this morning between too much excitement and not enough sleep. I'll go right now and personally dig you better onions. I'd like your master to taste just how fine my vegetables are! Besides, I know Melios would be furious if he thought his eminent guest had not been served the best his estate has to offer. It's a matter of pride, isn't it?"

Peter agreed. "And we servants too play our part in upholding our masters' honor. I'm grateful for your help."

Chapter Thirty-two

The first voice Anatolius heard was Europa's, the next a man's, loud and threatening.

His kalamos slipped and a blot of ink splotched the final sheet of the baker's vexatious will. In an instant he was out of John's study and running downstairs.

He could almost hear Bishop Crispin urging him to leave the city.

"He can't see me? Trying to avoid me, you mean! Get out of my way, woman! I'm his client!"

The man shoved Europa aside and entered the house. He was a burly fellow dressed in a short tunic and leather breeches.

It was Little Nero.

Europa stared in obvious bemusement as Anatolius made appropriate introductions.

"Now are you satisfied?" the baker asked her, then turned towards Anatolius. "I'll wager you've got your hands full with this one!"

"I've almost finished drafting your will," Anatolius told him. "The last page needs to be recopied."

"So you claim," growled Little Nero. "Don't think I'm going to pay you extra for that either. There's changes to be made anyhow, so you can tear it up and start over. That's why I'm here. Don't gawk at me like that! You're happy to have the work and we both know it!"

"Changes? Why?"

"It's that other viperous son of mine, Situs. I thought he'd learn his lesson when I cut Titus out of my will. I made certain they both knew too, but no! It didn't do a bit of good. They still expect me to pay all their bills, and complain when I refuse. I swear my sons are nothing but buboes on my long-suffering backside!"

"If you'll tell me what amendments you wish to make—"

"Time's money! There's nothing to discuss. Disinherit Situs!"

"Yes, of course. Now, when you disinherited Titus the reason you gave was that he'd insulted you by reciting a certain poem at the baths."

"And what was more insulting, his mockery of me or the fact my son calls himself a poet?"

"And Situs has affronted you as well?"

"Exactly! I put him in charge of my largest bakery and the way he's run it into the ground has been an insult."

"I'm not certain that is what the law has in mind when it refers to insulting behavior. As I explained, you can only entirely disinherit a natural heir if you have good cause. As it happens, the emperor promulgated a new constitution explicitly setting forth what cases of ingratitude can reasonably be stated by parents against their children. They include—"

Little Nero clenched his fists. "Why do lawyers always want to tell you how it works? Does the butcher describe how he cut the cow's throat? If I visit a whore do I want to hear what sort of pessary she's using? Of course not! I'm not paying you to tell me about the law, you fool! I'm paying you to do what I tell you to do!"

"Yes, yes, so long as it is within legal boundaries. Let's see. Has Situs laid violent hands on you?"

"In my opinion what he's done with my bakery is a slap in my face."

Anatolius looked dubious and began to run through permissible reasons for disinheritance.

"Does he habitually associate with criminals, or has he brought criminal accusations against you? I doubt he's made any attempt on your life?"

"There, you have it! The perfect reason! The way he's running the business is killing me!"

"That would be difficult to prove, I fear. On the other hand, if he's informed against you or prevented you from making a will....What about this? Does he keep company with actors and buffoons?"

"No!" bellowed the baker. "I'm the fool who associates with buffoons. Or one buffoon at least. You! I'm not going to stand here pissing away nomismata. If you want your fee paid, then cut Situs out of the will." He turned on his heel and opened the house door.

"Where are you going?" Anatolius called after him.

"I'm off to see Situs. I'm going to tell him exactly what I think of him until he lays violent hands on me!"

Europa slammed the door shut.

"Don't worry," Anatolius told her. "He'll probably change his mind before I can think of a legal way to disinherit Situs."

Europa suppressed a giggle. "What an excitable man! Are all your clients like that?"

"No, thank Mithra! Don't worry about it. I'm keeping this old will handy, since going by past experience he'll change his mind before I get a new one half-written. You'll see!"

"I should think you'd have more sympathy for poor Situs, as if he hasn't suffered enough having Little Nero for a father, and now he's about to be disinherited."

Anatolius smiled. "His paternity is its own punishment, eh?"

Europa couldn't stop herself from giggling. "I'm sorry. I'm not laughing at the son's predicament, Anatolius, it's just, well, I didn't like to ask before, but what have you done to your hair?"

Anatolius' hand went to his bare scalp. "I had to shave it off for a difficult task to be undertaken."

"Those adorable curly locks." Europa turned the corners of her mouth down in exaggerated sorrow. "What a shame!"

"They'll grow back. I hope."

"What sort of a task requires a bald head? Does it have something to do with that ridiculous peacock costume?"

"Francio wouldn't appreciate you disparaging his taste in sartorial elegance, Europa."

Anatolius wondered how Francio was recovering from his encounter with the bowl of eel soup, and from there his thoughts turned to the intruders.

Rather than the baker, it could have been the same pair at John's door, calling to look for Anatolius.

They wouldn't have wasted time arguing.

He realized what he had to do. "Europa, there's something I must tell you."

***

Europa sat at the kitchen table and listened, as stony-faced as an unsympathetic magistrate, while Anatolius told her everything he knew about her husband's predicament, John's trip to Egypt, and his own efforts to solve Senator Symacchus' murder.

"In short, Thomas lied to me."

"No, Europa. He expected he'd be meeting a man with further instructions at the Hippodrome and then he'd be traveling for a while, just as he told you. Something to do with a relic, he said." Anatolius took a gulp of wine. He had already consumed a greater quantity than was wise. Raw as it was, for once it seemed palatable. "He was just pretending to know more than he did in order to get the job."

"According to what Bishop Crispin told you, Thomas threatened these people, whoever they are. He must have hinted that he knew enough to cause trouble if he weren't hired. Sometimes I think—" Her eyes brimmed with tears.

Uncertain what to say or do, Anatolius got up and looked out the kitchen window. Constantinople was not a large city. The murderer of the senator, the people with whom Symacchus had been involved, the answers to their questions, all quite possibly lay within sight. Yet despite its limited area, the capital was also a maze, not just of brick and marble, but of conflicting motives, ambitions, and lies.

"Be careful, Europa. From now on, if I'm not here, don't open the door unless you're certain it's me on the other side."

Europa peered into her cup. "I understand about your disguise now, Anatolius. You can't be sure if the bishop glimpsed you around the palace, and you certainly don't want him to be able to give a reasonably close description of his mysterious visitor to anyone, but did you think how recognizable those peacocks are?"

"I know, I know. I won't be able to wear them in public, or go out with my head uncovered until my hair grows back."

"What I meant is what if Francio decides to wear those clothes again?"

"I never thought of that! I'll warn Francio when I return them."

"It's all become very complicated."

"Yes, I've been out of humor trying to piece it together. So far I've got a murdered senator, this relic Thomas hinted about, and now it seems Hektor is involved."

"What makes you think that?"

Anatolius explained his discovery that Hektor had worked briefly for Symacchus and, it appeared, had been with the men who visited the senator's house on the night Symacchus had died and his servant Achilles had disappeared.

He drained his cup. The wine was having its usual effect, which was to say as one cup followed another his understanding of the problem at hand became clearer and clearer and then, just as he was about to grasp the very essence, the precise explanation, just as he glimpsed it slipping around the next corner, a heavy, soporific fog rolled in.

"It sounds to me as if you've managed to make a good start on solving practically everything," Europa said.

"Practically everything is still nothing."

Europa began to giggle again. "I'm sorry, Anatolius, but I can't help it. Without your hair you look just like a poor shorn lamb."

Chapter Thirty-three

Cornelia pulled off her tunic and hung it on a peg. The bath was little more than a roofless cubicle with a slab of limestone in one corner. Slabs of the red sandstone that showed up all over the oasis protected plastered walls to waist height.

It wasn't much better than bathing in the Nile, Cornelia thought, but at least she didn't have to share it with passing crocodiles. The only wildlife visible inhabited eroded hieroglyphs in the sandstone—a flock of geese, a falcon, a snake or two. She bent to examine the opening where water drained outside. No scorpions lurked there.

She stepped up onto the slab, lifted the large jug she carried, and let water trickle down over her shoulders. The limestone felt hot against her soles, the water tepid.

There was no way to escape the heat. At least the water sluiced away the sand that accumulated on her skin, finding its way to the corners of her eyes and the back of her neck. She could feel the fine grit when she ran a hand along her arm.

When the jug was empty she stretched her hands up over her head, reaching toward the brilliant blue square of the sky. She shifted her feet, as if the motionless stone beneath them was the back of one of the bulls she had ridden in her days with the troupe.

She wondered if she would ever do that again.

Possibly not. While she was still slim and well muscled, her reflexes were becoming slower.

She was soon dry and reluctantly slipped back into her clothing and went into the house.

She stopped abruptly.

Thorikos scrambled up from his seat. "I can see you're angry, Cornelia, but spare me the scorpions!"

"Scorpions? How do you know about them?"

"Well, I peeked in that jar in the corner. I assure you I knocked quite loudly before coming in, and there didn't seem to be anyone here and—"

"So you invited yourself to enter and looked around?"

Thorikos looked ashamed. "I was curious to see what it was like. I've been inside Melios' home, but I haven't been inside an ordinary house, you see, and…."

"It's not exactly one of the wonders of the world!"

"Oh, that's true, but I'm most interested in learning how other people live."

"That's why you visited us, to see the inside of the house?"

"Actually, I was just passing by and thought I would ask if there was anything I could be of assistance with…." Thorikos was flustered.

"And perhaps get a glimpse of the house as well? It's a long walk from the pilgrim camp and rather out of your way," Cornelia pointed out.

"I went to visit Melios but he had a visitor. I thought it best not to wait."

Cornelia gave Thorikos a questioning look.

"Melios was having words with someone. By the tenor of the conversation, I doubt he'd be in the mood for visitors."

"Who was it, Thorikos?"

"It was that charioteer fellow. I heard racing mentioned. They sounded like a couple of partisans arguing the merits of their respective factions. Exactly what was being said I couldn't say."

Thorikos shifted his feet. "I wonder if you can help me, Cornelia? It's about my health. Ever since I set foot in Egypt I've been plagued with the most dreadful headaches. I happened to mention them to Hapymen. Would you believe it, it seems he's very knowledgeable about these matters?"

"I'm sure he didn't refer you to me for help."

"It's about the remedy he suggested. He said the only certain cure was to rub my head with a concoction made of a fried mixture of fish and, I regret to say, a cat."

"That surprises me," Cornelia admitted. "Many Egyptians still consider it a sacred animal."

Thorikos looked mournful. "Indeed. You would not believe the difficulty I had, trying to buy a suitable cat today. What's worse, while the settlement was swarming with them when we arrived, most of the nasty things appear to have gone into hiding. I've not been able to catch one of the few roaming about either, despite no lack of trying."

"Yes, I can see the scratches on your hands. At least the fish will be easier to obtain."

"Alas, not so. The sellers in the market are as sly as the cats. They think they can name their own price."

"They may do so, but won't necessarily obtain it. Obviously word's got around of your quest and you've been here long enough to be known by sight. Naturally it will cost you more to purchase fish than the amount anyone else in the settlement will be asked to pay."

"Exactly so. Still, provided it is not too outrageous I can afford to buy a fish. Getting a cat is the problem. I trust this will not offend you, but I glanced in one or two rooms and happened to see a cat mummy. I was wondering if I could purchase it?"

Cornelia curbed her tongue. Thorikos did look extremely unwell. "I am afraid Cheops is not for sale. I must say I've never heard of such a remedy."

"Is it possible Hapymen was having a jest at my expense? Perhaps I misunderstood my instructions? He has such a thick accent."

Cornelia laughed. "Of course! Could it be he didn't say you needed to anoint yourself with a mixture of fried cat and fish but rather meant cooked catfish?"

Thorikos stared in amazement. "Catfish? I never thought of that!"

"No matter. Both you and the local feline population would be better served if you treat your headaches with an infusion of willow or even a poppy potion. And here's another suggestion."

"What is that, Cornelia?"

"Don't creep into people's houses unannounced. It may be bad for your health."

***

John and Peter stopped in front of the weird agglomeration of stone, mud, and marble that stretched back into the rubble at the base of the Rock of the Snake. Peter gaped at the limbs of broken statues that formed the doorway, but before John could rap on the door Dedi stuck his sallow, bristly face into the sunlight.

Dedi gazed at his visitors and his fish-like mouth formed a smile that showed off his wildly askew teeth. "Lord Chamberlain, I'm pleased to see you, and your servant too! Tell me, has Melios been scared to his senses by the flying demon I sent?"

"I cannot say," John replied.

Dedi pursed his mouth in annoyance. "Melios should consider the situation more closely, excellency. A wise man would have long since given up claims to my land. Never mind. Come inside."

As had been the case during John's initial visit, they sat in the first room of the tunnel-like house.

"I fear I can only offer you beer today," Dedi apologized.

Peter took the proffered cup, sampled its contents, and grimaced.

John took a sip. "You'd get used to it in time, Peter. I did. It was only after I reached Constantinople I began to drink Egyptian wine."

"What is it you want to see me about, Lord Chamberlain?"

"The flaming demon. I believe you just admitted you were responsible?"

"Admitted? I am proud to say I was responsible. It was my final warning to Melios. If he does not accede to my wishes I will be forced to fill the sky with a hundred fiery demons. No, a thousand! And worse besides! Much, much worse!"

The magician's voice rose in anger. "This settlement belongs to Mehen! His shrine was here long before Melios' feeble god arrived on the scene!"

John slapped several burnt feathers on the table. "It appears that Egyptian demons have plumage remarkably resembling that of hawks."

Dedi snatched the feathers away. "What vile trap is this?"

"It's a common magician's trick," John replied.

"Melios is trying to discredit me. Any fool could release a burning bird!" Dedi picked up a feather and waved it at his visitors. "Do you think I don't have the power I claim? I'll show you soon enough!"

He muttered what sounded suspiciously like gibberish, then cried out, "Mehen, take this cursed thing away!"

He clapped his hands together. When he drew them apart, the feather was gone.

"It's up your sleeve," John remarked. "You're dexterous, I'll give you that. If you were thinking of removing it from Peter's ear, don't bother."

Peter clapped his hands to his ears, looking terrified.

"It's only sleight of hand, Peter," John told him.

Dedi slumped back down onto his stool. "You're shrewd, Lord Chamberlain. I can see I will have to be honest with you." The magician took a long, noisy slurp from his cup. "You have been to the shrine above us. You have looked upon the maze."

"The entrance to the maze," John corrected him.

"As you say. You will agree that this is an ancient place, the source of enormous forces?"

"If you mean the talking snake, it's obvious it has a dried monkey's head fitted with a wig."

"I won't deny that I sometimes resort to illusions. In the great city you come from there are fabulous churches, so I am told. Their ceilings and walls appear to be populated by saints and angels, their space ablaze with gold and gems and colored marbles. In a word, these incredible structures might have come straight from the hand of the Lord himself. But, in fact, they were erected by the emperor to demonstrate heavenly beauty and power in a way that the populace can understand."

"You are saying you perform your tricks to demonstrate the power of Mehen?"

"That's right. And why not? Can you imagine the destruction if a real demon descended on Mehenopolis?"

Dedi waved his hands and the burnt feather materialized, an arm's breadth above the table, and floated gently downwards. Peter quickly drew his cup away.

"Remember," Dedi continued, "Mehen works through the appointed guardian of his shrine."

"By which you mean yourself? How were you appointed to such high office?"

"Mehen called me, Lord Chamberlain. Years ago I was a traveling magician, wandering about performing for a few coins."

"Or frightening ignorant people enough so they'd give you more than a few if only you'd be on your way?"

Dedi reddened with anger, but ignored the comment. "Then something insisted to me that I travel along the Nile. I realized I was being drawn somewhere, as inexorably as the waters of great rivers are attracted to the sea. When I arrived here I camped just outside Melios' estate, undecided as to whether I should continue on my journey. Ah! But then I awoke in the gray light before dawn next day with a heavy weight on my chest. It was a coiled snake, the very one you saw a few nights ago."

The magician waved an excited hand. "Then, once I learnt the ruined temple was dedicated to Mehen, I immediately knew I had been sent a sign and that this was where I was meant to be."

"So why hasn't Mehen sent an enormous snake after Melios?" John asked pointedly.

"Doubt what I say at your own risk, Lord Chamberlain. The power of Mehen is everywhere in this place. There isn't a structure in the oasis that doesn't contain brick or stone from the temple ruins, all of them imbued with the Snake God's power."

John noticed Peter staring uneasily at the feather on the floor. "I gather the pilgrim business is lucrative, Dedi. Hardly surprising, is it, with a constant stream of travelers in need of shelter, making offerings, buying supplies and mementos. Naturally you would make such claims."

"I can see you don't believe me. Then consider Zebulon. Why does he never win that game he plays? It's because of his religious beliefs and his blasphemous use of Mehen's likeness, of course!"

John stood up. "You keep talking about Mehen and his power, Dedi. What I see are shabby illusions any fumbling magician could perform, all of them easily explained. You may be able to mislead many, but—"

Dedi leapt up, as if intending to restrain John from leaving. "You question my powers? Well, why haven't you been able to explain why Melios' sheep cut its own throat?"

Peter looked horrified. To hear his master addressed in such an insulting fashion!

"It was just another trick, Dedi." John's tone was withering.

"You know it wasn't!" Dedi waved his hands frantically. "You're mocking me! Very well, I'll prove my powers beyond any doubt. I'll force another sheep to kill itself."

John took a step toward the doorway. "That's hardly necessary, Dedi. As I said—"

"I must insist, Lord Chamberlain, if that is what it will take to convince you!"

John sighed. "Very well, then. It shall be arranged as you wish."

Chapter Thirty-four

Felix strode across the track at the Hippodrome, past the spot where the senator had lain.

He felt out of place on the floor of the stadium. He was used to looking down from the tiers of marble seats which, vacant, now rose all around like marble cliffs.

He had already talked to every person he could find who might have known something about the deceased senator. The conversations had failed to bear out Anatolius' conviction that a pointer to the murder might be found among Symacchus' house guests. No one recalled anything noteworthy about the visitors, except that most were Egyptian, but as Felix endured much unenlightening gossip, it occurred to him to explore a different connection.

The Hippodrome might well have been chosen for the fateful meeting simply because it was temporarily unused and only lightly patrolled. Before the plague, however, the races had rivaled the Great Church as the attraction every traveler insisted on seeing. Would Symacchus' guests have been any different?

Rounding the spina, Felix saw a man with a spear standing in the middle of the track. Heavy-jowled, with a thick neck and hooded eyes, he wore a tunic resembling a stained sack. He pushed the spear tip into the dirt gently, as if probing with a surgical instrument. He withdrew it, shuffled forward, and prodded again.

For a few arm's lengths behind him, the hard earth appeared dimpled, riddled with punctures. There were a couple of larger holes, of the sort a dog might dig, with soil piled beside them.

As Felix approached, the man began to dig more vigorously. He bent down and plucked from the ground what looked like a clod of earth.

"Droserius!"

The man turned at the sound of his name.

"Captain! It's you. I was afraid it was one of your men interrupting my work again."

"I've explained to my patrols that you have legitimate business here, Droserius."

"Yes, very legitimate, but they are always curious. Mostly looking for tips on the chariot teams for when racing resumes. Look, I've unearthed another crime."

He tapped the clod of earth against his spear. Dirt fell away, revealing a metal cylinder as long as his finger. Tossing his weapon aside, he gently unrolled the thin lead sheet. "Remarkable how people still dare to break the law by putting curses on the race teams, isn't it?"

Droserius rubbed his find on his tunic, leaving yet another streak of grime, and handed it to Felix.

It was a curse tablet. A demon with a contorted face, a long tail, and a rooster's crest had been crudely incised into the lead, along with an inscription.

Felix squinted at it. "I release you, demon, from the bonds of time. I charge you, from this hour bring a pestilence onto the Greens. Torture them! Flay their horses! The charioteers Glarus and Primulus, crash them! Destroy them!" He didn't attempt to articulate the magickal incantation which followed: *Ziugeu. Diaronco. Baxcu. Oeeora. Cagora. Aaiereto.*

He handed the tablet back to Droserius. "It's easy enough to tell who's being cursed, but there's never any way to discover who buried the things. I hope you'll finish soon. There's nothing in here that needs guarding now, but when the races start—"

"Do you expect to have repaid me what you owe by then?"

"Surely you've already turned more than enough profit in this enterprise to allow me a fair amount of credit against that?"

"Perhaps."

"I don't want to be seen giving anyone preferential treatment, Droserius."

"Who is going to question the captain of the excubitors? Are you looking to be promoted? What position do you seek?"

"I wouldn't turn down a military command," Felix admitted.

"Why would you want to go rambling around the ruins of Italy? Or worse still, far-off deserts?"

"I've been stuck inside the palace for too long, spending all my time looking at walls. Some nights I dream I'm on a march with nothing but the hills around me."

"Never mind. It won't be long before the racing starts up again. That'll provide enough excitement for anyone." Droserius contemplated the lead sheet. "Charioteers pay good money for a curse tablet with their name on it. They can destroy it and avoid whatever's been wished on them. However, I may not be able to sell this one. Glarus is dead. His chariot's axle broke, and it happened right where we're standing. I saw it myself. It was as if an invisible hand erupted from the track and snapped it in half. Cost me a fortune. He'd just arrived from Thessalonika, and no one had heard of him. No one knew about his skill and so I placed a heavy wager on his first race."

"Whoever concealed that tablet here must have heard about him, else how could they know his name?"

"That seems obvious. I just hope it wasn't the fellow who made off with my money. I may have to put this back. I don't think Primulus can afford it. He's been down on his luck of late and now I see why. On the other hand, if he removed the curse he might regain his former promise. No one else would be expecting that, so it would give me some scope for wagering. However, I can't take any bets from you on his races, Captain. It wouldn't be ethical."

"I won't be wagering again, Droserius."

"No? It's always good to have a break once in a while. Whets the appetite." He closed his hand around the small cylinder. "I shall keep this one for now, I think. What stories lie beneath our feet, Felix. A secret history of intrigue and rivalry, of ill will and bad fortune. A gold mine to one who knows how to work it."

"I want to ask you about another sort of story, Droserius. It involves the murdered senator. Were you here the day Symacchus was killed?"

"As I've already explained to your inquisitors, I always leave well before sunset. All those empty seats seem filled with phantoms once the moonlight hits them."

"Do you know anything about Symacchus?"

"Only what everyone else knows, Felix. He was devout to a fault, wasn't he? I would not be surprised to hear the night you found him was the first time he'd set foot in the place."

"What about his guests? I don't imagine he discouraged them from coming to the races?"

Droserius picked up his spear and gestured with it toward the seats. "The Hippodrome holds thousands of spectators. How many of them could I know?"

"You and your cronies are on always on the lookout for wealthy foreign chickpeas. You wouldn't think a hawk could spot a dead mouse on a hillside, but it does. What about the question?"

Droserius laughed. "Now that you mention it, there was an Egyptian fellow who was staying with Symacchus. Some big fish from an exceedingly small pond. A place called Mehenopolis."

"What was his name?"

"Melios."

"You have a good memory." Felix was suspicious.

"It's hard to forget someone who owes you as much money as he owes me."

"He wagered heavily?"

"And lost. Hercules himself couldn't have dragged that fellow away from the races. And he never paid up. I got off lightly compared to some I could mention. This was a couple of years ago."

"Why did you trust him to settle his debt? He was, after all, a stranger to you."

"He was staying with the senator. A man like Symacchus wouldn't offer hospitality to a dishonorable man. Or so I thought." Droserius thrust his spear into the ground.

"Did you lend Melios money?"

"I have a weakness for assisting those who aren't rich enough to invest in their luck, as you know, captain. Besides, Melios said he was in the city to present a petition to the emperor concerning some grievance or other. As far as anyone could ascertain, that was true. There was a lot of money involved, so with the stroke of his pen, Justinian was going to gild the fellow's backside."

He paused. "I thought he was a good risk. I was wrong."

***

The body on the pallet lay as still as if death's vast weight had already settled into the flesh. Glittering like gems sewn to the edge of a courtier's robe, the gaze moved back and forth while the leaden face remained immobile.

"I thought I was climbing the ladder to heaven and you were a demon tollkeeper."

"It's me, Tarquin. It's Hektor. Remember we were friends when we were both court pages? I've had an accident." Hektor turned his head to one side, to give the dying man a better view of his profile.

"Hektor?"

"I found you not far from the docks, huddled in a doorway. The Lord must have directed my steps."

"You speak of a Lord? The one you offered the chicken to that night when we were young? The dark one? No, you can't persuade me. This is a snare. Don't hurl me into the pit, I beg of you." Tarquin's hands, curled into claws, trembled.

"You're not dead, Tarquin. You're safe with me in the Hormisdas. What happened to you? I thought you'd been taken into the household of—"

"He tired of me. They all tire of me eventually, and yet what other way did I have to survive? Am I to burn in the eternal flames for it? Have mercy!"

"I'm not here to throw you into the flames, Tarquin."

"I didn't want to die on the street. I had nowhere else to go."

"You haven't died and you won't." The swellings on the sick man's neck showed the lie. Hektor looked round as the door behind him creaked open, letting a shaft of light into the dim, smoky room, accompanied by a burst of noise from the crowded corridor beyond.

Bishop Crispin shut the door behind him. "Ah, finally I've tracked you down, Hektor. Where have you been keeping yourself?" His gaze moved to the pallet.

"As you see, I've been tending to an old friend."

"Oh yes. Very praiseworthy. Now, I must ask you about a peculiar visitor of mine. A bald-headed fellow dressed all in peacocks. Does that suggestion anyone you know?"

"He doesn't sound like anyone at court." Hektor frowned. "Then again, I no longer spend much time among those who indulge in such sartorial vanities."

"Of course not, but I'd hoped you might recall this man. His demeanor struck me as suspicious."

Hektor stared thoughtfully into the gloomy recesses of the room. "I may need to take some action," he muttered.

Crispin stepped nearer to the sick man. He looked down at Tarquin, then up at Hektor, distress in his face.

"I fear there is nothing to be done."

Even though Hektor's words were spoken softly, Tarquin heard them. "What's that you're saying? I am going to die here?"

"Let's not speak of such things. You need to rest."

"Yes, yes, but before that I must tell you. I've had a vision, a dream. Hektor. You will be rewarded for your works. You won't die on the street, Hektor. Heaven has told me so."

***

A young man in a flowing cloak forced back the bull's head and buried a dagger in its neck. A snake, a scorpion, and a dog joined in the attack on the dying animal.

Felix stood in the shadows and contemplated the bas relief at the front of the mithraeum. It depicted Mithras slaying the Great Bull, the moment of creation.

He turned as Anatolius entered the narrow underground chamber. "Sorry about asking you to meet me here, Anatolius, but under the circumstances I thought it best if we weren't seen talking."

"You've discovered something useful?"

"I think so." Felix glanced around, with the instinctive caution of the military man. They were alone. The guttering light from an oil lamp sitting on a stone bench animated whorls of yellow stars painted on the vaulted ceiling. "I've been making discreet inquiries about Senator Symacchus' Egyptian visitors. I've heard enough gossip to enliven dinner parties for the rest of my life."

"But what did you find out that would be useful to us?" Anatolius broke in.

"Apparently most of the senator's guests were distant relatives or friends and acquaintances of distant relatives, who'd heard that the senator's door was always open to Egyptian travelers who arrived in Constantinople, be they businessman, dignitary, or pilgrim."

"That's common knowledge."

"I'll wager it isn't common knowledge that one of his visitors, a rascal named Melios, ran up big debts gambling on the races and returned to Egypt without paying!" Felix went on to detail the story Droserius had told him

"How reliable is your source?"

"He got his knowledge first hand."

"First hand? He's a gambler, you mean. Is that how you obtained this information?"

Avoiding Anatolius' gaze, Felix studied the bas relief of Mithra as if he'd never seen the god before. "Sometimes you can't be too dainty about who you talk to when you're investigating. You know that as well as I do."

"You've gone back to wagering, just like I said!"

Felix grunted and looked at his boots. "Just a coin here and there, for the sport. At least you won't find me fleeing the city with creditors at my heels baying for my blood. Besides which, it was necessary for the task in hand."

"Was there any mention of relics in connection with this Melios? I can't see how he would have anything to do with this whole business."

"As I said, Symacchus' guests were a boring lot. Melios was the only one I was able to find anything out about."

"He was from Egypt, of course. Where?"

Felix furrowed his brow. "Droserius did tell me. Some long name. I'm not sure. Mehen something or other, if I recall."

"Mehenopolis?"

"Yes. How did you know?"

"That's where John was sent. So there must be a connection."

Anatolius let his gaze wander to the sacred scene behind the altar. There was always something to ponder anew about the symbols of their religion—a raven, a scorpion, a snake, a lion and a cup, an ear of wheat growing from the tip of the bull's tail, the god's two torch bearers.

There was as much written in these images as in all of Justinian's legislation.

The over-riding message, however, was plain. All life had sprung from the Great Bull's death.

"Anatolius," Felix said quietly. "Tread lightly. And now I have a question for you. Is there a new requirement for a lawyer to be bald? Although it's not a bad idea at that, since it prevents disgruntled clients from grabbing his hair, the better to cut his throat."

Chapter Thirty-five

"And this business with the sheep was just a trick, Lord Chamberlain? Imagine, Dedi trying to wrest my position away in such a fashion." Melios' words smelled of wine. His wig was askew and he kept turning the side of his face with the clouded eye straight at John in a disconcerting manner.

He appeared to be as upset and angry as Dedi had been by the end of John's visit.

It was only a few hours since John had returned from Dedi's house and informed Melios about the proposed show of power. The headman must have begun fortifying his courage immediately.

The sun had set. The two men stood outside the barn and overlooked the final preparations. Guards had been posted to keep the curious away. Servants bustled about carrying out orders relayed from John by Melios. The hubbub was reminiscent of a marketplace. The odor of burning torch resin hung on the air.

"No magick is involved," John reassured the headman. "By dawn we'll have discovered exactly how it was done and you'll be rid of Dedi for good."

"Even so, I've ordered everything with a sharp edge locked up." Melios shuddered and put a hand to his throat.

"When I spoke to Dedi, I indicated that a man such as myself, from Justinian's court, could not be misled by some Egyptian chickpea. I intentionally hurt his pride by saying this in front of Peter, my servant, who was somewhat puzzled to be asked to accompany me on my visit. I've since explained to him why I wished him to be in attendance. My intent was to anger Dedi so much he would insist on another demonstration in order to convince me of his powers. Beyond that, when people are angry they become careless."

"Yes, I'm sure you're right."

They walked over to the barn.

"The whole place will be lit up as brightly as the inside of the Great Church tonight," Melios said. "For that matter, I have arranged to have so many guards here, the area will resemble the Hippodrome on race day."

John refrained from mentioning that some claimed more crimes took place in the Hippodrome during the racing than in the rest of the city. "That reminds me, Melios. You had an argument with the charioteer. Why?"

"Whoever said so is mistaken. I haven't argued with Porphyrios. I've hardly seen Porphyrios. Now if you'd said Scrofa, I admit I've exchanged hot words with that rascal. He's been content to skulk about out of my sight since then. Oh, he didn't like it when I told him about my acquaintance with the emperor! Let me tell you…."

Suddenly Melios' voice was echoing much too loudly in a sudden silence. The clamor from the workers had ceased abruptly.

Dedi had materialized out of the growing darkness. He carried a short wooden post, split halfway down. Its wickedly sharp blade pointing upwards, a sword was wedged into the cleft, and kept in place by a rope tying the split halves together.

Servants and guards alike moved out of Dedi's path.

The magician addressed John and Melios. "Let's get on with it! You know the routine, Melios! We've done this before, haven't we?"

All the color had drained from the headman's face. Caught by torchlight, sweat stood out on his forehead like drops of liquid fire.

"Yes," Melios wheezed. "Let's not delay. This time it is going to be different. Isn't it, Lord Chamberlain?" He instructed a guard to unbolt the door.

Torch light flickering through the slitted windows bisected its empty interior. Charms hung on the gate of the pen at the far end.

Accompanied closely by John and Melios, Dedi carried his deadly device into the enclosure and tied it securely to the gate. Then John ushered his two companions outside.

"Where's the sacrificial beast?" Dedi asked.

"Hapymen is bringing it now," Melios replied. Turning to John he went on. "Don't imagine I would allow my animal to be unprotected, Lord Chamberlain. You observed the amulets, and exactly as on the previous occasion Zebulon has blessed the beast and Hapymen has made a protective garland."

"All your precautions will be as ineffective as the last time," Dedi told him with a sneer.

"I am of the opinion we didn't use enough flowers of Paion on that occasion," Melios replied.

A loud, agitated bleating announced the arrival of a small, gentle-faced sheep led by Hapymen. A heavy garland of ruby globular blossoms intertwined with numerous leaves and sprigs of herbs hung around its neck.

Melios began to open his mouth, then clamped his lips together tightly, turned, and lurched off toward his house.

"My master does not appear to be feeling too well, excellency," Hapymen observed.

"We can proceed without him," John replied. "As soon as I've searched inside one last time, the animal is to be placed in its pen. I shall then seal the door, and it will not be opened again until I personally do so."

"As for me, I'm off to get a good night's sleep," remarked Dedi. "We'll see if all these precautions can overcome the power of Mehen."

***

As the night advanced stars blazed forth, brilliant against the clear sky. John had arranged the guards in two concentric circles. Those in the inner ring closely surrounded the barn, while others formed a human perimeter further out.

It was impossible for Dedi or any accomplice to reach the barn without being seen. Therefore, John thought, the magician was bound to fail and be forced to admit defeat or, more likely, concoct some excuse or other that would deceive no one.

On the other hand, Dedi might well make a reckless attempt from frustration and anger, in which case he would be caught and exposed in the act.

John strode around continually, keeping his own watch and making sure the guards were awake and attentive. Surrounded by armed men in a pool of light in the middle of darkness, he recalled his days as a mercenary.

How many sleepless nights had the younger John spent on watch in an encampment near enemy territory?

This time there were no bands of enemies waiting to ambush during the night, only a charlatan who called himself a magician.

John was not certain what would happen once Dedi was exposed. The magician would be forced to admit how he had accomplished the first killing. Would the answer somehow lead to the information Justinian sought in Egypt?

He would consider the question in the morning.

The hours advanced. John had always thought, whenever he stood watch, that the quality of time changed at night. The hours did not flow forward as they did during the day, but rather lay upon the world in a still pool, until daylight forced them into motion again.

He spoke a few words of encouragement to a boy leaning on his spear. The boy smiled, surprised that the tall, lean Greek could address him in fluent Coptic.

John made another circuit around the barn.

All was quiet. Occasionally a torch popped and threw off a gout of sparks. John half expected a second flaming demon to come shrieking out of the sky, or some other similar diversionary tactic.

He crossed the open space to the verge of the garden, where the smells of smoke and livestock were replaced by that of vegetation. The chirp and buzz of insects within the dark plant life grew louder.

Pale moonlight formed a patch of white behind the trees.

No, it was a robe.

John plunged toward it.

The figure turned to flee. John leapt forward, put his shoulder into the man's back, and drove him face down into the soft ground, crushing most of a fragrant bed of flowers.

John yanked his prey over. "Thorikos!"

"Lord Chamberlain...I...uh...."

John dragged the traveler none too gently to his feet. "What are you doing here?"

"I meant no harm!"

"You're fortunate I saw you before one of the guards decided to test his aim and the sharpness of his spear."

"Yes, I see that. My apologies, excellency."

"And why did you attempt to flee?"

"Well, I...er...realized I was trespassing and might not be welcome, although I came here with the best of intentions."

John treated Thorikos to a stream of Coptic invective that, although only barely understood by its recipient, was still more memorable than many of the sights the traveler had seen during his journeying.

Thorikos suddenly put his hand to his belt. For an instant John thought he might be reaching for a blade. Instead, Thorikos let out a faint cry, bent over and began feeling through the dark vegetation around his feet.

With a gasp of relief, he finally straightened up, holding out a smooth, rounded piece of bone. "Thanks be to the Lord! I thought I'd lost it, excellency. It's a saint's knucklebone."

He stuffed the bit of bone back into his pouch. "You see, Lord Chamberlain, I purchased it at an outrageous price at the pilgrim camp, having heard about the demonstration planned for tonight. I thought it might be useful in helping protect the animal."

"A touching thought, Thorikos, but surely you don't believe it's really the knucklebone of a saint?"

"Of course not! It probably belonged to some lesser holy man. Nevertheless—"

A series of frantic, high-pitched bleats resonated from the barn.

Cursing, John raced back.

He ordered the guard away and yanked the bolt open himself, breaking the wax seals he'd placed on the door.

As he reached the pen, he saw the sheep staggering. Its front legs folded, the crimson-chested animal pitched forward and rolled onto its side.

The sword blade anchored on the wooden post glistened wetly.

The ground was speckled with blossoms redder than the flowers in the garland around the dying creature's neck.

Chapter Thirty-six

Europa nervously cracked open the house door.
"Anatolius? Why are you back so late? I was beginning to get worried—"

The door was kicked violently inward, catching her on the side of the head and flinging her onto the tiles. Dazed, she tried to push herself up. All she could see from her prone position were boots stamping across the wildly spinning floor. Too late, she remembered what Anatolius had told her—not to open the door unless she was certain he was on the other side.

She lay still, peering through half-closed eyelids.

The intruders had leather leggings.

Except, comically, for one, who wore yellow hose and soft leather shoes.

The floor spun faster. The yellow hose no longer seemed so humorous.

She pretended to be unconscious. The thin trickle of blood seeping toward the house door would help the illusion, she thought. The shoulder of her tunic was already soaked. Scalp wounds bled profusely.

"Search the upper floors," someone ordered. "The men must be elsewhere, otherwise the racket would've brought them down here by now. Still, we better be certain they aren't hiding, trying to be clever."

There was a muffled query.

"You've had your instructions," snapped the man in charge. "Don't hesitate to do it, and don't ask me again."

Europa tried to control her breathing. As the floor gradually stopped turning she became aware of an agonizing pain in her side, centered on a hard lump. She hesitated to reach down to investigate. Had she broken a rib?

No, it wasn't a rib.

Through slitted eyelids she watched the yellow hose approach.

"If they aren't here now," said their wearer, "they'll be back soon enough. Then we'll finish our business and be off."

The intruders intended to kill Anatolius and Thomas, Europa realized. Thomas was safely away, but Anatolius should have returned long ago.

Yellow hose's shoe prodded her roughly.

She gasped.

"Ah, so you're still alive," he said.

The man in the yellow hose wore a brown robe. The face was a visitor from a nightmare, half human, half demonic.

It was Hektor.

Anatolius had warned her the former court page wanted her father's house.

Would he kill for it?

It seemed so.

"Should I finish her off, sir?" asked a gruff voice.

"It seems such a waste," Hektor remarked. Looking down, he addressed Europa. "Tell us where Anatolius and Thomas have gone. I'm delivering a homily on divine grace later this evening and I don't want to be waiting here all night."

"We can handle the task of persuading her, sir," the gruff voice suggested.

"And would you deal with that task as magnificently as you and your idiot friend handled your assignment at Francio's house? Unfortunately, the only man I can trust to do any such job correctly is currently in Egypt. Go up and help the others search. I'll call you when you're needed."

After the man had gone upstairs, Hektor kicked Europa more vigorously in her ribs.

She sat up groggily.

"Where do pagans suppose they go after they're dead?" Hektor asked her with a vicious smile.

"Your intention is to kill me?"

"I prefer to think of it as sending you to join your father."

Europa's hand moved swiftly, reached behind her, grabbed the clay scorpion on which she'd fallen and flung it straight into Hektor's face.

The protective charm disintegrated, showering bloodstained fragments onto the tiles.

Then Europa was on her feet, running across the atrium.

Behind her Hektor screamed, "Your death will be slow now! I'll make certain it's slow!"

Europa plunged into the darkness of the garden.

Past the pool she ran, toward the unused wing of the house.

Shouts and the clatter of boots followed.

She raced down a corridor and into the room containing the bath.

She was shaking. Her chest burned and her head pounded.

She surveyed the small space. The round bath, the lascivious mosaics, the enormous Aphrodite holding her marble mirror, the circular hole in the domed ceiling through which moonlight slanted.

She ran around the edge of the bath, took a breath, tensed her muscles, and jumped.

No sooner had she landed on Aphrodite's mirror than she leapt up lightly, gripped the goddess' smooth shoulders, climbed onto them, and launched herself upward again.

For an instant she dangled at arm's length from the rim of the aperture in the ceiling, until her feet found the head of the statue.

With a final despairing push she pulled herself out into moonlight and slid down the far side of the dome, hidden from anyone in the garden.

She could not linger. Her pursuers would doubtless now be racing back through the atrium and around to that side of the house.

She dropped to the ground and ran through shadows to a stand of firs some distance away, from which she surveyed the cobbled square separating the house and the excubitors' barracks.

Anatolius usually took the path leading around the corner of the barracks.

How could she warn him?

It seemed strange that none of the excubitors were investigating the disturbance at the Lord Chamberlain's house, hardly a spear's throw from their lodgings.

But then Hektor was known to be Theodora's creature. No doubt orders had been given no notice was to be taken of anything that might happen that night in the Lord Chamberlain's dwelling.

Making a quick decision, she slid away into the deeper concealment of the confusion of shrubbery behind her.

***

Anatolius let out a sigh of relief as he finally came within sight of the barracks. He hadn't intended to be away so long, and doubtless Europa would be getting anxious about him.

All the way back, as shadows massed under colonnades and spread out into the streets, he had felt nervous. Every beggar in a doorway had been lying in wait for him, only pretending to be asleep.

Now he was safely back on the palace grounds.

As he approached the barracks, a figure leapt from the bushes bordering the path.

His blade was in his hand before he recognized a familiar face.

"Europa!"

"Quick," she whispered. "Into the bushes. Hektor and his men are waiting to ambush you at the house."

Anatolius grasped the situation immediately. "There's no point calling the excubitors out if he's involved. We'll have to go to Francio's house."

They ran through deserted imperial gardens, taking the most direct route to the Chalke. As they loped along, Anatolius prayed Hektor had been over-confident and had overlooked stationing any of his men there.

Soon they slowed to a walk and approached the great bronze gate of the palace. The guard on duty looked them over and then stood aside to let them pass.

Suddenly, he lowered his spear into their path, barring their way.

"Anatolius! It's you!" The guard grinned broadly. "You're panting as hard as if you've just run twice around the Hippodrome. After the thief who stole your hair, were you? All the ladies will ignore you now!"

He laughed and raised his spear.

Then they were safely out of the palace grounds and moving swiftly along the Mese.

Anatolius led Europa into a series of alleyways and narrow spaces between buildings, through squares too small to allow a cart to turn around, and along decrepit, roofless colonnades. Their route twisted and turned.

"Are we lost?" Europa wondered.

"Don't worry. I've been this way plenty of times. Besides, you can never really get lost in the city at night. Not with the Great Church for a beacon."

Anatolius looked up toward the slice of night sky visible between the brick warehouses pressing in on either side. "See, just over there the sky's brighter. That's the glow from the windows in its dome."

There was no sign of pursuit.

When they reached Francio's door, Vedrix ushered them inside.

Francio had recovered sufficiently from the attack of the eels to be up and about again. He clucked sympathetically at the sight of the blood-bedaubed Europa.

Anatolius explained the situation.

Francio tapped his nose in annoyance. "So, it seems my visitors gathered together a few of their friends and paid a call on you. They are going to start a fashion for swathing the head in strips of white linen." He ran a hand over the wrappings still adorning his head. He was dressed, uncharacteristically, in matching white.

"We'll get that attended to right away. You'll be as stylish as I am in no time," he told Europa. "Might I suggest you adopt the same sort of headwear, Anatolius, until your hair grows back?"

"We don't want to put you in danger, Francio," Anatolius said. "But if we could—"

"I'll hide you in the servants' quarters."

"Felix has given me some useful information. I'm going to risk paying Bishop Crispin another visit. I think I can change his mind about talking to me."

Chapter Thirty-seven

From the flat roof of the guest house the oasis appeared as a choppy sea of palm fronds, interrupted by fields outlined by irrigation ditches and the few dusty streets of Mehenopolis. Beyond, dun-colored desert sands shimmered in the heat.

"I was happy we slept up here last night," Cornelia said to John. "The stars were magnificent. We'll have to continue sleeping on the roof. It'll be like old times, lying together beneath the heavens."

"Not exactly like old times." John had turned on his stool to face the upthrust cliff of the Rock of the Snake.

"We can only be what we are. If we spent our time regretting the endless things we're not, we'd never do anything else. I found this philosophy most helpful when Europa was difficult to manage."

John stared fixedly toward the ruined temple. "Our daughter is the best reason we have to return to Constantinople as soon as possible."

"Thomas can take care of her."

John turned his gaze away from the rock outcropping. He had erred in not explaining the situation to Cornelia immediately, when he spoke to her on the ship. His first thought had been to protect her peace of mind. It had been a misjudgment he had not been able to bring himself to correct. Now it was time.

She listened in silence while he told her how he had followed Thomas, discovered him in the Hippodrome next to the senator's body, instructed him to flee, and then drawn the excubitors away.

"I'm sorry I didn't tell you everything," John concluded. "I thought it would be simpler, for all of us, if I kept it to myself."

Knowing Cornelia, John feared she might be angry.

"Why would Thomas kill a senator?" was all she said.

"He didn't. The matter was deliberately arranged to make him appear guilty."

John explained how he had seized the opportunity to create a pretext for the emperor to exile him without raising undue suspicion.

She leaned over and kissed him.

He looked at her in surprise.

Cornelia laughed. "Now, John, admit it. Your first thought in the Hippodrome was to save Europa's husband, wasn't it?"

"Thomas is a reckless fool!" John paused and then smiled faintly. "Then again I was a reckless fool once myself. If I'd not insisted on seeking out silks for you and thereby strayed into Persian territory, if I hadn't been captured and taken away...."

"We would have long since quarreled bitterly and gone our separate ways, young hotheads that we were," Cornelia said firmly.

John was silent. Again his gaze went toward the ruins atop the outcropping thrusting up into the brilliant blue sky. "Melios is frantic over this latest death. He's now talking about using the banquet he planned to officially announce that he's entering a monastery."

Before Cornelia could reply, Peter climbed up through the trapdoor to the roof, bearing a platter of fruit.

"I apologize for the meager fare, master. I fear tonight I'll only be able to serve the remains of yesterday's evening meal, as it's difficult for me to cook right now."

As Peter put his burden down on the rooftop beside them, they saw his hands were covered with huge blisters.

"Did you burn yourself?" Cornelia asked with quick concern.

Peter reddened. "I was careless while preparing a meal, mistress. I've obtained a healing salve from Hapymen. He also kindly provided this fruit for you. Hypatia often claimed melons are plumper and grapes more succulent here than anywhere else, and going by these examples, I believe she's correct."

Cornelia sampled a few grapes and said she agreed.

"Though I must say, mistress, I have not been impressed with some of the vegetables. The lettuce, for example…and the onions too," the elderly servant rushed on. "The larger ones have a tendency to develop too strong a flavor. Hapymen cautioned me before I cooked them and just as well. Otherwise the entire dish would have been ruined. As you see, their juice irritated my skin very badly."

"You'll be back to your pots and spoons before your fire gets cool," Cornelia said.

Peter hesitated. "Master, could it be—"

"No, it's nothing to do with magick," John reassured him quickly.

A subdued rumbling caught their attention. From their elevated position they could see a cart bearing the body of a sheep trundling toward the gate of the estate.

"Is it the poor beast that died last night?" Cornelia wondered.

"It must be," John confirmed. "Melios said he intended to send it to the pilgrim camp."

"Nothing is allowed to go to waste in an oasis," Cornelia observed. "Not even a sheep done to death by magick. All those amulets and the protective garland you described didn't do it much good, did it?"

Without replying, John leapt to his feet and vanished through the trapdoor.

He sprinted outside, ran past two naked children playing in the dirt, and hailed the driver of the cart.

The driver halted at John's command, and watched him as, without a word, he began to examine the garland of wilted flower and greenery still encircling the dead sheep's neck.

As he suspected, several squill bulbs had been halved and were tightly attached to the underside of the collar, arranged so that their cut sides pressed against the sheep's throat.

Chapter Thirty-eight

On his way to the Hormisdas Palace to seek out Bishop Crispin, Anatolius was forced to dodge out of the way of a cart full of plague victims.

He was startled by the laboring donkey as he approached a bend in the wide path, where overgrown shrubbery blocked his view. He stepped back into a bed of herbs. The fragrance rose around him but failed to mask the odor of death as the cart creaked past, drawing with it the usual cloud of glistening flies.

The dead were not stacked in a jumble of limbs but neatly laid out, each granted the relative dignity of its own space.

Perhaps it was because they had all died on the palace grounds.

Deaths had become fewer, but whether that was because the plague was ebbing or due to the much reduced population, no one could say. Many who had survived this long had become used to its presence and thought of the plague as they did of death itself, a visitor who would call on them eventually—but probably not today.

The driver offered no greeting. A sunken-eyed, expressionless man with waxen skin, he was distinguishable from the corpses in his cart mostly because he was upright.

As the cart jolted away, a scrap of jewelry fell off the back, glittering momentarily in the sunlight. It landed not far from where Anatolius stood. He stepped back onto the path and picked it up.

It was a silver earring, rimmed with chips of red glass and inset with a delicate, enameled rose.

Anatolius contemplated it as he walked on. What would be the use in returning the earring to its dead owner? Whatever beauty it might have graced had been withered by death. Why had she worn it the day she died? Was it a favorite piece? A gift from someone she had loved? Was he dead too? What about the silversmith who had created the jewelry? Or had it been an heirloom?

Was there anyone left alive to whom the scrap of silver, glass, and enamel meant something, Anatolius wondered, or had its story been swept away by the plague, like so many others?

"Salutations, sir."

The greeting startled him.

"Hypatia!"

John's former gardener stood beside an unruly cluster of shrubbery, a pair of shears in her hand, staring at him with bemusement.

"My lack of hair and peacock-infested garment is a long story, Hypatia," Anatolius said with a smile. "They've served me well today, however, because I thought it prudent to take a back way through the grounds and thereby have found you."

The Egyptian servant's tawny skin looked browner than he remembered. She must have been spending her days in the sun.

"I see you were able to get your old job back," he went on.

"It wasn't difficult, sir. Look at the overgrown state the gardens are in! Today I'm supposed to cut back the Golden Gate here, before it closes completely."

Only now that she mentioned it did Anatolius realize the shrubbery had been pruned to resemble the great gate of Constantinople. The shortage of gardeners, not a besieging army, had reduced it to ruin.

Anatolius took a last look at the earring in his hand and gently tossed it into the shrubbery forming the gate.

Hypatia gave him a quizzical look.

"Something I noticed in the path. I didn't want anyone stepping on it."

"How is mistress Europa, sir?"

"She's managing well enough," Anatolius replied after a slight hesitation. "Thomas is away. Europa and I are living elsewhere right now. I ought to warn you, Hypatia, Hektor's succeeded in taking John's house."

Hypatia's hand tightened around the handle of her shears. "I'm extremely sorry to hear that."

"Believe me, Hypatia, it will be only a temporary situation. I hope you'll come back when everything's been straightened out. We all hope you'll return."

Hypatia began to clip the shrubbery energetically, even violently, or so it seemed to Anatolius. "I have heard the Lord Chamberlain is dead, sir. Is it true?"

"Just loose tongues idly wagging. How can anyone know what is happening so far away?"

Leaves and twigs flew, but the servant made no reply.

***

Bishop Crispin met Anatolius in a corridor near the front of the Hormisdas.

"Back again, my garishly garbed friend? Apparently you are in a great hurry to join whatever god it is you worship."

The corridor was made nearly impassable by boards leaning against its walls and further obstructed by bundles of belongings where Theodora's assorted heretics had constructed shelters or simply laid claim to space, like street beggars. The stench was nearly as bad as that rising from the cart Anatolius had seen not long before.

"It would be as well I don't take that journey until you've heard what I have to say, or I can guarantee you'll be following me shortly." Anatolius had to raise his voice to be heard over the unintelligible chanting of a hirsute fellow in a bright yellow loincloth sitting nearby.

"You are clearly deranged, young man. Your threats are but empty words. Still, I am bound to listen to those who seek an audience."

He grabbed Anatolius' elbow and directed him through an archway to an atrium whose walls were lined with classical statues, and beyond that into what had once been a series of private baths. The walls which had separated baths from changing rooms and exercise areas had been torn down, leaving an empty marble box illuminated by light from the apertures in several domes. Former rooms were marked by the marble benches, tables and statuary which had been left sprouting incongruously from the floor. Many of these traces of former glory formed the basis for the same sort of crude dwellings to be seen in the corridor. Some enterprising lodgers had made homes out of the dry bath basins by laying boards over them.

"Renovation work here is unfortunately not one of Justinian's priorities," Crispin remarked. "He'd much rather build something new and magnificent. Now, why have you returned? More pilgrim flasks, is it? You strike me as an aristocrat, but no one here recalls a bald-headed fop dressed in peacocks. At least you're a more convincing fraud than that big red-headed oaf with whom you say you're working."

"Then you've met my friend?"

"Not necessarily. Might it not be that he's been described to me? Your blundering acquaintance pretended to knowledge he did not have, as I told you at our last interview. I repeat I have no business which involves you, nor am I in need of whatever services either of you propose to offer."

"Did it not occur to you that I might not be a friend of orthodoxy? You suppose my associate and I are selling you our sealed lips. You think we know nothing, but there are certain matters of which we are aware, which we may be persuaded to reveal at the appropriate time. The question is to whom?"

This appeared to give Crispin pause. "So now you pretend to offer...what?"

Anatolius decided to test the conclusions he'd made.

Mithra, let the words be right, he prayed, and then began.

"I understand your suspicions. After all, Senator Symacchus' servant Achilles died because his careless mouth alerted my friend to a certain matter. Then the senator was murdered because he was thought to have become untrustworthy in that his servant should never have known anything about the affair in the first place."

"You and your associate have some strange notions." Crispin delivered his retort in even tones, but Anatolius thought he detected a slight movement in the narrow face, as if the bishop's jaw tightened. "I am a guest of our beloved empress, who shares my religious views, as everyone knows. I would not seek to offend her in any way, let alone engage in any sort of matter. What is it you're talking about? You have been vague about the details, I notice."

"Let me be plain. You were able to convert Symacchus to your religious views. Justinian sent him to you to argue theology, but the senator was a well-read man, open to new ideas. I believe his late wife, being Egyptian, was herself a monophysite, so naturally he would already have some sympathy for that point of view." Anatolius could see from the expression in Crispin's eyes that his deductions were correct. He pressed on. "More importantly, like you, I move among those who share the same beliefs."

"Then I congratulate you on your courage in remaining in the city, young man. However, you have yet to state this business of yours."

"Symacchus was seeking a relic in which you had an interest," Anatolius went on. "The man I know was to assist in this quest, but before he received his instructions, the senator was murdered. When we met recently, I showed you an artifact similar to that which my colleague was to use to establish his identity to the senator's intermediary."

He paused. "Although you tried to conceal the fact, it was obvious the token was familiar to you. I realized you would wish to appear ignorant to see if despite your assumed indifference and advice to depart the city I returned to offer our assistance. And here I am."

Chapter Thirty-nine

"Have more wine, Melios! You're not going to let a dead sheep cast a pall over the festivities, are you?" Zebulon gestured to Hapymen, who promptly filled the headman's cup from a blue glass jug.

Melios' gathering in honor of his esteemed visitor, John, Lord Chamberlain to Emperor Justinian, had been under way for some time. However, to judge by Melios' demeanor the departed animal might have been bleeding to death in the middle of the table. The headman, though dressed for the occasion in a voluminous toga and Egyptian wig, looked glum.

John wished he could reveal what he'd deduced, but it would have to wait a little longer.

Melios was flanked by John, Zebulon, the traveler Thorikos, and several middle-aged men in expensive garments, who had been introduced to John as wealthy local landowners. They sat at one of three tables of unmatched heights arranged to form three sides of a square.

Eye-watering smoke drifted from ill-trimmed wicks in silver lamps set around the room. Beneath the odor of cooked meats, spices, and fruit lay the less appetizing smell of too many guests dining in too small a space.

John glanced around the noisy gathering. Dedi was missing. Naturally, he would not be welcome, and neither would Scrofa the tax assessor. Apollo was not present either. Perhaps one did not invite itinerant beekeepers to formal banquets any more than one invited women.

John mentioned his surprise that Porphyrios was nowhere to be seen.

"Such stories he tells about the races in the Hippodrome," put in Thorikos. "He could entertain us half the night."

"He was invited but declined, excellency." Zebulon answered for Melios, then changed the subject. "Barley beer is excellent for every day, but for celebrations we have something much better. This pomegranate wine is made on the estate. Isn't that right, Melios?"

Melios drained his cup and set it down awkwardly. It tipped over, spilling a few drops of wine and several soggy petals, an ingredient not present in John's cup.

"Aren't those lotus blossoms?" asked Thorikos. "Do they perhaps guard against headaches caused by too much wine? I've been having the most dreadful headaches."

Zebulon placed a finger to his lips. "Be discreet, my friend. I minister to the soul, but there are times when the body must be cared for just as much. Let us not be overly critical of our host for seeking to enhance the soporific effect of what he's imbibing."

"You may recall I had a wine-importing business," Thorikos remarked to John. "There was never any call for Egyptian wine. Wretched stuff, generally speaking. Now I see how it can be made palatable."

The mixture of wine and petals seemed to gradually lighten Melios' mood even if it did not make his eyelids heavier. He began to speak in slurred tones about his visit to the empire's capital and his opinions of various classical authors.

John, whose preference for less elaborate dishes gave him a distaste for the rich and over-spiced offerings at imperial banquets, enjoyed the comparatively plain fare.

Melios' guests, having already been served platters of smoked fish and lentils, followed by roasted quails garnished with fat cucumbers and chopped lettuce, had just completed consuming a concoction described to John as moon fish sauced by mulberries.

"The next dish is of particular interest to learned men such as you and I, excellency," Melios remarked. "We are about to dine on the empire's most esteemed leeks, for as Pliny observed, the best of those are grown in Egypt."

"You have certainly plundered heaven, earth, and the waters for your guests, Melios," John replied.

"While it is surely but a small thing compared to the wonderful performances at even the humblest gathering at the palace, excellency, when we have finished this dish and while we enjoy more wine and some tempting dates and figs, I hope you'll find our special presentations entertaining."

In due course, Melios gathered the attention of his guests by clapping his hands several times. "Now, my friends," he said, when quiet had fallen, "to complete the evening I have arranged entertainment—"

He was interrupted by enthusiastic shouts of approval. When the noise had died away into the shadows in corners not fully reached by flickering lamplight, he continued with a slight smile. "As I was saying, I have arranged entertainment of a classical nature."

An equally loud burst of groans met this announcement.

Melios ignored the interruption and pressed on. "First, let me present Thorikos, a traveler who has journeyed through great and terrible dangers, the like of which—"

"You mean he passed through Alexandria?" a man at the far end of the table shouted.

Their host flushed, straightened his wig angrily, and glared at his unruly guest. "Thorikos has graciously agreed to sing for our delectation. In honor of our guest from court, he has selected a composition by Emperor Justinian himself."

Thorikos stood and commenced to sing "Only-Begotten Son" in a well-modulated voice. John recognized the words

Peter sang while scrubbing the floor or chopping vegetables. He was surprised at the choice, since it was clearly a celebration of orthodoxy and unlikely to be well received in a land notorious for its heretical religious thinking.

No sooner had Thorikos finished and sat down again when, at a signal from Melios, one of the company left the room briefly to return with a double flute of yellow wood.

He stationed himself in the oblong space fenced in by the three tables and began to play a melancholy tune, while the rest of Melios' guests clapped slowly in time.

As the final sad notes rippled away, Melios leaned over to John and spoke in an undertone. "That was one of our traditional airs, excellency. It's the melody for an ancient hymn once sung in the temple on the Rock of the Snake, but the words have long since been forgotten. Tonight it serves as a fitting lament for my poor sheep and for my time here as headman, for as I told you I intend to make a certain announcement at the conclusion of this gathering."

"Indeed." John glanced at Zebulon, wondering what the cleric thought of a pagan dirge being performed immediately after an orthodox hymn.

Zebulon, however, was busy consulting his wine cup.

The flute-player was now joined by two other musicians with sistrums. They began to play a livelier melody, whose soaring notes were soon taken up and lustily sung in the language of the country. John realized it was an example of the type of song men sang while working in the fields, raising water in shadufs, or in this particular instance while harvesting crops. In this almost forgotten part of Egypt, grateful thanks were being rendered to the Nile for its annual life-giving inundations, but the song was closely akin to the songs reapers had sung in the Greek fields of John's youth.

For a short time he allowed the locked door to his past to be opened, admitting memories he had seldom examined in the years since his life had been brutally changed.

Once, in this very country, he had dreamed of returning to Greece with Cornelia, to live out his days as a farmer.

Would that ever be possible?

Perhaps not, he told himself. Fortuna decreed their destinies, and it was possible neither he nor Cornelia had been marked to till the soil.

He pulled his thoughts away from the dead past and unborn future, and back to the present.

Why, he wondered, did Melios' guests sing the praises of the Nile in a settlement nourished by the wells of an oasis?

One possible answer appeared on the heels of his thought.

A girl, clothed solely in a fishermen's net and doubtless intended to remind spectators of that very river, had appeared.

Accompanied by flute and sistrums, she performed a dance consisting mostly of languorous gestures and back bends as her audience loudly voiced its appreciation of her interpretation of the rise and fall of the Nile's life-giving waters.

"Most interesting, most interesting, Melios, although not what I would call entertainment of a classical nature," murmured Thorikos.

At that point Hapymen made his contribution to the festivities by grasping the net and hauling the brown, writhing girl out of the room to loud, good-natured complaints from the dancer's audience and calls for her return.

The musicians resumed their seats as Melios rose unsteadily to his feet, bowed slightly in John's direction, and then addressed the gathering.

"My friends, this evening I had hoped to recite my panegyric to Emperor Justinian, of whom I was most honored to make some humble personal acquaintance during my visit to our empire's great capital, as you all know. Alas, recent events have doomed my efforts to complete it. However, I shall soon have ample time to accomplish the task. I have made an important decision which I wish to share with you—"

Realizing the headman was about to announce his flight to a monastery, John got to his feet. "My apologies, Melios, but before you make your news known, there is something I would like to say."

Melios blinked in confusion. The firm pressure of John's hand on his shoulder convinced him to sit down.

A buzz of excited conversation broke out and John waited until the company had quieted before he began.

"I promised Melios, our most gracious host this evening, an explanation of certain rather strange events that recently took place on this estate. I'm referring to the fate of two sheep."

With a glance down at Melios, who now looked extremely uneasy, John continued. "The first death occurred before my arrival. The second, as you are all doubtless aware, occurred last night. The unfortunate animal was confined to a closely guarded and locked barn and was, furthermore, protected with various charms and a blessing as well as a collar of certain flowers and herbs said to provide protection. Nevertheless, like the first, it was an apparent suicide, having cut its own throat. Dedi, who claims to practice magick, has taken credit for both mysterious deaths."

An uneasy murmur rose around the tables.

John held up his hand for silence. "Melios, am I correct in saying Hapymen provided the collar?"

Melios nodded silently.

Zebulon observed pointedly it was wiser to put one's trust in heaven than in amulets or charms and here was a perfect example of misplaced faith.

"I have personally examined the dead animal," John continued. "Dedi does not possess the powers he claims to hold. You have my word he cannot harm any of you, unless of course he attempts to sink a blade between your ribs."

Melios gasped. "But excellency…."

"The protective garlands that Hapymen—who also assists Dedi on occasion—so handily provided for the animals had several cut bulbs of squill laced into them. You may recall telling me a preparation from the same plant, administered for your rheumatism, had blistered your skin, Melios. It did the same to my servant's hands when he mistook squill bulbs for onions and chopped some in order to cook them."

John glanced around the room. "The sheep was encumbered with a heavy garland fastened tightly around its neck, and naturally soon experienced such intense irritation of the skin of its throat it attempted to alleviate the itching by rubbing itself on the only sharp thing available to it."

"The sword!" Melios breathed. "Summon Hapymen here!" he shouted. "And as for—"

He was interrupted by a thunderous knocking on the house door.

Guests began to rise to their feet, hands on blades, as a terrified servant rushed into the room.

"Master, we've just received word! The tax assessor's been found drowned!"

***

"At first I mistook it for a log," Porphyrios told John. "But there was something familiar about the shape…. He was floating face down. Must have fallen in and drowned. I was about to go for help when one of the villagers came by, so I sent him to raise the alarm."

They stood beside the ditch, staring down at the drowned man whose sightless eyes regarded the starry sky with a steady gaze. Behind them lights moved in the darkness and the low muttering of an unhappy crowd came to them on gusts of a rising wind. Melios had instructed his guards to block the road, to prevent anyone interfering with the body. The headman had chosen to keep his distance as well.

John bent down for a closer look. Scrofa had obviously been dead for more than a day.

"Scrofa wasn't a popular man, excellency," the charioteer continued. "I fear the authorities will be bound to suspect murder, and whatever the truth of it there will be reprisals on Mehenopolis. Fortunately I'll be on my way soon."

"You've been able to obtain what you sought?"

"A charm against curse tablets? Sadly, no. Dedi refused my request. It's probably just as well. I'm inclined to think he's not as powerful as he claims to be."

John moved his lantern above Scrofa, illuminating first the waxen face, wet hair clinging close to the skull, then the torso, and on down across legs whose red-splotched ankles testified to the powerful grip of the charioteer who had dragged the unfortunate tax assessor ashore.

Finally John stood and looked toward the settlement. "I see Melios has obligingly sent someone to take Scrofa back."

"He'll be more welcome there in his present state than he was when he strolled this way," Porphyrios remarked.

The charioteer turned and saw the approaching donkey, ridden by a young servant. "Well...um...Lord Chamberlain," Porphyrios stammered, "I'd better be off."

"Not yet!" John grasped the man's bulging forearm. He could easily have wrenched away, but his attention was engaged by the small beast which had reached them.

"Do...do you...er...want me to assist the young man in getting the body on the...?"

"That will not be necessary, Porphyrios," John replied quietly. "However, you will explain immediately why a charioteer is terrified of donkeys. I noticed your reluctance to approach one during the fire, and now I recall you sat at the back of the cart that brought us here from the river. It was less fear of the inhabitants of the beehives piled up behind the driver than of the donkey trotting in front. Am I not correct?"

"Please...please...Lord Chamberlain...if you will allow me to step away...I'll explain...just...just...."

John released the man's arm and walked along the road a few paces. Porphyrios followed obediently.

"Does your fear extend to horses?" John asked.

"I avoid them as much as possible, but donkeys most of all."

"It must be difficult at times, particularly when traversing crowded city streets. What is your real business in Mehenopolis?"

"Although I was never a charioteer, excellency, I am in fact employed by the owner of a racing team. I was dispatched here to collect a large sum from Melios. He lost several huge wagers betting on races at the Hippodrome during his visit to Constantinople."

He gestured to his belt. "I told him these reins would end up tied tightly around his neck, to frighten him into settling the debt. He asked me for a day or two to find what he owes."

"I observed the painting of the Hippodrome was much more recent than the rest of Melios' frescoes," John replied. "Even so, it's been a year or two since his visit. Why is your employer in such a hurry to collect the debt now after waiting so long?"

Porphyrios looked back at the donkey as it disappeared into the distance bearing Scrofa's lifeless form. "It came to his ears Melios petitioned the emperor about a tax dispute. Few are able to reduce their taxes, and Melios had drawn attention to himself. Once the imperial tax assessors had the headman in their grasp, there wouldn't even be bones left for the rest of his creditors to pick over."

"And so he wanted to collect his debt from Melios before Scrofa could take any assets that might be available?"

"That's correct, excellency," the other admitted miserably, "but unfortunately the assessor was already at work in the settlement when I got here."

"However, with Scrofa now gone, you've got a better chance of collecting on Melios' debt. At least until the next assessor arrives. How very convenient for your employer—and not a curse tablet in sight."

A look of distress crossed Porphyrios' face. "I never thought of that, but yes, I suppose it's true. Scrofa's death does look suspicious, doesn't it? Maybe the emperor—"

The charioteer was interrupted by a sudden shout from a man running toward them.

"Save yourselves while you can, sirs! Dedi's set loose another demon! This time it's walking the streets!"

Chapter Forty

"Then your conclusions proved correct?" asked Europa.

"Of course Crispin wouldn't admit anything," replied Anatolius, "but from his reaction I could see I was on the right track. He claimed he had to attend a service and could not spare more time. Then he said he'd send for me in due course for further conversation, as he put it."

Francio laughed. "Watch out! He might try to persuade you to his religious viewpoint, Anatolius."

The trio were seated in Francio's dining room. Anatolius had just completed a description of his visit to the Hormisdas and gone on to explain how he had reached his deductions concerning the events that had led to two deaths and John's journey to Egypt.

Europa picked up her spoon and pointed it at Anatolius. "So your reasoning was the wording of the will demonstrated Symacchus, probably the most orthodox man in the city, viewed Crispin with great esteem whereas most would expect him to consider the bishop a raging heretic? And it was from this you deduced Crispin had converted Symacchus, who began aiding him in an attempt to obtain a relic from Egypt? And how did the senator hear about this relic?"

"According to Diomedes, from Melios, one of the senator's many visitors from that country."

Francio asked who Melios might be.

Anatolius beamed. "Ah! Mithra smiled on our labors, for Felix discovered this Melios lives in the very settlement where John and the others went!"

Francio stared down at his plate, as if reading some meaning from the geometric pattern in the ceramic. "I've thought of another possibility, Anatolius. The senator might have been disposed of because he had rashly spoken with Thomas, a man who lives in the Lord Chamberlain's house."

"And John is Justinian's closest confidant," Anatolius agreed. "Eliminating Thomas by arranging for him to be caught with the senator's body would also mean grave suspicion would be cast upon John for harboring a murderer. I doubt whoever was responsible could have foreseen John himself being accused of the senator's death, but it must have been an even better result from their point of view."

"You're forgetting the most important thing," Francio pointed out. "This mysterious murderer will doubtless attempt to kill anyone who knows anything at all about what's going on, which now includes all three of us. Dear me, this isn't the sort of conversation to whet one's appetite, is it?"

Europa ignored the remark. "What could this relic be and why do they want it? The churches here are already bursting with old bones and such like."

"I'm hoping John can enlighten us when he returns," Anatolius replied. "It can't be a coincidence Justinian sent him to the very settlement where Melios lives."

A savory odor filled the air as Vedrix carried in a silver bowl filled with meat in a dark sauce. A ladle protruded from the steaming mixture.

"Let us put aside this gloomy conversation and celebrate your successful visit to the bishop." Francio gestured at the bowl. "Please help yourselves from this most amusing dish. The markets might be empty but the spice of imagination is inexhaustible!"

Anatolius peered into the bowl and blanched at the sight of tentacles coiled artfully around lumps of meat floating in the thick sauce.

"There wasn't much to be purchased today," Francio went on. "A rather mature octopus, a couple of fig-peckers, and an under-nourished partridge. So my cook and I devised this cunning dish. I call it The Wreck of the Ark."

Europa gingerly ladled out one of the lumps and dropped it onto her plate. She poked at it dubiously with her spoon. "What's that, Francio? Partridge?"

Francio leaned for a closer look. "I'm not certain. Oh, there's also something in it that Vedrix caught in the garden, so that could be a tasty tidbit of weasel."

Europa put a hand up to her mouth. "A weasel?"

"I wouldn't swear to it on oath in a court of law, you understand."

Europa pushed her plate away.

"Condemned without a trial," Anatolius remarked. "Barring Francio's testimony, I believe I could have conclusively proved these lumps are all portions of a succulent hare."

Francio looked disappointed as he traded plates with Europa. "There's more than one in this city tonight who'd be glad to have weasel boiled in sauce."

Anatolius rescued one of the fig-peckers and a bit of tentacle from the wine-dark sea. "Surely vegetables are still available, even if there isn't much meat?"

"Vegetables? What sort of meal can you make with vegetables? A peasant's meal!"

"We've had this discussion before," Anatolius grinned. "Justinian manages perfectly well without eating flesh."

"That's why he's ruled by Theodora," Francio observed. "A little red meat in his diet might do the emperor a great deal of good." He popped a portion of suspected weasel into his mouth and chewed. "You don't know what you're missing."

"Nor do I want to." Europa dropped her spoon.

"What's the matter?" Anatolius asked.

"We really don't know what we're missing, do we? We don't know what's happening to everyone. Where's Thomas? What's become of my parents? What about poor Peter, not to mention Hypatia?"

"You're safe here, Europa," Francio said. "My home is an island of sanctuary in a perilous sea."

"What will you do when Crispin decides to summon you to another interview?" Europa asked Anatolius.

"The bishop is nothing if not cautious. It'll take a few weeks for someone to go to Egypt and back in order to consult his contacts there, whoever they might be. We'll just have to hope John returns to Constantinople before then."

Chapter Forty-one

"I've been called many names in my time," Thomas observed, throwing back another hearty gulp of wine, "but never a demon."

"It's your red hair," John explained. "Many in Egypt consider it ill omened because their evil god Set's hair was the same hue."

"People will kill you for the strangest reasons. I suppose that was the intent of the fellow with the knife who waylaid me as I passed by some ruin or other. I don't think he intended to trim my beard."

They were sitting on the guest house roof, enjoying the light breeze that had sprung up after sunset. Several lamps cast flickering light, pale imitations of the vast starry vault overhead.

"I suspect the local residents wouldn't normally have reacted the way they did," John replied, "but there have been some strange events recently, and old fears once raised take a long time to die down again."

Thomas refilled his cup and gazed into the night. "The comical thing, John, is that I traveled to Egypt to save you. Anatolius sent me, but I'd better tell you the story from the beginning."

John and Cornelia listened closely to Thomas' narrative, starting with when Isis' employee Antonina had told him the client who'd been talking about relics was a servant of Senator Symacchus, thus setting in motion the chain of events that led to them sitting atop a mud brick house at the edge of the empire rather than in John's house in the grounds of the Great Palace.

John restrained himself from chiding Thomas for his reckless stupidity. "So you went to the senator and offered your services in obtaining some mysterious relic?" he asked when Thomas paused.

"That's right. He gave me this and instructed me to be at the Hippodrome at sunset on a given day. I'd know the man I was to meet because he'd be carrying the matching piece."

He drew from his garment the token in question and handed it to John. "The figure's been snapped off along with the top part, as you see," he continued. "There'd be no chance of someone duplicating the missing bit. Very clever idea, wasn't it?"

"As you say, Thomas. Further instructions were doubtless to be given at this meeting?"

"That's what I was told. I do have some experience in these matters so I was not suspicious when Symacchus insisted on utilizing an intermediary. Now it's obvious he didn't seek my expertise, but rather my execution." He frowned. "But how did you contrive to arrive in the Hippodrome on my boot heels, John?"

"You'd been going about with the look of a man with a guilty secret," John replied, "and in Constantinople it's wise to know everyone's secrets, particularly when the person involved is your daughter's husband."

"Of course, I should have told you," Thomas admitted. "But I thought if I could help them obtain this wretched relic, the service would be worth a fair amount of money."

"Strangely enough, we might be searching for the same thing, Thomas. Justinian is of the opinion those working against him seek something of value in Mehenopolis. Could it be this relic you heard about?"

"The orthodox have strange beliefs," Thomas replied. He looked down into his cup. "It may be it wasn't just my behavior which caused you to follow me to the Hippodrome, John.

Mithra might well have been dictating your steps. I hope He will look out for Europa and the others. It's extremely dangerous for them right now."

"I doubt Mithra has any interest in assisting Justinian! As to those you left behind, Anatolius is much more capable than he often appears and Felix is on the spot too. Now what's this about you traveling here to save me?"

"An assassin's been sent after you."

"I'd be more surprised if one hadn't followed. Naturally, I've been on my guard."

Cornelia's face registered dismay. "John, the intruder on the night of the fire! It must have been the assassin! But who—"

"It was Scrofa," John replied.

"The tax assessor?"

"He managed to arrive here just before we did, but that's not surprising considering we were delayed in Alexandria. When I examined his body earlier tonight, there were marks on the man's ankles I subsequently realized were strongly suggestive of scorpion stings. Remember, Peter drove the intruder away by throwing his jar of scorpions at him."

"That's something I would have paid a coin or two to see!" Thomas grinned.

"Furthermore," John continued, "despite Scrofa telling Cornelia he wished to talk to me, he made no effort whatsoever to do so, and I am not that difficult to find. He was overheard asking Melios about my movements. Then too Cornelia told me she'd seen Scrofa on Melios' estate the night of the fire."

Cornelia gasped. "It's just as well Dedi's demon set that blaze. If we'd gone straight home…."

John stood up. "Cornelia can tell you about our adventures, Thomas. Justinian sent me here to investigate suicidal sheep and that I've done. However, since I'm marked for murder, it shows that, just as he suspected, there's something here of much greater value. And the most important thing in Mehenopolis is whatever is at the center of the maze up there."

He looked toward the black bulk of the Rock of the Snake, outlined against the sky by an absence of stars.

"Dedi knows a great deal about that," he continued, "so I'm off to interview him right now."

***

John followed the trembling light of his torch. The pop and hiss of the burning resin carried in the quiet night.

The path was deserted. Once, he thought he heard the crunch of a footstep other than his own. He swung around.

No one was there.

When he approached the bench by the well, he half-expected Zebulon to call out an invitation in a game of Mehen, but the cleric was not to be seen.

John traversed the pilgrim camp and arrived at Dedi's dwelling. Its owner was not in residence.

John knocked twice, then pushed the door. It swung open. Perhaps the magician trusted his fearsome reputation to keep intruders out, rather than relying on locks.

The disembodied marble limbs in the doorframe seemed to grasp at John, animated by the motion of the torch he thrust inside.

"Dedi?" he called out.

No answer.

John stepped through the doorway.

The room appeared no different from his last visit.

He decided to take his opportunity to look around.

Bundles of herbs hung from the ceiling in the room opening off the first. It smelled of gardens drowsing in the last hot days of summer. Chests were piled against its wall. The room beyond contained more of the same as well as several amphorae, and from it other rooms marched back tunnel-like.

John continued on, finally arriving at a narrow chamber where a metal grate not unlike those used to protect shops in Constantinople was set in the floor.

He bent and shone torchlight through the grate.

A grotesque visage stared back.

Glassy eyes glinted from folds of shriveled flesh, and bloodless lips drew away from black gums to reveal uneven teeth.

It was the false head of Dedi's reptilian oracle.

John moved the torch further down and saw the snake itself, coiled up beneath the grate.

The creature didn't move. It appeared to be asleep.

Did Hapymen make a potion to keep it docile?

Beyond, John could see a dark archway opening into a shadowy ascending tunnel.

He pulled at the grate. It opened slowly upwards, making an alarming racket.

He began to step down, over the somnolent snake.

Then a shadow flickered on the wall beside him and before John could decipher the meaning of it his breath was cut off.

John's torch hit the floor in an explosion of sparks.

Reflexively he grabbed at the cord around his neck.

Someone had taken advantage of the noise of the grate opening to creep up behind him.

He managed to get his fingers under the cord. His attacker was not skilled in garroting and had not tightened it immediately.

Patches of darkness flashed across John's vision.

He allowed himself to relax and slump forward, then twisted convulsively, slammed his assailant into the wall.

His ears rang. He lurched out of the attacker's grasp.

Something hit him hard in the stomach and he crumpled.

"You fool! You've killed him!"

It was Dedi.

"No! He's just unconscious! I hit him with the end of the spear, not the point."

That was Hapymen.

John kept his eyes closed.

"And you...why are you here, Porphyrios?"

"I followed him from Melios' estate. I realized the Lord Chamberlain had guessed the truth, Dedi. He as much as told me he thought Scrofa's accident was too convenient."

"It wasn't an accident?"

"Of course not. Why shouldn't I have drowned him? And you as well?"

"Don't move," Dedi said, "or Hapymen will put his spear through you as quick as he'd gut a fish. Consider this. If you murder the Lord Chamberlain you'll spend the rest of your life looking over your shoulder, and it probably won't be a long span at that."

"Doubtless you're wagering your own on surviving long enough to tell the authorities I was responsible for Scrofa's death?" Porphyrios sneered.

"Are you ready to bet yours on how fast you can disarm Hapymen? It's one thing to kill a sheep. I'm not a murderer. Then again, I know why you came to Mehenopolis. I'd be doing Melios a service if I allowed Hapymen to kill you."

"How could that be?"

"More than one person overheard you threatening the head-man, including Hapymen here. I have no notion how much Melios owes your employer, but for a start, that stretch of land he and I have been arguing about for years is going to be mine. I'm not letting it be taken to pay Melios' creditors. It would hardly be fair. I wasn't the one gambling at the Hippodrome, was I?"

"Very well," Porphyrios replied. "Your logic persuades me to spare John's life—for now."

The conversation continued, but blackness washed the corners of John's mind. He couldn't make sense of the words. He felt himself being rolled over.

"Tie him up, Hapymen," Dedi was saying.

"Was it wise to let Porphyrios go?" Hapymen sounded worried.

"Another corpse would be difficult to explain, but more importantly Mehen has arranged for us to capture the Lord Chamberlain."

"But you can't kill him, master, for the same reason you gave Porphyrios!"

"Just make certain the knots are as tight as possible," was the curt reply.

John felt rope coiling around his body, pinning his arms to his sides. A foot was placed on the small of his back and the bonds tightened.

"I'll tell Melios the Lord Chamberlain's disappearance is Mehen's doing," Dedi explained, "but that I can placate the snake god and get his guest back. For a price, that is, and the cost will be the strip of land I want. How can he refuse? John is his guest and Justinian will hold him personally responsible for his safety. Naturally Melios will agree to any terms."

John was dragged across the uneven floor.

"And I'm happy for the opportunity to teach the great Lord Chamberlain a lesson in humility as well," Dedi added.

The dark waters lapping at the edge of John's thoughts welled up abruptly, and this time he could not hold them back.

Chapter Forty-two

A loud thump from a bedroom sent Peter rushing down the hallway.

"Master? Is that you?"

He found Thomas picking Cheops up off the floor. "Sorry, Peter. The door was open and when I saw it, I couldn't resist looking closer at the famous cat mummy."

Thomas laid Cheops back on the pallet. The whiskered face glared at him with fixed, eternal, feline fury.

The sun was high enough to send a brilliant shaft of light through the window slit high in the plastered wall. John had been gone all night and now half the morning. Peter briefly clasped his blistered hands together and muttered a prayer for protection of his master.

"It makes me nervous waiting around, even for divine intervention," Thomas said. "John wouldn't be talking to Dedi about whatever's in that accursed maze for this long. It's time for action."

He slapped the pommel of his sword just as Cornelia stepped into the bedroom.

She shook her head. "No, Thomas, you'd better stay right here."

"Mistress," Peter ventured. "I believe Thomas is right. Something dreadful must have happened."

"I should've insisted on going with him!" Thomas muttered. "Nothing speaks more persuasively to a rogue like Dedi than a sharp blade!"

He stepped forward, but Cornelia blocked the doorway. "You intend to venture out after your reception last evening? It would be better to remain indoors until John decides the best course of action. We won't know what it is until he gets back."

Thomas grumbled, but accepted the wisdom of her words.

"If Dedi's up to further trickery there's no point confronting him. He'd be expecting it and doubtless have some story or other prepared," Cornelia continued.

"But mistress—"

"Don't worry, Peter! John may well have had a sudden notion of other paths to explore and decided to pursue his investigations further, the middle of the night or not. You and Thomas stay here, in case he returns while I'm gone."

She pivoted and vanished down the hallway.

Thomas looked glum. "Cornelia's right. Everyone is so excitable here, and you never know what might happen. Even so, all this skulking about is getting tiresome. Ever since that night in the Hippodrome I might just as well have been locked in one of Justinian's dungeons."

Peter suggested Thomas might feel better after he'd had something to eat. A hearty meal was his solution to many problems of a worldly nature. He retreated to the kitchen and began to sort through vegetables.

His thoughts returned to John. Something terrible had befallen the master. Peter was as certain of it as if he had been granted a vision.

Perhaps heaven had spoken to him?

Would a vision come from outside? Could one's thoughts be mistaken such a visitation? Might it appear to him as a phantom or a disembodied voice?

John had gone to question Dedi about whatever was in the maze.

What could be hidden there? Most likely some blasphemous artifact. Hadn't the place been a pagan shrine?

Yet a fragment of weathered wood might still be a piece of the True Cross even though sold by a charlatan.

Peter had witnessed the crippled pilgrim cured. The man was carried into the shrine and walked out.

One of faith might brave the maze and be rewarded with what he sought.

Peter dropped the leeks he had been holding and strode out of the kitchen.

***

John came awake at the bottom of the sea.

He was drowning.

Then he realized he could breathe, although with difficulty since his throat was swollen.

Impenetrable darkness surrounded him. Not a hint of illumination revealed his surroundings. He was aware only of powdery dust against his cheek.

He remembered being bound.

During the process he had recalled the trick Cornelia had insisted on teaching him, one learned from Captain Nikodemos on the *Minotaur* during their journey to Egypt.

She had been thinking of employing it in an act to garner a few coins in some village square. Nikodemos used it to win bets.

John wondered if it might not be worth much more.

His life.

His captors thought he was unconscious. They didn't notice he kept his arms rigid, and slightly away from his body. Dim light helped conceal the maneuver. It had gained him enough slack so that now he was able to work one arm free, scraping skin off his wrist, and then the other.

After what seemed like a long time he extricated himself completely and got to his feet.

How strange that Nikodemos had been a Mithran.

A soldier of Mithra served the god, not the other way around, but perhaps sometimes....

John blinked, and ran a hand across his eyes.

He could not see his fingers.

He groped at the dark, found no obstruction, and took a step forward, half expecting to trip over some obstacle.

He thought uneasily of Dedi's snake. His boots could be close to a reptilian head for all he knew. For that matter, the place of his confinement could be crawling with scorpions.

He took another reluctant step forward and his outstretched fingers encountered a rough vertical surface.

Not mud brick. Stone.

Gingerly, he reached up. The ceiling barely above his head was also constructed of stone.

He stepped carefully to one side, his outstretched hand again eventually meeting what he supposed was another wall. Moving slowly in case Dedi had set a trap, he made a complete circuit of the space in which he found himself.

There were openings in each wall although no door frames, and neither did his fingers encounter any ridges in the walls where blocks had been fitted together. The walls not only felt uneven, they also bulged slightly outward—or perhaps the corner angles were not square.

Initially he supposed he was disoriented by the darkness, or dizzy from near strangulation. However, after brief consideration, he was realized where he was.

Dedi had thrown him into the maze.

Doubtless it would feed the magician's vanity to hear John beg to be rescued.

He didn't know that John would never do so.

John rubbed his neck.

Porphyrios had intended to kill him, having already murdered Scrofa. By his own admission he was in Mehenopolis to protect his employer's interests. If he hadn't been thrown into a panic by a harmless donkey, he might never have blurted out his true reason for his presence there, not to mention his confession to the death during his conversation with Dedi.

John considered what to do.

At some point he expected Dedi to return, hoping to hear him plead for an escort back to daylight. Could John feign unconsciousness and helplessness and thereby take the magician by surprise?

Should he wait in ambush until he saw the light from an approaching torch?

That would work if Dedi arrived alone.

It might also be possible if the magician were accompanied by Hapymen, provided the servant was unarmed.

Yet John did not care to simply wait and see, the more so since his blade had been taken.

He felt his way to the nearest doorway, tore a small scrap of material from the bottom of his tunic, and dropped it in front of the opening.

Now he would be able to tell which rooms he had already visited.

Then he began to explore.

Hours later he rested, his back against another rough-hewn wall. Phantom lights, void of color, slid across his vision.

He had not glimpsed a hint of illumination and had soon lost track of the number of rooms he had traversed. Some featured four doorways, others two or three. A few were dead ends. He had not been able to glean anything useful about the maze from the bits of cloth he had scattered and subsequently re-encountered.

Thirsty now, he tried to swallow.

As he had done more than once in his wandering, he placed his ear to the floor and then the wall.

And as before he heard no sound, felt no vibration. There had been no sign of life in the endless empty rooms.

He had not encountered a draught.

How many rooms could the maze possibly have? Dozens? Hundreds?

He thought of the sheer size of the Rock of the Snake.

What if the maze had been carved deeply into the outcropping itself?

The unwelcome thought came to him that he might well die of thirst if he was not soon rescued or found the way out.

His hand moved reflexively in front of his face, as if to brush away the blackness.

Yet pilgrims had to be rescued from the maze. Therefore it must be simple enough to navigate it by torchlight.

John guessed there must be markings, perhaps painted, showing the route in and out. He had already run his hands along enough walls and around doorways to know there were no carvings that would serve the same purpose.

The uneven walls, some bulging slightly outwards while others curved inwards, made the unseen rooms he had traversed all the more disconcerting.

He stood, unsteadily. His throat worked spasmodically and painfully.

He ran his palm along the nearest wall.

There was something different about it.

The wall did not so much bulge here and there as curve along its entire length.

Noticeably.

What did it mean? That was the problem to be solved. A riddle, almost a game.

Like Zebulon's game of Mehen.

No, John thought, Mehen's maze was exactly the same as Zebulon's board. It was hewn out in the shape of a coiled snake.

Why not? Wasn't the shrine of which the maze formed a part dedicated to Mehen?

Despite the confusion of doorways, the path to the center, like the path to the center of Zebulon's board, wound continuously inward.

The trick was to move inward without deviating.

He was certain of it.

And once he got to the heart of the maze he could easily work his way back out.

John trailed his fingers along the wall until he reached a doorway and stepped into the next room.

Working his way around he found the wall on the far side from the entrance seemed more curved than that in the room he had just left.

If he was not moving toward the center, he reasoned, he would soon reach a dead end.

Then he would simply try another direction.

He felt his way through the opening to the next room. Again he placed his left hand on the wall to the left of the doorway, followed it carefully around two corner angles and located the next doorway.

There was no way to measure the passage of time.

Occasionally John stopped to rest. He could feel his heart pounding. It wasn't from exertion, but rather that the darkness pressing in from all sides, blinding his eyes, blotting out the world, was too like his dreams of drowning.

More than once it occurred to him that he could be wrong about the shape of the maze. He might simply be wandering deeper into abandoned catacombs far away from the chamber that pious pilgrims sought.

Yet it now seemed as if the curvature of the walls was increasing and the rooms less wide.

Soon he was certain of it.

He must be fast approaching the heart of the maze and whatever lay there.

He sought the next opening.

And found a door.

He pushed it open and could see again.

Ahead lay a long, narrow hallway with light at the far end.

Several strides took him around a corner, under an archway, and into a chamber whose fitful lamplight had spilt out into the corridor.

He had arrived at a circular room.

Clay lamps, arrayed on the floor along the foot of its uneven walls, cast shadows into a dome crudely chiseled from the native rock. Light danced on a tall pole topped by a horizontal cross piece displayed on a low wooden pedestal set against the wall opposite the archway.

A serpent, thicker than John's leg, climbed around the pole, its glittering coils moving ceaselessly.

John realized the reptile's apparent motion was an illusion created by the flickering lamps, for the upper part of the snake's body and its head rested on the horizontal bar and their position remained unchanged.

Now he saw the truth of it.

The artifact Thomas had been given in Constantinople was not a cross with the top and the figure of the Christian's gentle god broken from it.

Clearly it was a reproduction of this effigy—one from which the serpent had been detached.

This then must be the thing Justinian's enemies sought.

A representation of an ancient god.

Dedi claimed to derive power from it, but he was a charlatan, wasn't he? The cures the pilgrims sought were empty promises, weren't they?

John looked up at the serpent.

It had been fashioned of copper. The black pits of its eyes fastened on him.

John suddenly felt cold. There was some quality beyond mere darkness in the shadows of those eyes. It was as if a hole had been punched through the brightly frescoed wall of reality to reveal a void beyond the world.

He reached up and touched the snake's glittering coils.

There was a faint crackle and the tip of his forefinger felt as if it had been stung by one of Apollo's bees.

It must have been his imagination.

He laid his hand against the serpent.

It felt warm.

No doubt warmth from the lamps had heated the metal from which it was constructed.

There was no doubt if any pilgrims reached this circular sanctum they would be suitably impressed and overawed, yet how could the strange artifact triumph against imperial troops or aid a plot against Justinian?

John looked behind the pedestal on which the idol stood and found what he had expected.

A wooden trapdoor.

No doubt the tunnel below led back to Dedi's dwelling.

The lamps guttered and smoke swirled. A figure stepped into the chamber.

It was Peter.

"Master! I…I made my way through the maze by faith, it seems…."

Peter's words trailed off as he saw the effigy. He fell to his knees, sketching a cross with a trembling hand.

His eyes glistened as he looked at John. His voice was a ragged whisper. "It is Nehushtan."

"Nehushtan?"

"The brazen serpent, master. When the chosen people wandered in the wilderness the Lord sent fiery serpents among them. Moses prayed to Him and was commanded to make a serpent and display it upon a pole, so that whoever beheld the image would be healed. But when it came to be worshipped as an idol in the days of Hezekiah, it was destroyed. Except it was not destroyed, master, for here before us is Nehushtan itself."

Chapter Forty-three

"I told Senator Symacchus I had a lot of experience when it came to relics," Thomas grumbled, "and didn't I end up with Nehushtan almost in my grasp? If only the senator had believed me—"

"There are safer ways to make a living than chasing after such things," Europa interrupted. She gave her husband's arm an affectionate squeeze.

She and Thomas were seated in John's study in Constantinople, along with John, Anatolius, and Cornelia. The clang of pots accompanied by a hymn drifted down the hallway. Peter was reclaiming his kitchen.

They had talked for a long time, trying to piece together what they had learned separately.

"So really you were pursuing an investigation for the emperor, John." Anatolius' tone betrayed his irritation. "At least you returned from Mehenopolis more rapidly than you arrived there. I was afraid that before you got back Crispin would summon me to a meeting, and then what would I say?"

"I'm certain you'd have invented a reasonable story," John said.

"Luckily I didn't have to! Now, let's see if we agree on what happened. Bishop Crispin learned of the existence of the relic in the maze from Senator Symacchus, who'd been trying to convert him to orthodoxy. Symacchus, who came to sympathize with the monophysites, had been told about it by his Egyptian guest, Melios."

"I'll ask Peter to show you the pilgrim flask Hapymen presented to him before we left," John said. "It's identical to one you described in the senator's collection. According to Hapymen, the wavy line you thought was a river was intended to represent Mehen. No doubt the senator's matching flask was given to him by Melios when he visited Constantinople."

"So the monophysites, having learned of the relic, realized bringing the brazen serpent of Moses to Constantinople would demonstrate clearly to everyone that the Christian god was on their side of the theological dispute."

Thomas guffawed. "Which, since they already had Theodora as their champion, would've forced Justinian to change his beliefs!"

"Almost certainly," Anatolius agreed. "And then who would have held the real power in the empire? Fortunately for Justinian, Crispin and whatever other clerics were involved were good at plotting, but reluctant to set events in motion. That changed when Hektor arrived on the scene. He isn't one to hesitate."

John nodded. "I'd guess that Hektor originally got in touch with Senator Symacchus because he'd briefly been his reader and Hektor was attempting to establish himself as a pious Christian for his own purposes. When he realized the opportunity he'd stumbled over he must have been jubilant!"

"Doubtless they intended to use Apollo's services to smuggle the relic out of Egypt?" Europa asked.

"I believe so. Melios admitted Apollo had performed similar services for him. I believe that Zebulon also had a hand in the same trade. He probably still has contacts in the religious community in Antioch. More importantly, the relic is not much taller than a man. It would fit into a large enough hive or could be cut in half and placed in two."

Thomas gave a snort. "I would've just put it in a crate and shipped it."

"Caution and secrecy are always the best policies when plotting against the emperor," John said. "Even Hektor was cautious, in his own way. He had to remove Symacchus and his servant Achilles, to make certain their indiscreet chatter didn't cause further trouble. He also arranged that the meddlesome adventurer who'd appeared on the scene was to be found in circumstances where he would be held responsible for the senator's murder. That he turned out to be Thomas, with myself on his heels, was just a stroke of unexpected good fortune."

Anatolius frowned. "I suppose Hektor and his accomplices came to the senator's house that evening in order to take Achilles and dispose of him. I've given it some thought. It wasn't just the matter of what he revealed at Isis' house that condemned him. Remember, Achilles was sent to alert Felix because Achilles was expendable, and furthermore wouldn't be recognized as a known associate of Hektor's."

Thomas leaned over to John's desk and plucked up the small enameled artifact which had been the cause of so much misery. "So it turned out this is not a broken cross as we all supposed, but a copy of Nehushtan with the snake removed?"

"Indeed. The original would be a particularly impressive relic to bring into the city with the plague still raging," John observed. "Consider. It cured the sick centuries ago and is still believed to be as powerful now as it was then."

Thomas laughed. "You're thinking about the crippled beggar, the one Peter kept telling me had been healed after going into the maze? It seems more likely Dedi arranged for one of the villagers to pretend to be lame, so he could point to him as an example of a so-called miraculous cure."

"That might be so," John admitted.

Cornelia looked away from gazing out the window. "What do you mean, John? You're not suggesting the relic is anything but a forgery, are you? Remember, the beggar wasn't in the maze for very long, yet it took you hours to find your way to the center and out again. The people carrying him should have stayed inside an hour or two at least. That speedy cure was a bad slip on Dedi's part, I'd say."

John agreed it was so. "Still, you have not seen Nehushtan as Peter and I did."

Cornelia smiled. "You sound so solemn, I could almost suspect you believe in the power of this relic!"

"I'm not certain what I think about it. Religion defies proof, unlike murder. I've already explained why I believe Scrofa was sent out to kill me."

Anatolius looked puzzled. "I don't understand. If it was Porphyrios who tried—"

"He obviously didn't know how to use the weapon very well. He must have taken the cord from Scrofa's body after he killed him. Maybe he thought he'd hide his tracks by using it. I'm convinced the plotters ordered Scrofa to kill Symacchus and Achilles as well. They were killed the same way."

"That makes sense. But if Porphyrios murdered Scrofa, why didn't you bring him back in chains?"

"He was gone by the time I got out of the maze. Not only had he admitted to at least one murder, but he'd also tried to kill a Lord Chamberlain. Then there's the question of his employers' money. He hadn't been able to get it, but I have no doubt that once they hear he's run off, they'll be convinced he absconded with it. He'll spend the rest of his life looking over his shoulder until someone catches up to him."

"So everything has been neatly solved," said Thomas.

"Except for the most important matter," John pointed out. "There remains the real reason I went to Egypt. The plotters have not been exposed. For that, I will need your assistance, Anatolius."

Anatolius looked at John in surprise. "What do you mean?"

"You mentioned you've gained Crispin's confidence?"

"Temporarily at least. He's half-convinced I know something about this relic, which is probably the only reason I'm still alive."

"Then you must arrange matters with him. He wanted to present Nehushtan to the emperor, and so he shall."

Chapter Forty-four

The audience gathered in front of the ivory double throne occupied by Justinian and Theodora could not have been more unlike the crowd atop the Rock of the Snake, except that they had assembled for similar reasons.

Glancing around, John recognized senators, aristocrats, and assorted palace officials. Shielded by lesser clergy, the Patriarch—whether by design or accident—stood as far from Crispin as was possible. Hektor had, John noted, stationed himself mid way between the bishop and Theodora. Armed excubitors flanking the imperial couple and stationed around the walls outnumbered the distinguished guests. Felix stood beside the throne.

Work on the hall had been completed in John's absence, and now that night had fallen, light from hundreds of lamps set on ornate silver stands or hanging by ceiling chains gilded the panes of the high windows. John glanced upward at the enormous cross that glittered through the mist of smoke. Although it was rendered in nothing more than gold and gems, he had the uneasy feeling it was on the verge of crashing down on the assembly.

He stepped toward the throne.

Justinian nodded almost imperceptibly, acknowledging John's low bow, while Theodora gazed down at him with the fixed, incomprehensible stare of an ancient statue.

"My dear Lord Chamberlain," the emperor began in thin tones John doubted were audible to most of the gathering. "We are pleased to extend our gracious thanks for your unceasing labors on our behalf. We were much relieved to hear the sheep which concerned us was not in fact suicidal, but merely the victim of a cruel trickster."

He leaned forward and continued. "Furthermore, Lord Chamberlain, you have intrigued us with the information that this strange man concealed a far more important secret."

"Yes, Caesar. The magician Dedi is the guardian of an astonishing relic."

"We understand Bishop Crispin knows something of this?" Justinian turned his bland, bucolic countenance toward the bearded monophysite.

Crispin bowed. "That is so, excellency. It has pleased the Lord to deliver unto His followers a sacred artifact as irrefutable proof our understanding of His true nature is correct, and one which I venture to suggest will not disappoint your expectations. The man who brought it to the city awaits without."

John glanced around. Theodora's expression remained unchanged, while a smirk of satisfaction crossed Hektor's ruined face.

"Very well," Justinian replied. "Then it is our wish to observe and examine it."

As the emperor uttered the words he cast a quick sidelong glance toward the impassive empress.

John signaled to the excubitors guarding the bronze doors at the other end of the hall, which immediately swung open to reveal the diminutive figure of Dedi.

The magician was dressed in plain white garments appropriate for the solemn task before him. He approached the throne slowly, almost hesitantly. An hour before he had appeared supremely unconcerned about attending an audience with Justinian, but,

John supposed, coming face to face with the man who held the power of life and death over everyone in the empire was enough to give even a boastful Egyptian charlatan pause.

When Dedi reached the imperial couple he bowed clumsily.

"And this is the rogue who was responsible for the death of the sheep?" Justinian asked.

"Yes, Caesar. However, Dedi now brings two gifts and begs for the favor of performing for your imperial highnesses, possibly thereby earning your gracious pardon."

Theodora gave a vicious smile. "Perhaps this little man believes he can mislead our beloved emperor and myself as easily and conveniently as he did ignorant peasants?"

Justinian waved his hand. "Indeed, indeed. The tale you have told intrigues me, Lord Chamberlain. We shall not rush to hasty judgement. Bishop Crispin, you assured me I would not be disappointed. We shall see. However, it seems this man has brought two gifts. What then is the second?"

Crispin looked startled, but quickly recovered his wits. "I believe Dedi wishes to present it personally."

An excubitor appeared with a lidded basket which he placed at Dedi's sandals.

Dedi drew himself up. "Here is a wonder to behold, most gracious one. A rare and fine example of a beast many have sought but few have found! That semi-mythical beast, the radish-colored cat."

There were a few nervous laughs from the onlookers.

"There's no such thing," someone remarked too loudly.

"Pliny would surely be amazed," another voice added.

Crispin directed a furious scowl toward Hektor.

Dedi waited for the murmuring to die down, then opened the basket and extracted a small kitten.

Theodora's caw of laughter rang out. "You fool! It's gray!"

Dedi bowed yet again. "But highness, do not radishes turn gray as they age and mould?"

Justinian chuckled as Theodora allowed herself an admiring smile at the magician's impudence. "You may be lacking in stature, Dedi of Egypt, but you have a lion's courage!"

Dedi handed the squirming feline to an excubitor.

"A clever gift, and one for which we extend our gracious thanks," Justinian told Dedi. "And now, as regards the other matter…." His gaze flickered toward Bishop Crispin.

"That was my personal gift to you, excellency," Dedi replied with another bow. He favored the royal couple with a crooked-toothed smile.

"Then now let us see this artifact of which we have heard so much," Theodora said firmly. "We trust we will not be disappointed."

"No true believer will be disappointed," Dedi replied. "First, however, we must take precautions, for there are wonders that would blind if seen in the light."

As he spoke attendants began dousing lamps until there remained lit only those suspended from the ceiling. In the smoky haze they glowed dimly, tiny suns glimpsed through fog.

The excubitors stationed near the emperor and empress moved closer, wary of the increased darkness. Felix peered around, alert for trouble.

Two servants hauled a crate to the foot of the throne.

Justinian gestured in Crispin's direction. "Come forward now and tell us what we are about to witness."

The bishop made his way with obvious reluctance to Dedi's side. He looked down at the closed crate with an uncertain expression.

When he spoke his voice trembled, as if with some powerful emotion. "Caesar, my followers and I are blessed to present to you, heaven's representative on earth, the brazen serpent Moses raised up in the wilderness. Nehushtan!"

With a flourish Dedi slid aside the top of the crate, reached inside, and pulled out a shadowy form.

Fitful light glimmered on loose coils and caught an eye in a withered human visage.

Gasps of awe and terror erupted from the audience.

They fell quickly silent as it became apparent that what the magician held was a stout stick around which coiled a somnolent snake fitted with a blatantly counterfeit human head.

Bishop Crispin turned pale as a few muffled oaths of a decidedly unecclesiastical nature were heard.

Dedi moved the stick back and forth, imparting a semblance of life to the comatose reptile. He grasped the snake under its false head and made it bow to the imperial couple.

Justinian roared with laughter before glancing at Theodora. "We haven't seen anything so entertaining since that dwarf mime of yours disappeared!"

Theodora rose from her seat. "Who is responsible for this insult?" Her venomous gaze fell on Hektor.

The former court page turned toward Justinian. "Caesar, as you can see, the information I gave you was accurate. There was indeed a threat from Egypt, only it has come to nothing. This Nehushtan is of no use to anyone."

Justinian, still seated, glanced briefly at Theodora. Then his gaze passed over Hektor as if he were not there and came to rest, instead, on Felix.

"Captain. Execute Hektor immediately."

Epilogue

"I only wish I could have handed my sword to you, John. Not that I minded putting an end to the villain myself."

Felix took another sip of wine and stared thoughtfully at the wall mosaic in John's study. "The strangest thing was when I returned to the reception hall after escorting Hektor to the dungeons for execution as ordered. Bishop Crispin kept muttering something about how it was turning out to be true, that Hektor wouldn't die on the street. What do you suppose he meant?"

John shook his head. "Who can say? Now we know that Hektor alerted Justinian to the plot, which is probably why the emperor gave me so little information. I suspect Hektor didn't tell him everything he knew."

"Hektor was trying to wager on both teams at the same time," said Felix. "I know what I would've laid a coin or two on, and that's that when a scapegoat was needed it wasn't going to be Theodora's prize bishop."

Anatolius spoke up. "I almost feel sorry for Crispin. I'm not sure he believed me when I told him my associates had Nehushtan. However, since I obviously knew about the plot and he was ordered to the audience with Justinian, he had little choice but to go along and hope for the best. He couldn't have expected anything as ludicrous as that snake on a stick. I wish I had as much hair." He ruefully patted his scalp, now covered with short, dark fuzz.

"Dedi's snake oracle appears much more convincing presented in front of an ancient temple ruin in the middle of the Egyptian night," John observed.

"I'll have to take your word for it," Anatolius replied. "Dedi will doubtless boast to the end of his days of his great success performing for the emperor and empress."

"No doubt he saw it as the opportunity of a lifetime. As indeed it was, particularly since he escaped with his life. Francio's guests will enjoy his act."

Anatolius' gaze went to the window. "See how the sky is purpling, John. We should leave soon or we'll be late. Francio's been planning this recreation of Trimalchio's feast for some time, and I don't want to miss any of it."

"Just as well Francio hasn't set eyes on Cheops," said Thomas. "I'm afraid he might have been tempted to add ancient feline to the menu."

Laughter from down the hallway mingled the voices of Europa and Hypatia, now back in residence, with the deeper tones of Peter.

"Whatever is going on in the kitchen?" Felix wondered. "It sounds as if Peter is declaiming something of great import."

"I believe he's entertaining the ladies with a magick trick he learned on the boat back," said John. "For the purpose of entertainment only, of course."

Thomas laughed. "It's the leaping coin illusion. Dedi showed him how to do it, as Peter wanted to amaze Hypatia when he returned. It's quite easy. All you need is a coin with a tiny hole drilled at the edge and a length of black hair or finely woven thread tied through it. A quick twist of the wrist and you can flip it out of a bowl as if by magick. It works wonderfully well, especially in dim light. In fact, I'm going to astonish Isis with it, assuming she'll allow me to return to her employ after such a long and unexplained absence."

Anatolius remarked that Peter sometimes surprised him.

"I expect Peter will chatter for months about our trip," John said. "On the boat back, he observed to me that right from the time we disembarked for Mehenopolis he realized Porphyrios was not what he could call reliable. He said he'd reached this conclusion because despite the supposed charioteer's statement about dogs running while they drank from the Nile for fear of being dragged in by crocodiles, a dog was standing quite calmly on the bank drinking from the river near where we landed!"

They went down to the atrium. Anatolius paused at the house door. "One thing more that I don't understand. Felix, at times it appeared to me as if you really thought John had murdered the senator."

Looking embarrassed, Felix tugged at his beard. "Yes, I could see you were puzzled. John indicated there was more to his exile than it seemed, but he was not very clear." He scowled briefly at John. "Officially he was being blamed for the murder. I wasn't certain how much to reveal of what I intended to do if we could not find evidence to clear him."

Anatolius gave the excubitor captain a questioning look.

"If we could not clear John's name—and Justinian would not—if John died for a crime he did not commit, I was prepared to take the first opportunity I had to kill Justinian. It would have been a dishonorable act to murder a man I am sworn to protect, but I knew John was innocent and as brothers in Mithra…."

"But John is so valuable to Justinian…" Anatolius argued.

John observed that many valuable subjects had been executed for lesser sins than supposedly murdering a senator.

"That's true," Thomas said. "I'd have expected Justinian to have Dedi dispatched on the spot for trying to foist that snake oracle off on him after all that talk about an astounding relic."

John chuckled. "I suspect Justinian realized Dedi's act could be used to discredit his religious opponents. Besides, the Christians' holy book claims Nehushtan was destroyed, and Justinian certainly wouldn't have welcomed proof the sacred writings were fallible."

"Then the emperor isn't likely to order anyone to Mehenopolis to seize whatever is in the maze, even if he guesses there's more to it than Dedi's performance suggests," Thomas observed. "Mind you, I wager Melios will go after it while Dedi is here, and then that'll be the end of Dedi's livelihood."

"I doubt if Melios has enough servants to fight his way through the pilgrims who'd rush to defend the maze," John said. "Besides, by destroying the relic he'd deprive himself and the settlement of a good source of income. For that matter, once Dedi gets a taste of performing at court he might not care to return to Egypt."

"It's enough to make my head hurt," growled Thomas. "I'm a fighter, not a plotter. Give me a fair contest, blade against blade, any day and none of this creeping around and skulking in shadows. Why, even the emperor's at it now! He needs a few good swordsmen, I'd say! They'd settle things a lot more simply, if not as daintily as some might like."

"Ruling an empire isn't so simple as it seems," John pointed out. "The imperial couple often hold themselves out in public as disagreeing on certain matters. It may be these are attempts to flush out hitherto unsuspected enemies foolish enough to declare themselves to one camp or another. Not to mention it keeps people off balance, always a good advantage to have."

Thomas frowned. "You mean Theodora wasn't really championing those heretics, or Justinian isn't as orthodox as he likes to appear?"

"All I can say is that Justinian requires the support of the orthodox, but he also needs the resources of Egypt, which is not entirely orthodox," John replied. "The emperor does not confide everything in me. Even a Lord Chamberlain can be trusted only so far."

"I'll wager the emperor and empress don't even trust each other," Thomas observed with a grin.

"That could be. Whatever the understanding or quarrel between Justinian and Theodora might be on this occasion, I believe they both keep secrets from each other. The real reason for my journey to Egypt is quite possibly one of them."

"We ought to get on our way," Anatolius interrupted. "Francio's expecting a good number of guests. I think he will get them, because according to Hypatia in the last few days—in fact, ever since Dedi's performance for Justinian and Theodora—they have admitted no further plague patients to the hospice."

"Strange indeed," John admitted as they crossed the cobbled square. "And yet, as followers of Mithra, should we not consider that as nothing more than coincidence?"

Glossary

All dates are CE unless otherwise noted.

APIONS
Extremely wealthy and powerful Egyptian family from Oxyrhynchus (present-day al-Bahnasa). A number of its members held high imperial posts.

ATRIUM
Court-like area inside a Roman house. Partly open to the sky, it not only provided light to rooms opening from it, but also contained a shallow cistern (IMPLU-VIUM) under a square or oblong opening (COMPLUVIUM) in its roof. While the IMPLUVIUM was also ornamental, its main purpose was to catch rainwater for household use.

BRITOMARTIS
Cretan goddess. She was called the Lady of the Nets because while fleeing unwanted amorous attention she leapt from a cliff, landing in the net of a fisherman in whose boat she escaped to safety.

BATHS OF ZEUXIPPOS
Public baths in Constantinople, named after ZEUXIPPOS. Erected by order of Septimius Severus (146-211, r 193-211), the baths were a casualty of the Nika riots (532). They were rebuilt by JUSTINIAN I. Situated near the HIPPODROME, they were generally considered the most luxurious of the city's baths and were famous for their statues of mythological figures and Greek and Roman notables.

BLUES
Followers of the Blue chariot racing faction. Great rivalry existed between the Blues and the GREENS and each had their own seating sections in the HIPPODROME. Brawls between the two sets of supporters were not uncommon and occasionally escalated into city-wide riots.

CHALKE
Main entrance to the GREAT PALACE. Its roof was tiled in bronze and the interior was decorated with mosaics of military triumphs, JUSTINIAN I and THEODORA.

CHURCH OF SERGIUS AND BACCHUS
Built in 527, the octagonal domed church is architecturally similar to the GREAT CHURCH. The two martyred saints it commemorates were popular in the east. It was built contiguously with the Church of Saints Peter and Paul, who were particularly venerated in the west.

COMPLUVIUM
See ATRIUM.

DALMATIC
Loose over-garment worn by the Byzantine upper classes.

DELPHIC ORACLE
Most famous oracle in Greece. Priestesses serving in the temple to Apollo on Mount Parnassus prophesied in a semi-conscious and incoherent state after inhaling vapors escaping from the earth and chewing laurel leaves. Their ramblings were interpreted by a temple priest.

EUNUCH
Eunuchs played an important role in the military, ecclesiastical, and civil administrations of the Byzantine Empire. Many high offices in the GREAT PALACE were typically held by eunuchs.

EXCUBITORS
GREAT PALACE guard.

FLOWERS OF PAION
Peonies.

FORUM BOVIS
See MESE.

FORUM CONSTANTINE
See MESE.

GARUM
Spicy, pungent, fermented fish sauce much used in Roman cuisine.

GOLDEN GATE
Principal gate at the southern end of the Theodosian Wall protecting the land side of Constantinople.

GREAT BULL
See MITHRA.

GREAT CHURCH

Colloquial name for the Church of the Holy Wisdom (Hagia Sophia). One of the world's great architectural achievements, the Hagia Sophia was completed in 537, replacing the church burnt down during the Nika riots (532).

GREAT PALACE

Situated in the southern part of Constantinople, it was not one building but rather many, set amidst trees and gardens. Its grounds included barracks for the EXCUBITORS, ceremonial rooms, reception halls, the imperial family's living quarters, churches, and housing provided for court officials, ambassadors, and various other dignitaries.

GREENS

Followers of the Green chariot racing faction. Great rivalry existed between the BLUES and the Greens and each had their own seating sections in the HIPPODROME. Brawls between the two sets of supporters were not uncommon and occasionally escalated into city-wide riots.

HIPPODROME

U-shaped race track next to the GREAT PALACE. The Hippodrome had tiered seating accommodating up to a hundred thousand spectators. It was also used for public celebrations and other civic events.

HORACE (Quintus Horatius Flaccus) (65-68 BC)

Eminent Roman lyric poet, satirist, and literary critic.

HORMISDAS PALACE

Residence of JUSTINIAN I and THEODORA before JUSTINIAN I became emperor.

IMPLUVIUM

See ATRIUM.

JUSTINIAN I (483-565, r 527-565)

His ambition was to restore the Roman Empire to its former glory, and he succeeded in regaining North Africa, Italy, and southeastern Spain. His accomplishments included codifying Roman law and an extensive building program in Constantinople. He was married to THEODORA.

KALAMOS

Reed pen.

LAKE MAREOTIS

Body of water south of Alexandria. During Roman times the lake was larger than it is today, stretching for nearly 60 miles. It was connected by canals to both Alexandria and the Nile.

LIBERTY CAP

Distinctive conical cap of soft material, worn by manumitted slaves with its peak pulled forward. Representations of Liberty often wear this type of cap.

LORD CHAMBERLAIN

Typically a EUNUCH, the Lord (or Grand) Chamberlain was the chief attendant to the emperor and supervised most of those serving at the GREAT PALACE. He also took a leading role in court ceremonial, but his real power arose from his close working relationship with the emperor, which allowed him to wield great influence.

MEHEN

Egyptian snake god who protected the sun god Ra by coiling around the solar barque in which Ra voyaged through the underworld each night.

MESE

Main thoroughfare of Constantinople. Enriched with columns, arches, statuary (depicting secular, military, imperial, and religious subjects), fountains, religious establishments, workshops, monuments, emporiums, public baths, and private dwellings, it was a perfect mirror of the heavily populated and densely built city it traversed. The Mese passed through several fora, including FORUM BOVIS and FORUM CONSTANTINE.

MIN

Egyptian fertility god.

MITHRA

Sun god who slew the GREAT BULL, from whom all animal and vegetable life sprang. Mithra is usually depicted wearing a tunic and Phrygian cap, his cloak flying out behind him, and in the act of slaying the GREAT BULL. Mithra was also known as Mithras.

MITHRAEUM

Underground place of worship dedicated to MITHRA. These places have been found on sites as far apart as northern England and what is now the Holy Land.

MITHRAISM

Of Persian origin, Mithraism spread throughout the Roman empire via its followers in various branches of the military. It became one of the most popular religions before being superseded by Christianity. Mithrans were required to practice chastity, obedience, and loyalty. Women were excluded from Mithraism. Parallels have been drawn between this religion and Christianity because of shared practices such as baptism and a belief in resurrection as well as the fact that Mithra, in common with many sun gods, was said to have been born on December 25th. Mithrans advanced within their religion through seven degrees. In ascending order, these were Corax (Raven), Nymphus (Male Bride), Miles (Soldier), Leo (Lion), Peres (Persian), Heliodromus (Runner of the Sun), and Pater (Father).

MITHRA'S TORCH BEARERS

Representations of MITHRA often show him accompanied by the twin torch bearers Cautes and Cautopates, statues of whom were also part of the sacred furnishings of a MITHRAEUM. Cautes always held his torch upright, while Cautopates pointed his downward. The pair are said to represent the rising and setting of the sun. Another interpretation is that they symbolize the twin emotions of despair and hope.

MONOKYTHRON
Similar to a stew or casserole, it was made from cheese, fish, and vegetables. More elaborate versions of monokythron (Greek, one-dish or one-pot, from the method of cooking) called for the addition of garlic, wine, olive oil, and more than one variety of fish to the basic ingredients.

MONOPHYSITES
Adherents to a doctrine holding that Christ had only one nature, and that it was divine. Despite condemnation by the church the belief remained particularly strong in Syria and Egypt.

NATURAL HISTORY
Encylopaedic work written by PLINY THE ELDER. It numbered over thirty volumes and its topics included botany, anthropology, minerals and gems, geography, medicinal plants, zoology, and the arts.

NOMISMATA (singular NOMISMA)
Gold coin in circulation at the time of JUSTINIAN I.

NUMMUS (plural NUMMI)
Smallest copper coin during the early Byzantine period.

PAION'S FLOWERS
See FLOWERS OF PAION.

PATRIARCH
Head of a diocese or patriarchate. The ancient patriarchates were Rome, Constantinople, Alexandria, Antioch, and Jerusalem.

PHAROS
Lighthouse at Alexandria. Regarded by the ancients as one of the Seven Wonders of the World, it was completed c 280 BC and destroyed by an earthquake towards the end of the 14th century.

PILGRIM FLASKS
Small clay bottles, brought back from pilgrimage sites as souvenirs. They contained holy water or oil from lamps at a saint's tomb, and were thought to have miraculous powers. The flasks typically were flat with a short neck and two handles.

PILLARS OF HERCULES
Strait of Gibraltar.

PLAGUE
Writings by Procopius (known 6th century) and John of Ephesus (c 505 - 585) provide vivid eyewitness accounts of the Justinianic plague. It appears to have broken out in Egypt or central Africa and, spreading along trade routes, arrived in Constantinople in the spring of 542. Sufferers generally died within three days of the onset of symptoms, which included hallucinations, fever, anxiety, chills, and swellings in the armpits, groin, or beside the ears. Some patients lived only a few hours after infection. In many cases, victims' bodies became covered with black blisters. In Constantinople

up to 10,000 people died each day, so that by the time the plague departed the population of the city had been reduced by 40 percent.

PLATO'S ACADEMY
Founded in 387 BC and situated on the northwestern side of Athens, its curriculum included natural science, mathematics, philosophy, and training for public service.

PLINY THE ELDER (Caius Plinius Secundus) (c 23-79)
Roman naturalist and author of the encyclopaedic work NATURAL HISTORY. He died during the eruption of Vesuvius, having traveled to the area to observe the event.

PUBLILIUS SYRUS (fl 1st century BC)
Syrian-born former slave who became a successful writer of, and actor in, theatrical presentations. He was also the author of a large number of maxims and pithy sayings. Several hundred have survived and many have entered common speech.

QUAESTOR
Public official who administered financial and legal matters.

ROMANOS MELODOS (known 6th century)
Hymn-writer and saint, Romanos Melodos (The Melodist) composed over a thousand works, of which about 60 have survived. His subjects included sacred festivals and saints' lives.

SAINT MENAS (d c 295)
Egyptian soldier in the Roman army who was martyred for refusing to renounce his Christian faith. His cult was centered at a healing spring at present-day Abu Mena, near Alexandria. According to legend, the site for his tomb was indicated when the pair of camels bringing him back for burial refused to go any further. PILGRIM FLASKS from his shrine were popular souvenirs, and the saint was depicted on them dressed in a tunic and cloak and standing between two camels.

SAMSUN'S HOSPICE
Founded by Saint Samsun (d 530), a physician and priest. Also known as Sampson or Samson the Hospitable, he is referred to as the Father of the Poor because of his work among the destitute. His hospice was near the GREAT CHURCH.

SPINA
Low platform separating the two arms of the U-shaped race track in the HIPPODROME.

STYLITES
Holy men who often spent years living on platforms atop columns. They took their name from *stylos* (Greek, column or pillar) and were also known as pillar saints. Constantinople boasted a number of stylites.

THEODORA (c 497-548)
Influential and powerful wife of JUSTINIAN I. It has been alleged she had formerly been an actress and prostitute. When the Nika riots broke out in Constantinople

in 532, she is said to have urged her husband to remain in the city, thus saving his throne.

TOOTH POWDER

Manufactured from such ingredients as shells or animal hoofs and horns, which were burnt and then ground into powder. Astringent substances were sometimes added to these mixtures.

TRIMALCHIO'S FEAST

Vulgar and extravagant banquet described at length in *The Satyricon*, written by Roman satirist Gaius Petronius (d c 66). Courses included pastry eggs containing small cooked birds, a hare fitted with wings to represent Pegasus, saffron-filled cakes, honeyed dormice sprinkled with poppy seeds, and bread served from a silver oven.

ZEUXIPPOS

Thracian deity whose name combined Zeus and Hippos (horse).

To receive a free catalog of Poisoned Pen Press titles, please contact us in one of the following ways:

Phone: 1-800-421-3976
Facsimile: 1-480-949-1707
E-mail: info@poisonedpenpress.com
Website: www.poisonedpenpress.com

Poisoned Pen Press
6962 E. First Ave., Suite 103
Scottsdale, AZ 85251